Death in Henry James

Death in Henry James

Andrew Cutting

First published 2005 by
PALGRAVE MACMILLAN
Houndmills, Basingstoke, Hampshire RG21 6XS and
175 Fifth Avenue, New York, N.Y. 10010
Companies and representatives throughout the world

PALGRAVE MACMILLAN is the global academic imprint of the Palgrave Macmillan division of St. Martin's Press, LLC and of Palgrave Macmillan Ltd. Macmillan® is a registered trademark in the United States, United Kingdom and other countries. Palgrave is a registered trademark in the European Union and other countries.

ISBN-13: 978–1–4039–9336–6 hardback
ISBN-10: 1–4039–9336–X hardback

This book is printed on paper suitable for recycling and made from fully managed and sustained forest sources.

A catalogue record for this book is available from the British Library.

Library of Congress Cataloging-in-Publication Data
Cutting, Andrew, 1966–
    Death in Henry James / Andrew Cutting.
        p.   cm.
    Includes bibliographical references and index.
    ISBN 1–4039–9336–X
    1. James, Henry, 1843–1916—Criticism and interpretation.   2. Death in literature.   I. Title.
    PS2127.D4C87 2005
    813'.4—dc22   2005043392

10   9   8   7   6   5   4   3   2   1
14   13   12   11   10   09   08   07   06   05

Transferred to Digital Printing in 2005

Contents

Abbreviations

Acknowledgements

I would like to thank Laurel Brake, Steven Connor, Pamela Thurschwell, Richard Salmon, Julia Kuehn, and Polina Mackay for their helpful suggestions in developing this book. In relation to archival sources, I received generous assistance from Susan Halpert, Greg Zacharias, and Susan Gunter. Most of all, thanks to my partner Terry for love and encouragement over the years.

The cover photograph of Henry James's life mask is reproduced by permission of Bay James and Houghton Library, Harvard University. The extract from Alice Howe Gibbens James's letter to her son appears by permission of Bay James.

Note on the Texts

My main discussion of issues raised by the different editions of James's texts concerns *Roderick Hudson* in Chapter 1. For other sections of my argument, the differences between editions are generally not significant for my purposes; where they are significant, I discuss them in my text. Otherwise, I refer where possible to James's novels, tales, travel writing, and criticism in the Library of America editions as the most readily available and relatively standard source of first book texts. For novels after 1899, for which there is currently no Library of America edition, I refer where possible to the New York Edition.

Introduction

Henry James's fiction is full of death. It drives the plot, colours the mood, and heightens the climaxes of his novels and tales. Among the cast of James's characters are suicidal artists, murderous lovers, adventurous heiresses, romantic consumptives, fallen soldiers, intrusive biographers, and faithful keepers of the flame. Death comes violently by poison, drowning, gunshot, fall, and execution, peacefully at home, or as a gothic spectacle. James gives us some of the most famous hauntings in literature, and by the end of his long career has explored again and again the relationships between the living and the dead. Jamesian death is varied and complex. It is not a passenger, contributing nothing of interest to his novels and tales – how could it be, as if separate from everything else that makes James one of the most critically contested of writers? Death informs James's narrative structures and strategies, his characteristic subjects and styles, and thereby invites the full range of critical approaches that have made James studies such a rich field.

No book-length academic study has been devoted to death in James's fiction. Instead, death has been scattered across other categories, the most developed of which is the ghostly.[1] The Jamesian ghostly avoids generic trappings, such as overtly supernatural manifestations, in favour of carefully controlled uncertainty and suggestive blurring of conceptual borders. With its characteristic use of unspecificity and absent centres, James's late style is especially uncanny. His novels and tales derive a haunted quality from being written from the point of view of outsiders, such as children, servants, sensitive bachelors, and Americans adrift in Europe. Many of his characters are haunted by the lives they fail to live, whether through choice, wounds, repression, or missed opportunity. Biographically, James himself seems to have been haunted by the Civil War in which he did not fight and the virile, American self he might have become had he not settled in England. Within literary history he is a marginal figure, glimpsed between two centuries and two national literatures, in none of which is he fully at home. Given the importance of haunting as a theoretical concept[2] and the enduring critical and popular interest in his famous ghost story, 'The Turn of the Screw' (1898), above all of his other works, it is not surprising that haunting has dominated perceptions of death in James.

A second established category of Jamesian death is the sacred: James's fiction uses the language of religion to give value to a secularised world, but without ever stepping over into religious conversion or belief.[3] The 'sacred' is here an umbrella term for sacrifice, renunciation, redemption, consecration, sacrilege, taboo, fetishism, and the cult of the dead. In the absence of religious guarantees of meaning, these elements of a religious framework contribute to the generation of narrative form and substance in James's fiction, so as to create life-values in the face of death and the passing of time. This process becomes more apparent in James's fiction as he ages and experiences bereavement; his novels and tales increasingly defend art and the past from the accelerating changes of modernity. Thus 'The Aspern Papers' (1888) is one of many works that defend the reputation of the writer against the invasive enquiries of a new breed of biographers and journalists, and in his final decade James went some way to preparing for his own posterity by creating the New York Edition (1907–9), burning personal papers, and writing his autobiographies.

A third dominant account of death in James's life and writing centres on his cousin, Minny Temple. She died from consumption in March 1870 while James was on the other side of the Atlantic, on a visit to England. He was about to turn 17 and she was 24. The letters that James wrote to his family in reply to the news, together with the retelling of this event in his autobiography, *Notes of a Son and Brother* over 40 years later, have been used by biographers to claim that Minny's death was a pivotal moment in James's career.[4] Elisabeth Bronfen cites James's letters as an illustration of her thesis that Western culture repeatedly projects the otherness of death into the death of a beautiful woman – from Cordelia to Marilyn Monroe. For James, 'distance allows the departed beloved to become an object entirely at his interpretative disposal and as such the central stake in his self-definition as an artist.'[5] The dead Minny becomes James's muse, inspiring not only some of his most famous heroines but also his whole life as an artist.

Already in this brief account, 'death' has taken on many different meanings. Haunting, the sacred, and the dead muse function as implicit master tropes of Jamesian death – a large territory that is not usually named as such. In this book, I move away from these established figures in order to open up the representation of death in James's fiction as a dynamic, fertile, and lively field for criticism.

The task is not to locate an essential, authentic, *Jamesian death-itself* under a single meta-argument. Death is not a phenomenon within life, capable of being grasped and explained, but rather an experiential void outside life that neither individuals nor culture can ever master. We never experience death itself, since we are always still alive even in the final moments of dying, and no one can write when they are dead. Hence, observes Garrett Stewart, death is a linguistic abstraction and the scene for pure 'rhetorical ingenuity.'[6] Faced by the 'referential vacuum' of death, language develops strategies for appearing to speak from a position of knowledge about it – from beyond the grave. Narrative fiction especially has developed a repertoire of literary devices for managing the 'intransigent abstraction' of death and turning it to fictional account.[7] For example, during the moment of his stroke the elderly James allegedly heard the phrase, 'so here it is come at last – the Distinguished Thing'; the writer reifies death so as to bring it within his power of naming.[8] For Stewart, the work of British novelists from the mid-Victorians to the modernists is particularly fertile in its development of various 'styles of dying.' James's novels and tales can justly be included in this outpouring of thanatographical invention.

The different phases and types of James's output and its embeddedness in changing cultural milieus suggest that Jamesian death will need to be mapped under a series of interrelated figures. Many of these are familiar, but others will be new. We are certainly not dealing with a monolithic theme limited to those novels and tales that represent death as a climactic spectacle grandly intruding into life. Like gender, sexuality, and modernity – concepts that have proved especially fertile for James studies – death is a pervasive register potentially informing every aspect of his writing. The organic quality of his style, in which *ideas* are integrated into a complex fabric of narrative structure, contemporary reference, and urbane style, means that *death* cannot be isolated without a degree of violence towards the characters and the whole textual game. Death can be a discrete motif on the surface of James's fiction, but it also functions at the level of a key signature setting the overall tonality. James's comedies include death so as to enhance the glitter of their style and to imply an anchoring in reality; *The Europeans* (1878), for example, opens with a description of a snowy graveyard and ends with the announcement, in the final sentence, of a death and a marriage. By contrast, the sense of the past becomes a surrounding medium in James's last fictions, so that a tale such as 'Crapy Cornelia' (1911) positively reeks of a lost era. Here the sense of global bereavement renders fatuous any demand for death to appear in spectacular fashion.

Even in works with climactic death-scenes, such as 'Daisy Miller: A Study' (1878), the representation of death is woven throughout all of the narrative's different levels and aspects. Along with 'The Turn of the Screw' and *The Portrait of a Lady* (1881), 'Daisy Miller' is one of James's most canonical works, by which he is often introduced to undergraduate students. A major reason for the accessibility of these three fictions is their prominent use of death. Death, like sex, sells books; the wealth of generic expectations around fictional death provides the author with many ways to surprise and satisfy the reader; and the power to represent death is a key stake in literature's claims to cultural importance and thus provides an exemplary site for critical discussion.

The death of the heroine at the end of 'Daisy Miller' provides the final stage upon which the tale's narrative and stylistic strategies display, in a climactic flourish and sleight of hand, the young author's ambition. This tale was James's first bestseller, giving him a taste of transatlantic stardom at the age of 35 after 14 years in the writing business. The account of Daisy's death is that part of the text where the narrative crucially tightens so as to arrive at closure. The final pages move swiftly: in an epiphanic moment of visual and moral perception amid the quintessentially Romantic scenery of the Coliseum, Winterbourne cuts Daisy socially; within the space of a few sentences, her fever occurs behind closed doors and she is pronounced dead without us seeing her illness or her corpse; at the internment, daisies nod around her grave; the briefest of remarks by his aunt and by Daisy's Italian friend, Giovanelli, seal Winterbourne's lips on the affair forever; and he returns to where he started, at Geneva. Although there is much more to discuss in the tale than Daisy's death, the final pages offer themselves particularly for rereading by virtue of their privileged position; more than any others they might seem to represent, with their account of Daisy's death, the essence of the tale as a whole, its interpretative ambiguity, and stylistic poise. The closing pages project the narrative beyond its literal ending by inviting the reader to imagine the meaning of Daisy's death. It comes as neither a complete surprise nor a foregone conclusion; the narrative has been building up to the death by carefully weaving its possibility in advance into the fabric of plot, characterisation, and tone, so that when the death arrives it can make sense. Numerous small signposts to the possibility of a tragic outcome give expression to a sense of fatality that weighs against the vitality of Daisy's youthful, American personality, which is built up with equally deft touches. Whereas she seems determined to live and yet dies at the end of the story, Winterbourne seems never to become fully alive but almost to have died in spirit before it began. The closing pages present her death as a condensed climax, over with all too quickly, while his moribund and chilly nature diffuses, purposeless and unfocussed, throughout the tale.

What is the justice, lesson, or tragedy, if any, in Daisy's death? What judgement does it pass on Winterbourne, or on James? How might it explain all that has gone before? These *basic* interpretative questions, left without clear answer from the narrator, help to define the pleasures of the ending and to explain the popularity of the tale. The openness of the ending flatters the reader's sense of his or her own fine perceptions in weighing possible interpretations, while the story can also bear complex theorisation and historical contextualisation beyond the brief formal analysis sketched above.

'The Turn of the Screw' is even more bound up with death. As Shoshana Felman explains in what has become a seminal reading of the tale, the narrative is written in response to Miles's death; it describes the return of the dead servants; and it reaches the reader via a double bequest: from the governess to Douglas and then from Douglas to the anonymous narrator. 'It is thus *death* itself which moves the narrative chain forward, which *inaugurates* the manuscript's *displacements* and the process of the *substitution* of the narrators.'[9] Each of the deaths contributes to the legendary ambiguity of the tale. For example, is Miles murdered by the governess, who crushes him to death, or does his heart fail because it was already weak? Is his death the result of a successful exorcism, or does it represent the repression of emerging homosexuality? Or does Miles not die after all, but recover and grow up to become Douglas?[10] This last interpretation is a strictly marginal one, as the mere fact of Miles's death is the point in the text where ambiguity becomes horribly lacking. 'We were alone with the quiet day, and his little heart, dispossessed, had stopped,' reads the final line.[11] Whether the ghosts were real or not, Miles's life has ended as surely as has the text. The stop cannot be undone; it has already happened ('*had* stopped') before these words can be uttered. Even at the very moment when the governess is aware that she and Miles are alone (no Miss Jessel, no Peter Quint), he is no longer there with her to form a 'We.' Simultaneously incontrovertible and radically incomprehensible, a void opens up on the page while we as readers are still moving in response. We are left with the business of interpretation upon our hands as the governess is left with the child's body upon hers.

In Felman's account, death is not *in* 'The Turn of the Screw' discretely, such that there are other discussable aspects of the tale that have nothing to do with death whatsoever; death defines the narrative's origin, distribution, and endpoint and is organically present in the narrative's very fibre and cell. This is more obviously true of 'The Turn of the Screw' than it is of 'Daisy Miller,' which implies that James's fiction is not uniformly deathly. 'The Turn of the Screw' uses framing devices and ambiguity to lure the reader into wallowing in morbid fears that trade off fin-de-siècle interest in the supernatural, revival of romance forms of fiction, and fears of cultural degeneration. These techniques and conditions can be generalised to only some of James's other writing, not to all – most obviously not to his earliest work, including 'Daisy Miller,' which belongs (leaving out of account its revision for the New York Edition) to a very different historical period and authorial phase. In miniature, these two tales nevertheless indicate how representations of death might span James's career. In their current canonical position, they are already models for death's importance in James's fiction and invite the more detailed study that this book undertakes.

How do James's novels and tales represent death? How do they respond to their author's experience of bereavement and awareness of his own mortality? What is peculiarly Jamesian about death in his fiction? How does all this change at different points in his career? How does death in James's writing reflect his position in literary history? These are relatively direct questions that we can expect to have complex answers, reflecting the complexity of James's work and its critical reception.

An enquiry into death in James's fiction is in many ways a rather traditional form of literary study. Death has long been recognised as a major literary theme, indicated for example by the title of Leslie Fiedler's classic study, *Love and Death in the American Novel*.[12] On the other hand, in the last few decades literary death has become intensively theorised and located in cultural history as part of the multi-disciplinary field of death and dying studies.

Death in Henry James draws upon and contributes to this field, but is first and foremost an author study. Its approach is always to start with specific examples of James's fiction and to discover how, if at all, death might be important in their composition, publication, and reception. For critical leverage, it turns to a variety of approaches, more often reflecting the prevailing strands of James studies than of philosophical, sociological, or psychological accounts of death and dying. Seeking to avoid abstracting Jamesian death, the argument embeds it in the complexity of the novels and tales themselves, their historical moment, and the readings they have attracted. The book's main thesis is relatively simple and, I think, uncontroversial: death is consistently central to James's fiction, as it is to the work of many other writers. The bulk of the book consists in demonstrating how the varieties of Jamesian death can be read as complex examples of the literary representation of death. For the most part, the result is a deepening of our understanding of James within existing borders rather than a repositioning of him upon the literary map; hence this book is not to any extent a comparative study. I am certainly not claiming that James has anything special to teach us about the experience of mortality in our own lives.

There are varieties of Jamesian death and these need to be understood in the context of specific texts, figures, and periods. Methodologically, this book is correspondingly varied; chapters tend to illustrate a series of approaches, sometimes quite briefly, rather than argue in detail a single, programmatic approach. However, it is worth stating at the outset that Jamesian death is not endlessly polysemic. For example, at the risk of generalising too broadly, we can say that James's fiction in all its modes and phases is concerned with showing both the reality of death and the blurring of boundaries between death and life.

In James's lifetime as they do today, science and religion defined fundamentally opposed positions on death. Death is an extinction of individual consciousness through irreparable damage to the physical body, or death is a release of the soul from the body to enter a new form of life. As a literary realist, James clearly leans towards the former position, and my sense is that this inclination prevails beneath the variations of particular texts and stages of James's career. James is not a religious novelist, and even in his most romantic, melodramatic, gothic, or ghostly representations of death there are layers of irony that provide implicit criticisms of the idea that death might ever be transcended. Whereas Flaubert's realism in *Madame Bovary* (1856) emphasises the physiological actualities of Emma's death and parades her emotional, mental, and sexual degradation, James's fiction consistently avoids such bodily detail and focusses more exclusively on social and psychological relations. Even so, his novels and tales manoeuvre their characters into conditions determined by social and material realities with which they must come to terms. Again and again, death is one such actuality: a reality felt and ultimately inescapable, however ingeniously represented. In James's fiction this reality of death is often highly mediated, filtered by a self-conscious style and by a point-of-view technique whose primary concerns are to register social, mental, and affective relations rather than the unmediated encounter with death. Such an encounter only rarely breaks through, as when it is deployed as a shock tactic at the end of *The Princess Casamassima* (1886), where the hero's body is discovered lying on a bloody bed. Even here, we will find, the encounter is described as if through half-averted eyes. James's filtering techniques and concerns constitute the dominant mode of his representations of death, but these representations nevertheless consistently work from an assumption of death's actuality and resistance to being imagined away.

Death in James's fiction is not just a single, absolute event at the end of a character's lifetime. It is also a gradual and partial process. 'While "we" nominally go on those parts of us that have been over-darkened become as dead,' writes James in his late essay 'Is There a Life after Death?' (1910). We lose those we love, we deteriorate physically, and so we die 'piecemeal.'[13] This insight becomes acute as James ages, but even in his earliest work there is no clear separation between life and death. Across his career, James's endings often strain to show how characters have experienced an emotional, moral, or social trauma comparable with physical death. At the end of *The American* (1876–7), for example, Claire de Cintré renounces love and the world by incarcerating herself in a Carmelite convent. This institution is repeatedly likened to a tomb, particularly in the episode where Christopher Newman, whose imagination has been primed with gruesome images about the nuns' ascetic lifestyle, listens to their dirge-like chant from behind an iron screen.[14] Other examples in James's fiction are less melodramatic, or shade off into subtle disappointments whose significance as a life-wound, or the creeping approach of death, depends on fine manipulation of the reader's perception and feeling. So long as physical death has not yet arrived, life continues to provide some ground for potential meaning, even if the effort of the narrative, as in *The American*, is directed towards demonstrating conclusively the irreversible limitations on this potential. Claire will never leave the convent for the remainder of her life. She enters a state of suspended animation, or still life; she is not yet finished being alive, yet her 'life' seems to be laid out in the past for evaluation, not for living in the present or future.[15]

'Life' is an horizon that, in general, James's characters never fully reach.[16] Marcher in 'The Beast in the Jungle' (1903) is the extreme example of the Jamesian *man who never lived*, and the pattern is also implied in Strether's famous advice to young Bilham in *The Ambassadors* (1903): ' "Live all you can; it's a mistake not to" '[17] – as if it is possible to be alive and yet not to live. The strict moral codes of late nineteenth-century society define a range of experiences, such as sexual freedoms, that are easy to associate with the 'life' that Strether – and, some would say, James – feels he has missed. (Today we are given a comparable message by product advertising that tells us of the life-styles we should be enjoying.) At the same time, James's writing gives off a sense of the plenum of life in many forms: the delights of the senses, intellect, society, and the arts all provide a ground for meaning and value. A sense of utter void informs fairly few of James's novels and tales, most obviously 'The Beast in the Jungle,' which actively explores how a life might be evacuated of meaning. More often, the idea of total negation – of a pure encounter with non-being or absolute annihilation – is neither confronted directly nor invoked with a high degree of explicitness. Instead, James's novels and tales consistently operate at some remove from a purely existential moment. At most they imply this moment while inhabiting a fictional space that is always already imbued with at least some meaningful relations between self and other, world and time.

If James's fiction is not yet existentialist, can we nevertheless place Jamesian death philosophically? The most influential thinking about death in the modern period has been Continental, from Hegel to Heidegger and from Bataille to Blanchot.[18] For almost the whole of his life James was immersed in and receptive to the intellectual currents of Europe, but he had a prior philosophical allegiance, as it were, through his brother, William, who was a central figure in American pragmatism. More importantly, philosophical ideas filter into James's fiction indirectly rather than drive the narrative programmatically. For example, in *The Princess Casamassima* the hero mentions Schopenhauer – a philosopher famous for his discussion of suicide – but this clue does not provide a significant explanation of the hero's death.[19] James is not a primarily philosophical novelist, any more than he is a religious one, though he can be read philosophically, sometimes to striking effect.[20] As the history of James criticism has already shown, his writing is malleable enough to be read in seemingly endless ways, if not always convincingly. It is tempting to read his twentieth-century fiction as anticipating later philosophical approaches to death, such as the existentialist concern with authenticity and nothingness. However, such an approach is in danger of distorting James's fiction, especially its historical specificity and literary resistance to explicit ideation.

In a letter to H. G. Wells near the end of his life, James famously claimed that it is 'art that *makes* life, makes interest, makes importance' (*L* 4: 770). This remark might be taken as an avowal of faith in a religion of art, capable of defying death, were it not that James's work repeatedly critiques aesthetic attitudes and ideals, such as the convention of the immortal artwork and Romantic myths of the artist as genius. Instead, art '*makes* life' not with absolute autonomy but within a contested ethical and cultural field of conventions and available positions.

My primary focus in this book is on the 'representation' of death – a term that belongs to both communication theory and politics. In order to be understood, James's representations of death need to draw on shared systems of meaning, ranging from the elementary levels of language and grammar up to discursive practices of genre conventions and character types. At the same time, his representations of death assume a power to speak for others and to tell their story. The author is the arbiter of his characters' fates and thereby participates in constructing social identities, such as the figure of the American heiress in Europe. This power is not entirely autonomous, but defined by systems of meaning shared between author and audience. The moral and aesthetic standards according to which James's fictions dispense death are partly created by the fictions themselves, but they can function only in relation to existing conventions and codes – otherwise they would not be understood or have a ground against which to innovate.

How far James's fictions *are* understood and by what audiences, what trade-offs they make between popular comprehension and more idiosyncratic representations of death, are large questions. As 'Daisy Miller' and 'The Turn of the Screw' show, James could use death in such a way as to create a bestseller. In other cases, such as *The Wings of the Dove* (1902), for which James was unable to secure serialisation and which proved a relative commercial failure in book form, the use of death serves to develop a niche readership. Each work invites detailed consideration of the interplay between the politics and poetics of representing death. Who dies in James's novels and tales? How, why, and for what audience? How does the representation of death enable James's fictions to construct their authority? How does death establish, develop, and defend *Henry James* as a literary brand?

The concept of authority here functions as a bridge between nineteenth-century debates around the role of the author within culture, expressed for example in Wordsworth's Preface to *Lyrical Ballads* (1802), and Foucauldian concepts of discourse as knowledge-power, belonging to a much later period and most forcefully applied to James in Mark Seltzer's *Henry James and the Art of Power*.[21] Seltzer sets out to show how 'both the content and the techniques of representation in James's works express a complicity and rigorous continuity with the larger social regimes of mastery and control.' James's fiction basically reinforces dominant ideology, but disguises this expertly: 'the Jamesian aesthetic is elaborated precisely as a way of dissimulating and disavowing the immanence of power in the novel.'[22] Other critics, such as Ross Posnock and John Carlos Rowe, have replied that, while James's novels and tales do perform an enmeshing of power and discourse, they simultaneously enable and require their readers to become conscious about this process. James's writings work hard to reveal the processes of power operating at the levels of inner consciousness, language, and social interaction; they offer a sceptical critique of bourgeois gentility; and James can justly be viewed as both a literary and a cultural critic.[23] I see the representation of death as an ongoing, contributory strand to this simultaneous performance and exposé of power. In this respect I discern three phases across James's career.

First, James's early fiction is written primarily for a New England audience centred on literary periodicals such as the Boston-based *Atlantic Monthly*. The *Atlantic*'s assumption of moral and intellectual pre-eminence at a national level was increasingly challenged after the Civil War by the growth of mass publishing markets that were geographically more diverse and in ethos more populist and commercial than the *Atlantic*. In this period, James's novels and tales use death primarily to construct an author-position of literary realism based on European models, but also asserting American cultural independence from Europe and actively experimenting with a variety of literary forms. Individual fictions, such as *Roderick Hudson* (1875), discussed in Chapters 1 and 2, show death being used not only to take up positions relative to specific topical concerns, such as the Civil War, but also to mark a departure into a distinctively Jamesian agenda, including the experiences of the American leisure class in Europe and the testing of the American artist.

A second phase can be roughly aligned with James's middle period, though this is not simply a matter of a one-way timeline but of relationships between author and publishing context that can recur and revert. *The Portrait of a Lady*, discussed in Chapter 5, is clearly a much more assured and authoritative piece of work than *Roderick Hudson*. Its use of death is constructed in more detail, blurring the boundaries between death and life and taking account more precisely of differentiations and topical concerns within its audiences (most obviously on national and gender lines: a more fully transatlantic audience and a more committed tackling of issues around marriage than in his earlier work). James's fiction in this period continues to arbitrate on death in a largely realist mode, via a narrator more omniscient than in later works such as *The Sacred Fount* (1900) that adopt a focaliser technique programmatically. Death continues to be a primary means to exert ownership of a distinctive James territory and also to extend it, for example to annex the representation of women's consciousness.

Thirdly, by the end of the nineteenth century, journalism and biography become bêtes noires of James's fiction. They become channels through which his novels and tales respond to democratic, mass-market challenges to patrician authority and high culture, relocated from post-bellum America to late Victorian and Edwardian England. Battles are fought in his novels and tales over the reputation of the dead. Sacrifices are made, even unto death, to preserve privacy, refinement, and the past from the assaults of publicity, vulgarisation, and modernity. Death is reconfigured into provisional forms of after-life. The sense of the past haunts characters struggling to come to terms with a desensitised, materialistic present. This does not mean that James's work after 1900 is merely defensive and nostalgic, retrenching into a shell of obscurity. His fiction, non-fiction, and New York Edition all imagine new territorial claims and revel in stylistic innovation even while looking elegiacally backwards.

This third phase, discussed via *The Wings of the Dove* in Chapters 3 and 4, is an obvious place to look for connections between James's representations of death and his responses to modernity. The last decade or so of James studies has seen a move to reread his modernism: no longer is he the aloof Master obsessed with form; now his writing is seen as responding in multiple, nuanced ways to the changes occurring around him in the contemporary scene. The travel writing, autobiography, New York Edition, and tales that follow his visit to America in 1904 have been recognised, in good part as a result of Posnock's study, as a fourth major phase. The roots of James's modernism can also be traced back into at least the 1880s. Indeed, James's earliest work in the 1860s, with its construction of an emerging American form of literary realism and publication in a dynamic and innovative periodicals market, have claim to be included in the arc of James's evolving relation with modernity. My own interest in modernist death in James's fiction focusses on his protracted representation of Milly Theale's demise. *The Wings of the Dove* seemingly avoids contemporary reference but actually registers many aspects of modernity within the subtleties of its style, structure, and characterisation.

One example is the role of the typewriter in its composition. James's switch from longhand manuscript to dictation, starting with 'The Turn of the Screw' in 1898, has long been recognised as a contributory factor in the development of his late style.[24] More recently, the switch has been theorised as a pivotal change to James's scene of writing, marking his response to the mechanisation of discourse production and the role of women as technical-cum-spiritualist mediums of discourse across the cultural landscape around 1900.[25] Usually discussion of such matters latches on to 'In the Cage' (1898), the companion tale to 'The Turn of the Screw,' in which an anonymous telegraphist tries to piece together meaning from the telegrams that she processes. In *The Wings of the Dove* the mechanisation of discourse is not displayed on the surface of the novel. Instead, I will argue that the presence of the typewriter diffuses into its notoriously difficult style and its attenuated representation of the heroine's approaching death.

The typewriter is here a special case of technology, which is in turn an aspect of modernity. The rapid digitisation of Western culture during the last two decades has inspired an emerging body of theory about new media and the relationship between technology and culture, and also a reappraisal of the late nineteenth century as the period in which our contemporary networked society was already foreshadowed. The social and cultural impacts of the Internet, for example, are remarkably similar to those of the telegraph.[26] Technologies such as the typewriter and telegraph do not have a simple deterministic role in bringing about modernity; they are enmeshed in all the other changes – to the human subject, society, cultural forms, and everyday life – that together produce and constitute modernity. And they affect the experience and representation of death. 'The realm of the dead is as extensive as the storage and transmission capabilities of a given culture,' writes Friedrich Kittler, explaining why the invention of photography, telegraphy, telephony, and other media undermined literature's power to represent the dead in the nineteenth century.[27]

Machines do not literally kill in James's novels and tales; instead, everyday technologies such as buses, photographs, and telegrams tend to indicate a vulgarisation of culture and individual consciousness that potentially entails a deadening and dehumanising of unique sensibilities and histories. At the same time, James's encounter with new technologies – including his use of a typewriter and, on a larger scale altogether, his 1904 tour of America – undoubtedly contributed to his burst of creativity after 1900, which is astonishing even if one dislikes his late style. Writing both against and with technology proves a way to stay alive as a creative practitioner. The fiction of James's early career, such as *Roderick Hudson*, assumes an enabling relationship with mid-century technologies of periodical serialisation and naturalised technologies of manuscript; they mediate the representation of death in a relatively transparent fashion and support him in becoming an author. The novels and tales of this period tend to frame death using the artistic technologies of the past, such as painting and sculpture, rather than new, overtly modern technologies such as photographs. By contrast, in James's later fiction, such as *The Wings of the Dove*, the medium of print is thickened by the presence of the typewriter and by anxieties about the changing status of literature in a century set to be dominated by journalism, advertising, and visual media. This thickened medium must also express a relationship to death deepened by bereavement and by questions of literary posterity and personal survival becoming more urgent as James aged.

Even more than modernity, sexuality and gender have become the central preoccupation of James studies during the last decade, and will clearly have a bearing on our understanding of death in James's fiction. How is death gendered in his novels and tales, and what connections can we find between death and sexuality? If Minny Temple's death inspires James's career, then her memory is substantially transformed into a varied cast of dead men, women, and children. In *The Portrait of a Lady*, for example, Isabel Archer is commonly cited as one of Minny's avatars, but it is her cousin, Ralph Touchett, who dies of consumption. In thinking about how death might contribute to James's fictional play with conventions of gender and sexuality, we will need to understand the role of other discourses through which gender and sexuality were constructed during the course of James's career. Thus in James's early Civil War tales soldiers are subtly feminised by dying at home in implicit contrast to tropes of heroic battlefield death, while the death of a reluctant British soldier in 'Owen Wingrave' (1892) can be read in terms of codes for homosexuality that did not develop until the nineties. Daisy Miller dies from malaria after visiting the Coliseum at night, but this cause of death does not in itself make her a feminine subject so much as it signifies the perils of Europe for the American tourist. By contrast, Milly Theale's unspecified ailment is the basis for a sustained exploration of feminine subjectivity and representation, reflecting both nineteenth- and twentieth-century perceptions of women's illness.

We might expect death in James's later fiction to evolve into increasingly 'queer' forms, along with his style and representation of self and other. Even in his earliest novels and tales, his major characters make remarkably few fertile marriages. Death often thwarts the marriage plot so that the characters' sexuality is not put to the test of a consummation. Many of James's protagonists will die as spinsters or bachelors, questioning heterosexual-familial assumptions about a valid life. Some, we suspect, will die as virgins. Others are in love with the dead. In the later fiction, the boundaries between characters seem so fluid that intimate psychic relations between them seem to persist across the boundary of death. 'The Altar of the Dead' and 'The Beast in the Jungle' – among James's most morbid and overtly necrophilic works – both illustrate all of these points.

Roderick Hudson and *The Wings of the Dove*, my two principal texts, allow me to explore connections between death, sexuality, and gender, along with differences of period, theme, and style. The next four chapters consist of sustained readings of death in these two novels, supplemented by discussion of, among others texts, *The Princess Casamassima* and 'Is There a Life after Death?' These chapters explore four distinct, if related, aspects of Jamesian death, as follows.

Chapter 1 argues that the writing of sacrificial death is fundamental to James's emergence as a novelist and continuing construction of his authorial position. Roderick is made a scapegoat in James's break-through novel and his death is then confirmed in its importance to James's retrospective appraisal of his career through the novel's position at the head of the New York Edition.

In Chapter 2, Jamesian corpses become complex figures of desire and transcendence, sometimes spectacular but more often withheld from the narrative gaze so as to create a sense of mystery. James's corpses include dead writers, dead texts (lost novels, worthless papers, and burned letters), and his own body (reproduced in a death mask and then cremated).

Chapter 3 examines how examples of James's later fiction, especially *The Wings of the Dove*, positively explore morbidity beyond its prevailing critical meanings around the fin-de-siècle and into the twentieth century. For some readers, a study devoted to death in James's fiction will sound inherently morbid but, after the queering of James during the last decade, it is surely outdated to desire to keep him clean of associations with an unhealthy interest in mortality.

In Chapter 4, I consider how some of James's twentieth-century fiction reimagines immortality in terms of new communication technologies, quasi-magical notions of consciousness, and publicity culture. Works such as *The Wings of the Dove* transform ideas of death into ideas of afterlife, and this transformation reflects both the rich cultural matrix of the early twentieth century and the strategies of a writer beginning to anticipate the end of his career.

The approach of the final chapter, on *The Portrait of a Lady*, is somewhat different in its style of argument. Locating death in this novel in terms of nineteenth-century statistical and demographic discourse, exemplified by the Victorian census, I end with a discussion of the possibilities for computer-aided analysis of mortality across James's fictional population.

Rather than share out space to a hit-list of obviously deathly works, the book concentrates on developing conceptual frameworks that readers can consider in relation to the many novels and tales that are mentioned only in passing. *Death in Henry James* is an introduction to conceptualising Jamesian death and is far from exhaustive; it offers relatively little in the way of comparative analysis with other writers, for example. Like sexuality, gender, and modernity, death is a pervasive register of James's fiction that invites multiple interpretations and revaluations, and I hope readers will take up some of the loose ends of my argument.

In order to redress the relative neglect of death by James's critics, this book promotes death as a prime mover behind James's creativity. 'Death, we might say, was the spur,' suggests Lyndall Gordon.[28] But what, then, caused death to be so important for James: insecurity about his gender and sexuality, ambition for social recognition? Marxist, feminist, and psychoanalytic criticism each claims to possess fundamental explanations about the origins of culture. A comparable claim can feasibly be advanced in relation to death, though not in a spirit of competition against these other forms of explanation. Writing and reading works of fiction is a way to distract ourselves from our awareness of mortality, and literary fame is a powerful model of longed-for immortality. Death is 'the ultimate condition of cultural creativity as such,' suggests Zygmunt Bauman. 'It makes permanence into a task, into an urgent task, into a paramount task – a fount and a measure of all tasks – and so it makes culture, that huge and never stopping factory of permanence.'[29]

Fuelled by feminist and queer theory, interest in the fin-de-siècle emergence of alternative sexualities, and question marks over James's private life, sexuality has been perhaps the major strand of James studies during the last decade. This focus reflects trends in scholarship and criticism more generally and the widespread changes in sexual attitudes and behaviour since the 1960s. Whether this book will be an isolated study of its subject or the first of many probably depends on whether a similar change occurs, both among academics and in society at large, in relation to the cultures and taboos of death. At this point, all we can say is that death has long been a central concern of literary criticism and theory, and not for nothing. Far from being an old-fashioned theme removed from the cutting edge of James studies, death deserves to be recognised as one of the most powerful and challenging conceptual categories through which to approach the task of reading this canonical author's work.

1
Violence Ashamed: Sacrifice in *Roderick Hudson*

Roderick Hudson makes an example of its eponymous sculptor as a failed artist in order to promote, by contrast, its author as a model of artistic success. By scapegoating Roderick, the novel ingratiates itself with the community of readers of the Boston-based periodical, *Atlantic Monthly*, in which it first appeared, in serial form during 1875. From being a neophyte, James becomes an established author empowered to dispense death. The writing of sacrificial death exemplified by this early novel is not a one-off event, but continues to be central to James's construction of his authorial position across his career.

To select *Roderick Hudson* for detailed attention is to restage James's decision to place the novel as the first volume of the New York Edition, a position that indicates its importance for his own retrospective perception of his career. In scope of conception and quality of execution, *Roderick Hudson* marks a closure of ten years' literary apprenticeship. In his New York Edition Preface, James figures this novel as his emergence into a 'blue southern sea' of literature proper, whereas all of his earlier work, consisting of short stories and non-fiction, had 'but hugged the shore.'[1] This is the judgement of an author who has built a successful career in part on his early hero's grave. *Roderick Hudson* is not solely responsible for James's success, nor the only foundation of his career, but it is clearly a pivotal text by means of which he leaps from being a writer of tales, reviews, and travel sketches to being a novelist worthy of a higher level of critical and popular attention. *Roderick Hudson* is of a different order of success from his first novel, *Watch and Ward*, published in *Atlantic Monthly* four years earlier in 1871. Following F. R. Leavis's praise in *The Great Tradition*, *Roderick Hudson* has consistently been recognised by critics as James's first book-length synthesis of his major themes and first success in the novel form.[2]

What James's Preface and many subsequent critical readings tend to neglect is the extent to which the novel's success hinges on Roderick's death. As we will see, the Preface directs the reader's interpretation away from the *need* for Roderick to die and towards the technical deficiencies with which this character's fall is represented. Similarly, critics typically relegate the fact of Roderick's death beneath questions about the novel's overall moral meaning or value in discussing other agendas, such as gender or transatlantic relations. By contrast, I see Roderick's death as the lynchpin of the novel: the primary matter requiring critical attention because the generative centre of the narrative's various strategies. *Roderick Hudson* is first and foremost a novel *constructing a death*, a death designed to promote its author by positioning him relative to topical issues and to a contemporary literary field. Roderick's death resolves the novel formally, and this fact is not trivial in so far as it seals the novel as an example of aesthetic and commercial success. His death is the raison d'être and destination of the narrative. It provides a platform on which the novel can explore its many other concerns, such as aestheticism and the experience of the American leisure class in Europe. His death is the basis on which this particular novel has come down to us as the breakthrough work of a canonical writer.

I examine Roderick's death on three occasions: the novel's first publication in 1875, its revision for the New York Edition in 1907, and its indirect rewriting in *The Princess Casamassima* in 1886. *Roderick Hudson* is unique among James's works in inspiring something approaching a sequel. The Princess (Christina Light) is not the sole character in James's entire cast to reappear, but she is the only one to play a major role on both occasions. The later novel continues her story, after an interval of several years, and again ends with the death of a budding artist. It does not explicitly acknowledge the earlier work; only the New York Edition Preface to *The Princess Casamassima*, written many years later, admits some connection between the two novels. It suggests that James's unfinished business is with Christina as a virtual person existing in her own right, in an extra-narrative 'limbo.'[3] The Preface severs her from the earlier novel and pointedly declines to consider how her reappearance in James's imagination during the composition of *The Princess Casamassima* connects the two novels and the fate of their heroes. Her reappearance, I will suggest, signals unfinished business of a more fundamental kind, namely with the process of killing off the artist-hero.

Roderick Hudson's success was initially in addressing the audience of *Atlantic Monthly*, and it is therefore to the first book edition that I refer as my base text.[4] The final section of this chapter sets James's novel in the context of this periodical's market position and the cultural values it represents in the decades after the Civil War. *Roderick Hudson* is by no means a merely reactionary work confirming James as an uncritical member of a literary establishment. Rather, it confirms James as a leading exponent of emerging American literary realism, which was in turn part of a bid by *Atlantic Monthly* to retain cultural authority in post-bellum America. Roderick is an ambivalent figure through whom James's novel negotiates a complex landscape of differing sensibilities. One aspect of this landscape is the aftermath of the War, and thus Roderick's death can be read as a critique of Unionist ideals of heroism continuing from some of James's earlier work for *Atlantic Monthly*. It is on a regional and class basis as much as on a national and aesthetic basis that *Roderick Hudson* marks James's graduation into a career as a novelist.

Fait accompli

How important really is Roderick's death to the overall effects of *Roderick Hudson*? Two aspects of the novel suggest only a secondary importance: the restriction of the point of view fairly rigorously to Rowland Mallet and the continuation of the narrative after Roderick's death. James's Preface claims that

> My subject, all blissfully, in face of difficulties, had defined itself – and this in spite of the title of the book – as not directly, in the least, my young sculptor's adventure. This it had been but indirectly, being all the while in essence and in final effect another man's, his friend's and patron's, view and experience of him. (*RHNY* xvi–xvii)

In James's retrospective reading, Roderick's death is in every way secondary to Rowland's consciousness. A cogent account of *Roderick Hudson* along these lines and directly questioning the importance of Roderick's death appears in Richard Poirier's classic study, *The Comic Sense of Henry James*.[5] Poirier argues that *Roderick Hudson* is primarily a contest between comedy and melodrama. The use of Rowland – reasonable, responsible, but also capable of imaginative insight – as a focaliser enables the novel to criticise both the stultifying conventions of society and the egotism of Romantic idealism. In the first half of the novel, Roderick's innocent optimism occasions admiring irony. In the second half, as the injuriousness of his self-absorption becomes grotesquely apparent, the comedy turns to satiric irony. Roderick's death imposes melodrama and, according to Poirier, provides 'nothing to laugh at.'[6] The values behind the earlier comic dimension survive this climactic moment of melodrama, however. They are the values of responsible imagination represented by Rowland, who acknowledges and tries to balance the claims of both morality and art. The final pages allow us to feel the pathos of Roderick's death, but it is a mistake to complain that the novel denies us access to his point of view. Poirier agrees with James's Preface that, ultimately, Roderick's significance consists solely in the drama of consciousness that he stimulates in Rowland. The whole weight of the novel's method, consisting of a performance of responsible imagination, demands that the reader recognise that 'what happens to Rowland in life is more important than Roderick's death.'[7]

Poirier, whose focus is on James's early novels, does not discuss the change made by the New York Edition to the final lines of *Roderick Hudson*. The first book text ends with Rowland declaring that his chief characteristic is not restlessness, as his cousin, Cecilia, suggests, but patience – presumably to win the hand of Roderick's fiancée, Mary. The New York Edition adds the sentence: 'And then he talks to [Cecilia] of Roderick, of whose history she never wearies and whom he never elsewhere names' (*RHNY* 527). This addition undermines Poirier's suggestion that Roderick has finished achieving his purpose as a means to Rowland's drama of consciousness. This nuance is implicit within the original version but it now becomes explicit at a key point in the text. Roderick is reinstated, once and for all, as the primary object of attention in the novel, dominating Rowland's subjectivity.

Secondly, Poirier's argument relies on a distinction between comedy and melodrama, but this binary opposition excludes laughter of the ludicrous, grotesque, and perverse. These are tones that Poirier does not hear in the novel, partly because they might appear to belong to a later period of James's career but also because they threaten the boundaries of Rowland's sane and purposeful consciousness.

A third factor that Poirier does not foresee is the way that Rowland has become a key case for studies of James's representations of masculinity. Many of these studies find latent homo-erotic associations in the novel's focus on, and greater realisation of, the male–male relationship than the male–female relationships. From such a perspective, Rowland can seem guilty of precisely the emotional self-ignorance of which Roderick accuses him in their final dialogue on the eve of his death. 'Roderick has rightly condemned Rowland for being out of touch with his passion and refusing to admit it,' suggests Kelly Cannon.[8] The novel is then far more substantially a critique of Rowland than Poirier admits.

Whereas Poirier's humanistic account of the novel as a moral drama declares the relative unimportance of Roderick's death, a contrasting strand of readings questions its endorsement of Rowland's point of view. For example, writing at around the same time as Poirier, Oscar Cargill argues that the novel demonstrates the danger of meddling in other people's lives. Rowland is unable to disentangle himself from the responsibility he incurs by encouraging Roderick's artistic inclinations.[9] Such counter-readings to Poirier's tend not to make Roderick's death the crux of the matter, or even address the death head-on. Hugh Stevens, a more recent critic, does not examine the final chapters of *Roderick Hudson* in any detail in the course of his extended discussion of the masochistic cruelty and violence that characterise the novel's erotic triangles.[10] Any account of the novel is likely to acknowledge to some extent the importance of Roderick's death to the ending, but the particular manner in which the death is represented tends to become secondary to discussions about the larger moral pointed by the novel. Thus Richard Ellmann frames the novel's argument in terms of a critique of aestheticism and concludes that Roderick's death is intended to punish what the young James saw as the failings connected with this movement.[11] He does not discuss Roderick's death in detail; this event is just the final stage of the novel's critique of dilettantism.

Yet Roderick's death is a cornerstone of the narrative, enabling such critical readings to fix the quality of the novel's universe. The insight that Poirier attributes to Rowland depends upon Roderick's dying – that is, putting beyond doubt his failure as an artist and confirming the accuracy of Rowland's judgement. By siding with the reading promoted in James's Preface and foreclosing the potential value of questioning Rowland's relative monopoly over point of view, Poirier effectively constructs an authoritarian version of the novel in which the meaning of Roderick's death is policed by Rowland. The novel's denial of access to Roderick's viewpoint and to the moment of his death is an ideological procedure, whose circuit is closed by the death. Poirier is correct to suggest that the novel does not provide easy means to imagine a viable alternative to Rowland's version of Roderick's death. The consistency of point of view is supported by consistency of style; there is no break in the surface of the novel's language and narrative mode. Instead, an 'outside' can be felt as a space, not entirely blank but actively constructed by the novel, especially by Roderick's death offstage.

The dialogue between Roderick and Rowland that precedes the death-chapter, as we will see, provides the basis for some degree of ambiguity. But instead of fostering this into a genuine sense of polysemy, the ending cuts off the possibility of alterity derived from this dialogue and renders it futile. Ambiguities in the chapter prior to Roderick's death resolve into a fait accompli: an unquestionable event that cannot be undone and is immediately absorbed into the past. Fit for regret and pathos, the death's chief function is to enable the sense of richly satisfying closure to attach, not to the death itself, but to Rowland's blighted future. The ending, characteristically Jamesian, is finely wrought so that the reader is brought to dwell on an effect of subtle and penetrating insight into its significance for the surviving characters. Roderick's death is thus the decisive manoeuvre in the narrative's endgame, designed to position the reader into a particular range of responses for the sense of closure.

In the turn of the final paragraph, the death seems to become the means to an end. Rowland has brought Roderick's body back from where he found it, up in the mountains. Mary throws herself upon her fiancé's corpse 'with a loud, tremendous cry' (*RH* 511). This sound becomes a *memory* at the start of the next paragraph, where, within the space of a sentence, the time and location shift to America, months if not years later:

> That cry still lives in Rowland's ears. It interposes, persistently, against the reflection that when he sometimes – very rarely – sees

[Mary], she is unreservedly kind to him; against the memory that during the dreary journey back to America, made of course with his assistance, there was a great frankness in her gratitude, a great gratitude in her frankness. Miss Garland lives with Mrs. Hudson, at Northampton, where Rowland visits his cousin Cecilia more frequently than of old. (*RH* 511)

By returning us to Northampton, where the novel began, the final paragraph makes the plot circular. The whole European adventure is sickeningly placed in parenthesis. The reporting of Roderick's death that has occurred in the preceding paragraphs (discussed in detail in Chapter 2) is indecently quick; there is no inquest and no questioning of the death as an accomplished fact. The absence and futility of such questioning – within the realist world of the narrative, Roderick's death cannot be undone – is condensed in the novel's closing lines, which subordinate Roderick's death to Rowland's continued hopes of winning Mary's heart. The New York Edition version, by contrast, returns to remembering the dead. 'And then he talks to her of Roderick, of whose history she never wearies and whom he never elsewhere names.' Rowland's courtship of Mary becomes an excuse to talk about the man who has been the real love of his life, and Rowland's conversations with Cecilia become a private inquest scene from which the reader is excluded. This revision suggests an increased sensitivity by James to the reader's desire to challenge the fait accompli of Roderick's death, together with a reinforced trust in the perverse narrative satisfaction the reader enjoys by not being able to fulfil this desire.

Without death, the failure of Roderick's artistic practice remains unproven. Were he not to have fallen from the cliff, or were the fall not to have proven fatal, there would still be a chance that he could have recuperated and become productive again, however spasmodically. In other words, he dies in order to prove that he has failed as an artist. He fails quantitatively, because he does not continue to produce. Yet the novel also implies a qualitative standard, by which Roderick's handful of large, idealised sculptures are superior to the feminine flower-paintings, diminutive watercolours, and cynical sculptures churned out by the other artists in the novel. During the course of his life, Roderick produces what we gather are at least a handful of sculptures, such as his Adam, worthy of serious critical consideration. Even one such sculpture potentially makes him an example of the varieties of artistic success. In order for his downfall to count as a cautionary tale at all, the narrative must imply that Roderick has really begun to be a significant artist. Thus the Preface observes: 'The very claim of the fable is naturally that he *is* special, that his great gift makes and keeps him highly exceptional' (*RHNY* iv). At the same time, the New York Edition plants more sense of doubt in the reader's mind over the worthiness of the Adam to be judged a serious effort rather than a youthful fluke. The two versions are:

> [I]t partook, really, of the miraculous. He never surpassed it afterwards, and a good judge here and there has been known to pronounce it the finest piece of sculpture of our modern era. (*RH* 234)

> [I]t partook really, in the case of this particular figure, of the miraculous. He was never afterwards to surpass the thing, to which a good judge here and there had been known to attribute a felicity of young inspiration achieved by no other piece of the period. (*RHNY* 103)

The addition of 'in the case of this particular figure' in the New York version strengthens the idea that all of Roderick's other productions can be discounted, without any other exception. 'The thing' suggests that the sculpture grew positively to haunt its maker. The change of tense from 'has been known' to 'had been known' implies that any generous judgements of Roderick's work lie in the past and have now been superseded. The sculpture no longer belongs to 'our modern era.' Perhaps we can hear a faint mocking of the patronising position from which 'felicity of young inspiration' is spoken, as if the narrator is quoting these words from some fusty, out-of-touch connoisseur. Nevertheless, overall there seems to be a greater distance between the narrator and the young Roderick in the New York Edition version.

In both texts, the qualitative superiority of Roderick's work over that of the other artists, Augusta Blanchard, Sam Singleton, and Gloriani, is not assured; through the foils of these characters the novel questions the integrity and value of Roderick's work alongside those of his person. Of the three alternative artists, Singleton provides the main contrast to Roderick during the chapters leading up to his death. His name suggests both single- and simple-mindedness. He is assiduous, methodical, cheerful, and prudent. While Roderick is busy sulking, Singleton is busy collecting material during the approach of the storm in which Roderick is to die. He returns to America presumably enabled to practise as a self-supporting artist. The quality of his work has steadily improved, and this improvement will perhaps continue, though there is no suggestion that Singleton will ever achieve greatness. Regardless of how modest Singleton's best will ever be, his example implies that Roderick, with what seems to be much greater talent, could have learnt some of Singleton's virtues and nurtured his talent more responsibly and profitably.

Roderick becomes instead a case in point of the failure of 'the continuity of an artist's endeavour' (*RHNY* vi) that James's inaugural New York Edition Preface presents as a major triumph of his own artistic practice. *He* has survived to revise *Roderick Hudson* and the other works of the collection and does so with an authority earned by the sustained, cumulative quality of his practice, so that the Preface seems to say, *look at Roderick, who so fails, and understand why I am so great.*

But what kind of moral does the story of Roderick's burn-out tell without the clinching proof of his death? The Preface tries to forestall some such objection by its remarks on the inadequacy of the novel's time-scheme, a mistake 'not in the least of conception, but of composition and expression' (*RHNY* xiv). This remark implies that, if the novel had been better executed, we would be in no doubt that Roderick's artistic practice is unviable and that his actual death is merely the inevitable physical expression of the irreversible collapse of his artistic will. That James did not attempt to fix the time-scheme in the course of revision suggests that, on the contrary, the problems may perhaps be more deep-seated than he allows. James's editorial policy in the New York Edition revisions, demonstrated for the first time in revising *Roderick Hudson*, is not to alter the plot, for example by introducing or removing characters. But surely this policy was not simply preconceived and then *applied* to the deficiencies of *Roderick Hudson*. At least as likely is that James's perceptions of the novel's deficiencies at the outset of producing the New York Edition in part *created* the policy. The project of the New York Edition needs Roderick to die again – to be made an example of, an example of how *not* to be an artist – but this motive disappears into a limitation of editorial intervention that seems perfectly rational on other grounds.[12]

'Really, universally, relations stop nowhere,' famously observes the Preface, and it is the artist's task to make some 'visibly-appointed stopping-place' *seem* realistic (*RHNY* viii–ix). To do so requires 'a difficult, dire process of selection and comparison, of surrender and sacrifice. The very meaning of expertness is acquired courage to brace one's self for the cruel crisis from the moment one sees it grimly loom' (*RHNY* ix). This is a strange definition of expertise, to say the least. One would think from this formulation that the author suffers more than his creation and that the 'crisis' is somehow not of his own making – that James's own 'sacrifice' and 'stopping' are more terrible than Roderick's, whose body is made by James's pen to crash to a shattering halt.

Even if we agree that, in order to count as an artistic success, Roderick should have learnt from Singleton and continued to produce, the despair into which he sinks prior to his death might yet have yielded to productivity. Who should say whether the melodramatic misadventures and despair of his youth might not, in hindsight, turn out to be the right course for his personal development as an artist? The unsustainability and failure of Roderick's artistic practice is finally provable only by his extinction. Instead, Roderick's death becomes retrospectively destined. Conventional signposts throughout the novel point to this outcome. One strand of these is Roderick's Romantic talk of a desire for death, for example at Lake Como upon the departure from too-beautiful Italy: ' "Dead, dead; dead and buried! Buried in an open grave, where you lie staring up at the sailing clouds, smelling the waving flowers, and hearing all nature live and grow above you!" ' (*RH* 470). Such comments can hardly be missed, though we cannot take them totally seriously in so far as Roderick is not imagining himself as truly dead. Such signposts are confirmed as accurate only once the ending seals, rather than pulls surprises on, the expectations that the signposts create. Indeed, the rhetorical exaggeration that characterises many of Roderick's speeches is inherently unreliable as evidence of his decline. For how can his melodramatic *simulations* of despair constitute proof of irreversible collapse, rather than of ongoing psychic struggle and experimentation from which he might yet recover?

The final conversation between Roderick and Rowland, which seems to trigger Roderick's suicidal mood and fatal, solitary walk into the mountains, includes ambiguous suggestions that Roderick might yet have a grip on life and on artistic practice. Following his death, these hints merely feed feelings of pathos – of what he might have done had he only lived – instead of consolidating into a serious consideration of the possibility that Roderick need not have died. The paragraphs following his death bribe the reader out of recriminations against the gratuity of the death with expertly controlled release of subtly modified, conventional pleasures of the sense of ending.

Accident, suicide, and murder

Relatively few characters in James's fiction unarguably commit suicide, are murdered, or die in a violent accident. This does not mean that the sense of violence – verbal, psychological, and moral – is not felt widely in James's fiction. The representation of Milly Theale's death in *The Wings of the Dove*, for example, contains a profound sense of her violation by her various experiences in Europe.

Legal processes intrude into very few of James's overtly violent deaths; usually no shadow of legal investigation or accountability even flickers across the narrative. Two atypical examples are 'A Round of Visits' (1910) and *The Princess Casamassima*: a man commits suicide rather than face the police, who arrive at his door to arrest him over financial fraud; the hero's mother is incarcerated for stabbing her husband. Both cases associate legal prosecution with shameful scandal. In *The Other House* (1897), the family doctor seems to be acting with integrity when he colludes in hushing up the murder of a child,[13] so that the death can be passed off as an accident; the murderess will be punished well enough by losing the man she loves. As in Newman's attempts to incriminate the Bellegardes among their social peers in *The American*, James's fictions tend to represent punishment as psychic and interpersonal, rather than institutional and social: the law is internalised rather than imposed externally.

To ask whether Roderick's death is an accident, a suicide, or a murder, or what combination of these, invokes these terms on a different level than the purely legal: a level familiarly known as poetic justice. As we will see, such verdicts, constructed between text and reader, depend on genre conventions and topical issues.

As a brief respite from recognising his own and Roderick's responsibility, Rowland imagines how his friend had been caught out by the storm, tried to descend, and slipped. To understand Roderick's death as purely accidental, however, evacuates meaning from his life; his death becomes the outrageous insult of a godless universe. Such a nihilistic vision is out of keeping with the tone of the novel and no match for the fictional convention of comeuppance. Accidents are not really accidents at all, but poetic justice demonstrating purpose in death. As the introduction to one popular paperback edition of *Roderick Hudson* puts it, 'we know it was no accident. [...] The reader's traditional expectations are satisfied, for a character cannot be allowed to act like Roderick without getting his just deserts.'[14] No belief in a divine power is needed to make this convention work; expectations of just desserts can be satisfied *as if* a divine agency still existed, such as in the person of the author.

In 1875, the 'traditional expectations' whereby an author dispenses punishments and rewards at the end of a novel were still under construction. The idea of 'just desserts' is not ahistorical, but reflects interactions between fiction, law, and religious faith during the novel's maturation in the nineteenth century. James dropped out of law school and can be seen as an example of those nineteenth-century novelists who, for Kieran Dolin, were interested in individual psychology and moral development but were 'largely unsympathetic to law, to its enforcement of public standards, its empiricism, its rationality and categorization.'[15] Influenced by the law but keeping a distance from it, fiction such as James's explores the complex interaction between ideas about justice, morality, individual psychology, and social control. *Roderick Hudson* does not foreground the law as a way of evaluating Roderick's death. For example, the climactic interview between him and Rowland can be read as a kind of trial, but this reading is not strongly encouraged by the text. To seek a verdict on Roderick's death is to read against the grain of the novel, which seeks to complicate our responses so that there appears to be no simple, legalistic way to judge the characters or the reasons for Roderick's death.

However desperate Roderick may appear on leaving Rowland, his intention to kill himself is not absolute; to suppose that he commits suicide as a wholly autonomous act implies a greater degree of conscious self-determination than he has previously shown. Rather, suicide would be a continuation of his Romantic egotism and heroic idealism. Suicide is clearly implied in the text by suggestions of Roderick's self-disgust and despair at the end of his final interview

with Rowland. His total failure as an artist seems to have been conclusively proved. ' "Certainly, I can shut up shop now," ' announces
Roderick (*RH* 502). He also declares a revenge motive for killing himself
when he observes that, following his death, Mary would idolise his
memory rather than start loving Rowland (*RH* 501).

Yet ambiguities in the climactic interview suggest that perhaps
Roderick does not leave it merely ready for suicide. When he says
that Rowland has given him ' "something to think of" ' (*RH* 502)
could not this be a creative idea for a sculpture? In the New York Edition
this possibility is accentuated: ' "You've given me an idea, and I now-
adays have so few that I'm taking this one with me. I don't quite
know what I can do with it, but perhaps I shall find out" ' (*RHNY*
512). The second sentence here could be read as another deluded
statement; Roderick is too far gone to turn *any* idea to good account,
and when he recognises this later he will only be pushed even nearer
to the edge. But this is to impose the retrospective judgement, rather
than allow the possibility that he did find something and was therefore
cut down even more cruelly by an accident. Also, why does not
Roderick simply take the money from Rowland and run to Interlaken?
His instinctive, mistrustful refusal is one of the most convincing
aspects of the conversation: ' "I have never yet thought twice of
accepting a favor of you," he said at last; "but this one sticks in my
throat" ' (*RH* 495). This moment of doubt could be a sign of genuine
moral awakening, rather than the prelude to an inevitable final
collapse. When Rowland names Mary as the object of his love, Roderick
replies ' "Heaven forgive us!" ' (*RH* 500). The next sentence is 'Rowland
observed the "us," ' but no further interpretation is offered for the
implications of the pronoun. This reticence potentially implies
Rowland's generous restraint in not immediately assuming the worst
of Roderick's inability to take responsibility for himself. But it also
suggests some room for uncertainty as to whether Roderick's self-
centredness might be genuinely shifting. Overall, this section of the
exchange conveys Roderick's sudden concentration of moral thought
and contrasts this with Rowland's reductive judgement of Roderick's
behaviour as 'egotism still: aesthetic disgust at the graceless contour of
his conduct, but never a hint of simple sorrow for the pain he had
given' (*RH* 502). Rowland's surrender to impatience anticipates
Winterbourne's similar dismissal of Daisy in the Coliseum; both
prove to have fatal consequences.

The text does not make it easy for us to read this scene as one of genuine moral awakening, however. It is reported through Rowland's eyes and, as I read it, ultimately rather reinforces than overturns his credibility as a witness. In particular, when Roderick suggests that Rowland has no inkling of the extent of Christina's regard for him (Rowland), this suggestion falls short and becomes a cheap shot. Roderick says he has ' "her own word for it" ' (*RH* 497) and claims that Rowland's ignorance on this point demonstrates his general indifference to women and incompetence to judge his friend's sexual needs. ' "There is something monstrous," ' Roderick declares, ' "in a man's pretending to lay down the law to a sort of emotion with which he is quite unacquainted – in his asking a fellow to give up a lovely woman for conscience' sake, when *he* has never had the impulse to strike a blow for one for passion's!" ' (*RH* 497). Rowland dismisses the point, but Kelly Cannon, as mentioned previously, feels that Roderick's comments genuinely have the power to expose Rowland as an incompetent judge. I am less convinced because the preceding chapters, albeit filtered through Rowland's consciousness, have not led us to believe that Christina's desire for Rowland's respect *is* of the sexual nature that Roderick is implying. Roderick has not been privy to those scenes between Rowland and Christina – in the church at Engelberg in the previous chapter and at Rome prior to her marriage in Chapter 20 (*RH* 484–8, 429–34) – in which Rowland is well aware that Christina seeks his good regard. The final dialogue between Roderick and Rowland does not probe this matter, but instead moves on to show that the revelation of Rowland's feelings for Mary catches Roderick unawares in a way that impugns *his* judgement to a worse extent than his friend's. ' "Isn't an artist supposed to be a man of perceptions?" ' Roderick observes (*RH* 502). Though the point of Rowland's lack of perception has not been proven, the moment passes as if resolved in his favour because Roderick's own pretence to superior perceptiveness is so much more undermined.

Roderick is characterised as trapped in varieties of self-dramatising rhetoric, of which the final interview merely provides a climactic example. Nothing has so far broken his Romantic delusion. Even as Rowland's plain speaking seems to break the spell, Roderick describes his awakening in language that suggests the continuation of his delusion and bankruptcy of any other language in which to conceive of his past, present, or future: ' "I am fit only to be alone. I am

damned! [...] There is only one way. I have been hideous!"' (*RH* 502).
Retrospectively these remarks become primary indicators of his suicidal
mood, rather than the last, transitional utterances of the rhetoric
from which Roderick was perhaps actually about to emerge.

The established patterns in the characterisation of both men thus
place limits on positive interpretations of Roderick's ambiguous
change in awareness prior to his death. After the event, the ambiguity
is not taken up again, but rather collapsed into the concentrated
effect of rich suggestiveness constructed in the closing paragraphs.

Despite Roderick's apparent despair and his own intuitions, Rowland
allows himself to be overruled by Roderick's insistence on walking
off alone. After the death, Rowland's sense of guilt is strongly
evoked, but this does not amount to a suggestion that a verdict of
murder is of any relevance. Roderick's death could be murder in so
far as his reckless climb was either incited by Rowland and the
women in his life, or, at a meta-narrative level, engineered by the
author. D. H. Lawrence's *Women in Love* (1916) provides some comparison here, though the two novels are very different in their style,
ideology, and contemporary reference. Gerald, the virile but inflexible
son of a colliery owner, fights with his lover while holidaying in the
Alps, climbs recklessly into the mountains, and freezes to death. 'He
could feel the blow descending, he knew he was murdered.'[16] Here
the event of 'murder' consists of the psychological registration, at a
particular moment, of the destruction of Gerald's will. Both Roderick
and Gerald are tormented by a lover (Christina, Gudrun) and oppressed
by a possibly homo-erotic relationship with a friend (Rowland, Birkin).
Each is also the sacrificial victim of his author's narrative requirements,
which ultimately have an ideological basis. One of Lawrence's targets,
made explicit in the polemic of his novel, is the mechanistic over-
consciousness of modern culture, its deadening effects exemplified
by the ice. James's targets are not polemically advertised; *to what* is
Roderick sacrificed?

Scapegoat

Roderick is to some extent a conventional sacrifice on the altar of
Victorian respectability, as indicated by the comeuppance quality
of his death. More specifically, his death is a carefully constructed
expulsion of an authorial alter-ego, explaining the retrospective

significance of the novel to James as he embarked on the New York Edition. The basic idea that Roderick might be a scapegoat – is made an example of – is a variant of commonplace ideas of the Romantic artist. These are illustrated by Fiedler's discussion of the image of Edgar Allen Poe as an archetypal outsider.

> In the nineteenth century, the alienated artist still functions as a scape-hero [...]. [S]ociety needs him still, demanding of the poet that he enact in his life the rejected values of heedlessness, disorder, and madness – and also that he permit himself to be abused and rejected for enacting them [...] and so free the community from the burden of its repressed longings and its secret guilt.[17]

Such an image of Poe is as much mythic, created by Poe and his critics, as biographically accurate. By contrast, James's status as an outsider does not so easily fit a Romantic myth. For one thing, he is writing several decades later than Poe, in a post-Romantic period. But also, he is less an outsider than someone on the margins. James's fiction offers subtle critiques of social, sexual, and gender norms in often genteel periodicals and, for the most part, is careful to avoid scandal.

Roderick Hudson's relationship with the myth of the Romantic artist as 'scape-hero' is ambiguous and subtly differentiated. If the character of Roderick seems a fairly clear-cut condemnation of exaggerated Romanticism, what is the author's stake in this judgement? The novel appears to side with Rowland and to position its author as a voice of moral sobriety, as we saw in Poirier's account of the novel and Ellmann's reading of the novel as a critique of aestheticism. But counter-readings imply that the author has an investment in Roderick's character, too: identifying with his position as a relative outsider and revealing by stealth the transgressiveness of Rowland's attraction to the young sculptor. *Roderick Hudson* accrues to its author some of the vestigial allure of the Romantic myth by re-enacting it, even while critiquing it so as to foster James's reputation as a literary realist.

René Girard's account of the scapegoat in *Violence and the Sacred* is a key example of how 'sacrifice' has become a highly theorised term.[18] Though religious and sociological in focus, Girard's study makes many points that can also be applied to literature. First, he argues that modern societies pride themselves on having risen above primitive forms of sacrifice. Most obviously, they have evolved powerful legal mechanisms intended to do away with the need for overtly retributive violence. The idea of sacrifice, however, is still important in various ways to modern society. Thus literature frequently uses ideas about sacrifice, both at the level of metaphor and in deep narrative structures. Secondly, sacrifice is a communal act designed to cut short cycles of revenge that would otherwise be never-ending. The sacrificial rite aims to 'achieve a radically new type of violence, truly decisive and self-contained, a form of violence that will put an end once and for all to violence itself.'[19] As a ritual, sacrifice by no means occurs once only in time. It becomes a form of institutionalised, repetitive behaviour, economising on violence by strategic deployment of super-effective interventions. This mechanism carries over to imaginary sacrifices in fiction from the rites that fascinated colonial ethnographers. Thirdly, sacrifice protects society by venting its internal violence on a scapegoat. In order for the sacrifice to be effective, the scapegoat needs to resemble the real target of violence but also to be marginal to society so that there is no fear of reprisal; the scapegoat must be a ' "sacrificeable" victim.'[20] Fourthly, the true basis of sacrifice needs to remain somewhat of a mystery in order for the sacrifice to be effective. A 'degree of misunderstanding' must prevail about the 'displacement upon which the rite is based'; what is needed is a 'fleeting, sidelong glimpse of the process,'[21] otherwise the scapegoating, whether in real life or in fiction, will be ineffectual, no one will be fooled, and the violence will be redirected towards its real object after all.

Interpreted on the basis of these points, *Roderick Hudson* is an example of sacrificial logic surviving beneath the veneer of civilisation. The sacrifice of its hero is not the act of a mere individual author, but of a community of readers and writers. Through fiction, this community scapegoats certain values, identities, and discourses. Roderick's exaggerated Romanticism, aestheticism, personal moral collapse, and (in some readings) dubious American masculinity seem the most obvious ways in which the novel constructs Roderick as a ' "sacrificeable" victim' against topical concerns and marginalises him from a society of more respectable readers. Presumably, whom Roderick most resembles – who would otherwise, according to Girard's theory, be in danger of becoming the target of this society's violence – is some better kind of artist and young American male; someone whose values and actions are superior to Roderick's but still questionable according to norms of masculinity, morality, culture, and nationality that the novel both internalises and partly disputes. Girard proposes that the real target of sacrificial violence must be obscure to the community on behalf of whom the violence is carried out. Perhaps an indication of this is the way that Roderick's body is discovered after the event, so that we do not see the hand pushing him in the back: 'it was as if Violence, having done her work, had stolen away in shame' (*RH* 510). Even when the corpse is discovered, its disfigurements are quickly hidden by sleight of hand (as discussed in Chapter 2).

According to Girard's theory, the sacrificial rite is sanctified by its economically defusing some other violence 'once and for all'; it institutes itself successfully as a repeatable mechanism. If we read *Roderick Hudson* in isolation, Roderick's death seems to be a climactic, highly individuated event, justified according to the narrative's internal logic and thus performing some moral purpose, rather than displaying violence as a gratuitous spectacle. Yet the success of the novel, riding on readers' acceptance of Roderick's death as a literary performance, sets up James more securely in the position of author, authorised to repeat such sacrificial deaths. The 30-year-old author of *Roderick Hudson* was ambitious for popular and critical recognition, and both the sales and peer esteem garnered by the novel constitute authorisations to repeat his brand of fiction and its various ideological manoeuvres. Killing off characters, such as Roderick, is one such manoeuvre.

The Princess Casamassima

To show how James's fiction might restage its sacrifice of Roderick, I now turn to another of James's sacrificial victims. Hyacinth Robinson shoots himself instead of carrying out the political assassination that he had promised to perform. An artisan bookbinder initiated by the eponymous Princess into an appreciation of high culture, Hyacinth is a kind of thwarted artist and thus to some extent a reworking of Roderick's character. *The Princess Casamassima* is rooted in a closely observed London scene, it is one of James's most naturalist novels, and Hyacinth is English, whereas *Roderick Hudson* is set in Rome, it is an early example of James's realism, and Roderick is American. Nevertheless, both characters are provincial types who come from divided families and who have their peak aesthetic experience in Italy. The later novel sees the reappearance of Christina, who is again made partly responsible for the death of a frustrated admirer. Roderick's death is neither mentioned nor suggested in *The Princess Casamassima*, which ends without giving any retrospective insight into Christina's repeatedly fatal touch. It is unclear from reading the two novels whether she in fact even knows about Roderick's death. No intimation peeps out of the later novel that Hyacinth's corpse makes Roderick momentarily present once again – a suggestion that would dizzyingly expose a repeat mechanism operating across James's career.

If *The Princess Casamassima* is a sequel to *Roderick Hudson* in its similarity of sacrificial thinking, this connection operates only within substantial reconfigurations of character relationships and narrative structure. Hyacinth is torn apart by the tension between, on the one side, his love of the fine things of life, represented by his allegedly aristocratic, English father and by his friendship with the Princess, and, on the other, his belief in the cause of the people, represented by his incarcerated, working-class, French mother and his friend, Paul Muniment. These oppositions bear limited resemblances to the distinctions central to *Roderick Hudson*, such as between Roderick's idealism and Rowland's sober patronage of the arts, though both Roderick and Hyacinth can be seen as aesthetes.

Crucially, unlike Roderick, Hyacinth is the main focaliser and thereby receives a much greater investment of the reader's sympathy. The climactic death again occurs offstage; we discover the hero's body without even hearing the bullet being fired. This time we experience a drastic deprivation of a consciousness to follow after the death. Having been with Hyacinth Robinson for most of the book, the point of view switches briefly to the Princess in the dread-filled lead-up to the discovery. At the last moment, the point of view switches again, to a virtual stranger, Schinkel, who represents the largely invisible revolutionary organisation that Hyacinth had joined. The lines from his point of view are more disappointed than horrified; they conclude the novel with a sickening reduction from the heightened, subtle consciousness that the novel has offered throughout its length to a relatively alien mode of perception. While the reader has been dropped hints of doom from early in the novel and the dread expertly mounts during the final chapters, the climax still comes as a blow, combining a rich mix of emotions into the pleasures and shock of ending. The mention on the last page of Hyacinth's landlady 'fetching the milk'[22] particularly stimulates a sense of the pathetic cosiness of the final scene. The cadaver is presented as a peaceful tableau watched over by a lighted candle of hope. Such details encourage the reader's desire to celebrate or sentimentalise Hyacinth's death. After the discovery of the body the novel ends abruptly; unlike *Roderick Hudson* it does not shift to another time and place where the death is already in the past, but instead leaves us at the scene of death where we must put together whatever meaning we can, on the spot.

The humanistic basis of a heroic interpretation of Hyacinth's suicide is stated most directly by Lionel Trilling in *The Liberal Imagination*.[23] Writing in the late forties, when James was being acclaimed as the great American novelist, Trilling argues that *The Princess Casamassima* is a clear-sighted diagnosis of the political and spiritual conditions of modernity. James, the master of moral realism, reveals uncomfortable truths that are neglected by the prevailing American intellectual tradition of liberalism. Hyacinth recognises a fundamental contradiction at the heart of civilisation, namely that social justice and the most glorious peaks of human achievement are mutually incompatible and equally compelling.

> Hyacinth's death, then, is not his way of escaping from irresolution. It is truly a sacrifice, an act of heroism. He is a hero of civilization because he dares do more than civilization does: embodying two ideals at once, he takes upon himself, in full consciousness, the guilt of each. He acknowledges both his parents. By his death he instructs us in the nature of civilized life and by his consciousness he transcends it.[24]

Roderick has never been the recipient of such eulogies. This is partly because, compared with the uncertainty of Roderick's fall, Hyacinth's use of the pistol is indubitably a deliberate act of self-determination. And Hyacinth is clearly a more sympathetic character, more dear to his creator. Even so, Trilling's glorification of Hyacinth's death downplays the extent of the ironic distance between the realist author and his protagonist. In his early, apprentice fiction, such as *Watch and Ward*, James notably fails to control this distance, but this is rarely a weakness of his mature work.

Trilling *rescues* Hyacinth, for his own purposes, from an ending that pointedly fails to endorse unambiguously the value of his suicide.

The light of Hyacinth's candle is hardly a beacon; it is 'so poor' that the Princess initially cannot see anything (*PC* 552). It is all too possible for the reader to interpret Hyacinth's death as an act of 'irresolution' – or, indeed, as meaningless waste and no kind of test of moral realism (a criterion of critical judgement and ideal of readerly activity that now seems particularly outdated, for better or worse). In classical myth, Hyacinthus is a prince beloved by both Zephyr and Apollo. He is killed when the jealous wind-god blows the sun-god's discus at the boy's head, whereupon Apollo turns drops of the boy's blood into the spring flower. Here Hyacinthus is the accidental, feminised victim of a squabble between powers far greater than himself. He is hardly a 'hero of civilization.'

Even though the point of view brings the reader closer to Hyacinth than to Roderick, Hyacinth's death repeats to some degree the scapegoating function of Roderick's. Both characters are marked by frustration and failure, contrasted with their author's implicit achievement and success. While *The Princess Casamassima* was not received to the acclaim that James had hoped, the narrative voice within the novel does not noticeably anticipate this disappointing reception, but despatches Hyacinth with relative confidence. If James identifies to a large extent with Hyacinth, then his character still does the dying for him. *The Princess Casamassima* is a long novel, and the end of its speech is correspondingly shocking. The shock is not just the deprivation for the reader of the chance to grieve through the absence of any scenes showing the aftermath of Hyacinth's death. It is also the withdrawal of all that the narrator possesses and that Hyacinth – the little bookbinder who never sees his own words in print – has been aspiring towards but not achieved. Compared with Roderick, the character of Hyacinth is certainly a more sophisticated construction of a ' "sacrificeable" victim.' James's narrative voice, 11 years on from *Roderick Hudson*, is both more urbane and more capable of suggesting sensitivity. The greater technical mastery of the later novel evokes death more powerfully but also constitutes a power more detached from what it represents. For example, when Rowland hunches over Roderick's body the implied howl of anguish, the silent scream, is both less subtly constructed and less alienated than the Princess's relation to Hyacinth's corpse. The class differences between her and Hyacinth are greater than between Rowland and Roderick; they are of different nationalities; Hyacinth has not occupied her life to the extent that Roderick has Rowland's; nor have the tensions between them been so suggestive of emerging forms of transgressive sexuality. Hyacinth has died intensely alone in a pitiful rented room, and to attempt to repair this, 'a convulsive movement of the Princess, bending over the body while a strange low cry came from her lips, covered it up' (*PC* 552). This movement recalls Mary's on receiving the body of her fiancé. As soon as the Princess hears the landlady enter the room, however – seemingly only a few moments later – she recoils from the body as if exposed in a fraudulent act of private contrition. By contrast, Roderick dies in a sublime confrontation with the grandeur of nature, Rowland is left alone with the body for seven hours, and this time does not feel too long for him to make what peace he can with himself.

Chapter 2 will have more to say about this comparison in its discussion of James's representation of corpses. One of the difficulties of reading *The Princess Casamassima* as a sequel to *Roderick Hudson* is the very different biographical and publishing contexts in which each novel was written. As Girard points out, scapegoating is a communal action, and thus the construction of a ' "sacrificeable" victim,' such as Hyacinth or Roderick, draws on specific topical concerns and on the values of particular audiences as much as on core myths of Western culture such as Christian sacrifice. For the original publication of *Roderick Hudson*, the primary audience was that of *Atlantic Monthly* – its readers, owners, editors, and contributors. What figures of sacrificeability most defined this audience in 1875?

War artist

When *Roderick Hudson* first appeared, the American Civil War was fresh enough in individual and cultural memory to be a major source of discourses of violence, death, heroism, and sacrifice. Such discourses took particular form among the community of readers and writers centred on Boston's *Atlantic Monthly*. This periodical was forthrightly antislavery, to a large extent a mouthpiece of New England's patrician class, and a champion of emerging American literary realism. These core characteristics generated a rich and sometimes contrasting mixture of discursive expressions. During the War, the deaths of Union soldiers are frequently represented in its pages as heroic martyrdoms, most famously in Julia Ward Howe's 'Battle Hymn of the Republic' (1862).[25]

By contrast, James's first story in *Atlantic Monthly*, 'The Story of a Year' (1865), shows a Union soldier dying far from gloriously: at home, from his wounds, and betrayed by his mother and fiancée. Two further stories, 'Poor Richard' and 'A Most Extraordinary Case' (1867), develop this aspect of James's early trademark as an emerging realist writer in the *Atlantic. Roderick Hudson* is not directly a critique of Unionist ideals of heroism as these stories are, since it is a narrative about the aftermath of the War written a decade after the cessation of hostilities. Roderick's death nevertheless takes up the threads of James's earlier critique of Unionist heroism among the targets of the novel's realism, which is more mature, sustained, and far-reaching than that of the early stories.

Atlantic Monthly was the primary publisher of James's fiction during his first decade as a writer. Between 1864 and 1874, half of James's published tales plus his debut novel, *Watch and Ward*, first appeared in its pages. For most of this period James was himself resident in the Boston region. From the late 1860s he developed a close friendship with William Dean Howells, soon to become editor of the *Atlantic*. This periodical[26] was an obvious forum in which a budding, Boston-based writer, coming from a relatively patrician background and ambitious to capitalise on his familiarity with European culture, would aim to get published after the War. Founded in 1857 as an upmarket journal dedicated to literature and current affairs, it entered a market of numerous weeklies and monthlies. These included the illustrated, New York-based *Harper's Monthly Magazine*, which had established itself during the early 1850s as the pre-eminent provider of popular literature, based on serialisations of British fiction such as novels by Dickens and Eliot. By contrast, *Atlantic Monthly* set out to voice New England's role as the cultural conscience of America: as self-appointed guardian with a mission to provide moral, intellectual, and cultural guidance. With its policy of fostering native writers, it was instrumental in shaping American literary culture, though in practice this was focussed on New England and was highly respectful of European culture. In its pages some of America's most prestigious and upcoming writers, including Ralph Waldo Emerson, Harriet Beecher Stowe, James Russell Lowell, Louise May Alcott, and Henry James, challenged the dominance of *Harper's* British writers. By 1875, when *Roderick Hudson* appeared, *Atlantic Monthly* also faced competition from *Scribner's Monthly. Scribner's* offered a combination of eminent and popular fiction from both America and England, was comparable to the *Atlantic* in moral tone, but struck a more popular note than its rival through the use of illustrations. Rather than turn to illustration, Howells continued the policy begun by his predecessor, James T. Fields, of fostering a new generation of young, native, realist writers in the hope that they would support the *Atlantic's* continuing claim to be the nation's foremost literary magazine. *Roderick Hudson* was a stake in this process, since James was recognised as one of these young, American realists. At the same time, the specific literary reputation of *Atlantic Monthly* – as opposed to that of *Scribner's* or *Harper's* – was likewise valuable for James's own campaign to be recognised as an emerging author of national importance.

Howells was himself to become the foremost practitioner and theorist of American literary realism by the 1880s, when James settled in Europe. In 1875, however, while American realism had become a characteristic flavour of many of the fictional contributions to *Atlantic Monthly*, this realism's aesthetic and intellectual credibility did not yet translate into any systematic overhaul of the periodical's prevailing values and beliefs. Since its founding, *Atlantic Monthly* had been enmeshed at the heart of a regional network of cultural power and production, comprising institutions, relationships, and practices that endured as much as they evolved. As a stroll around Boston and Cambridge makes clear, a host of movers and shakers lived within walking distance of each other and were connected in a social–cultural–geographical nexus. For example, *Atlantic Monthly* had a longstanding relationship with Harvard University; most of the periodical's founders, editors, and contributors were either alumni or professors. After the Civil War, the University made sure to celebrate its dead heroes as moral exemplars for the region. The year 1867 saw the publication in two volumes of the *Harvard Memorial Biographies*, a celebration of those noble few lost by Harvard in the War. The biographies were edited by Thomas Wentworth Higginson, Harvard alumnus, contributor to and sometime editor of *Atlantic Monthly*, and ex-colonel of the 54th Massachusetts regiment.[27] Memorial Day was a key event in the University calendar, and in 1878 the Memorial Hall was completed, containing marble tablets to the University's War heroes. Unionist heroism was thus maintained as a thriving discourse by one of the most powerful institutions in the region, with whom *Atlantic Monthly* had intimate links (though the periodical was by no means simply a mouth-piece of the University).

Discourses about the Civil War evolved and returned to topicality across James's lifetime. The War formed a backdrop to national discussions about culture and politics throughout America's gilded age and imperial expansion under Roosevelt. By the early years of the twentieth century, veterans had become leaders, fathers, grandfathers, and pensioners. Some of them had experienced the War as the high point of their lives and as a revelation of life-purpose; now they worried about what would become of the next generation, who had no Civil War to give them such a pre-eminent rite of passage. On the one side there were anxieties that American masculinity would degenerate into effeminacy and hedonism; on the other, that latent aggression would find unworthy channels, such as the starting of unnecessary wars. Thus Oliver Wendell Holmes Jr's address, 'The Soldier's Faith,' delivered to students on Harvard University's annual Memorial Day in 1895, champions blind military obedience as the way to bring out the best in American youth, whereas in 'The Moral Equivalent of War' (1910) James's brother William (a Harvard professor) argued for military service on pacifist grounds.[28] Henry James's fiction and non-fiction occasionally contributes to such debates fairly directly, for example in 'Owen Wingrave,' passages in *The American Scene* (1907), and large sections of *Notes of a Son and Brother*. We can also detect the influence of the War in many other examples of James's fiction, in so far as the War was fundamental to James's development as a writer. It was *the* formative historic experience of his life, as it was for many of his peers. As Eric Haralson suggests, the War was 'woven into [James's] fiber.'[29]

How, then, does *Roderick Hudson* represent the aftermath of the Civil War with readers of *Atlantic Monthly* in mind? How is Roderick constructed as a ' "sacrificeable" victim' against Unionist models of heroic sacrifice, such as those celebrated and maintained by Harvard's memorial programme?

In the expository opening chapters of the novel, Roderick's father is characterised as a Virginian drunk who leaves his wife to settle his debts (*RH* 184). This is a stereotypical characterisation of the debauched Southerner, to which Roderick largely succumbs: he drinks, womanises, and during his final conversation with Rowland he reverts to 'his fine old Virginian pomposity' (*RHNY* 504).[30] Mrs Hudson comes from a Massachusetts family of judges and barristers, but, catalysed by Rowland, Roderick gives up his legal career. His elder brother chooses to fight for the Union and dies in battle, leaving Roderick, as the only surviving child, to labour under the comparison. ' "My brother, if he had lived, would have made fifty thousand dollars and put gas and water into the house. My mother, brooding night and day on her bereavement, has come to fix her ideal in offices of that sort. Judged by that standard I'm nowhere!" ' (*RH* 194). Rowland finds two sculptures of the brother in Roderick's Northampton studio: one a portrait, the other 'a small modeled design for a sepulchral monument' (*RH* 190). The War is therefore central to the delineation of Roderick's character in the early stages of the novel. A conventional interpretation of such an exposition might be that it defines the development and crises that the character must undergo thereafter. A basic understanding of the novel would then read the beginning into the ending and conclude that Roderick's death is indeed the final outcome of the aftermath of the War on the Hudson family.

The novel is set contemporaneously with its publication, so that its 1875 readers would be in a position to identify with the novel's playing out of the pastness of the War and of the War's continuing capacity to haunt the characters. The War had not become a taboo subject for *Atlantic Monthly*, but had receded into a repertoire of historic settings and backgrounds, while other issues, such as America's relationship with Europe and the state of American literature, had become of greater interest. So the serial that immediately preceded *Roderick Hudson*, Howells's *A Foregone Conclusion*, concerns Americans in Venice in the year 1861, and James's review of the novel shows no interest in the War-time significance of this date.[31]

References to the War in the first two instalments of *Roderick Hudson* might sensitise contemporary readers by stimulating memories, or be read conventionally as mere historic colour. A determined reading will find Roderick's War-riven family background, not just as part of the initial impetus of the novel, but also as a sustained under-note throughout: woven into its fibre, as it were. The civil strife is internalised in Roderick's fraught relationships. The practice and ideal of sculpture, Mary and Christina, America and Europe – each of these oppositions transforms the North/South and parental division, as well as evoking that between realism and romance. Roderick's incapacity to resolve these divisions escalates and culminates in his death.

The novel is circular, in that the final paragraph returns the characters to America, but the ending does not explicitly remind the reader of the War as the root cause of Roderick's death. Like James's other novels, *Roderick Hudson* is not primarily concerned with historicising the contemporary scene according to specific chains of cause and effect. Instead, the sense of the past – of personal history and the history of civilisations – forms a complex ground of possibility for insight and action in the present. If Roderick goes to Europe to find death in the form of the weight of that continent's history, he also brings death with him in the form of America's more recent crisis. Thus we can read the bereaved trio of Rowland, Mary, and Mrs Hudson as figures resonating with the War through a series of final tableaux. Roderick's corpse is borne in state from the field, as was his brother's. Rowland's vigil with Roderick's corpse becomes a scene on the body-strewn battlefield. Mrs Hudson is the mother losing not one son to the War but two and numbed by the double assault of grief. Mary is the sweetheart caught up in a romantic fever of fidelity; not just any sweetheart adopting the conventions of nineteenth-century mourning, but specifically a War-sweetheart dignified by being deprived with the especial injustice of the War. (On the eve of his sailing for Europe, Roderick had become engaged to Mary in the garden at dusk like a soldier about to depart for war – indeed, as occurs at the start of James's first Civil War tale, 'The Story of a Year.'[32])

The tableaux that Rowland enacts are more diverse. The opening chapters of the novel tell us that, after an unduly disciplined childhood and an unpleasant dispute over his father's will, Rowland

> submitted without reserve to the great national discipline which began in 1861. When the Civil War broke out he immediately obtained a commission, and did his duty for three long years as a citizen soldier. His duty was obscure, but he never lost a certain private satisfaction in remembering that on two or three occasions it had been performed with something of an ideal perfection. (*RH* 176)

Rowland's readiness to enlist dispels any spectre of conscription. The emphasis on duty and the implication of modest tests of courage enable Rowland to escape without dishonour while avoiding heroism. He survives the War without significant personal cost; it occupies only these brief sentences in the four-page exposition of his early years. The tone of the last sentence in particular ('...something of an ideal perfection') is carefully poised on the verge of satire. Rowland survives to enjoy the benefits of battles in which so many others have died: battles fought financially by his father, emotionally by his mother, militarily by his fellow soldiers, and artistically by Roderick. His comfort is disturbed by visions of the real human cost to his mother, to Mrs Hudson, to Mary, and to Roderick. A variety of unresolved and conflicting War-survivor roles emerge for him. He is a deprived sweetheart, like Mary, yet this role is impossible within heterosexual norms. He is her demobbed suitor, but his suit is apparently futile. A stoic father figure, he has none of Mrs Hudson's parental rights. A passionate comrade-in-arms, he has mostly been excluded from the scene of Roderick's battles. And as a commanding officer he can offer no account of Roderick's honourable death in the field.

Noticeably absent from this reading of the War-tableaux of the ending is Christina. This does not mean that her character undermines a reading of *Roderick Hudson* as a War story. The opposition between her and Mary recalls and transforms the Unionist/Confederate divide. Christina's removal from the ending, whose climax she precipitates, indicates the disappearance of the Southern side of Roderick – licentiousness, drunkenness, pomposity, and so on; and of his European side, too, in so far as Mary claims his memory for the Northern side and for America, as she claims his body when it is brought down from the mountain. Christina's return in *The Princess Casamassima* suggests that her exit from the earlier novel is indeed too hasty; there is unfinished business between her character and Roderick's corpse.

As the comparison with his brother makes clear, Roderick is no soldier, but a poor imitation who can never hope to live up to an example held sacred in the memory of his mother and country. His brother will be remembered for his heroism and not for his faults, which he did not live to show, unlike Roderick. Roderick's initial drive and subsequent despair suggest that he is still trying to compete with his brother. This is a competition that he can never win, for how can the life or death of an artist ever be as heroic as the sacrifices made by those who fell in the War in the name of a just cause? Ideals of Unionist heroism trump in advance the myth of the artist as scape-hero.

To become an artist such as James becomes by the time he revises the novel for the New York Edition, Roderick should have internalised the sacrifice of his life to art and gone on living, rather than melo-dramatise his plight and end his life with a pseudo-sacrifice bound to fall short of his brother's death. Yet Roderick's body is borne down from the mountain on a 'rude bier' (*RH* 511) by a team of men, as if in honour from the battlefield. The Romantic myth of the artist who sacrifices his life to art has enough currency to reprieve Roderick's suicide from utter egotism, inadequacy, and folly. He is an American, after all; if there has been no nobility in his struggle, no element of genuine sacrifice in his life, then how can he have been an American, or someone worthy of our and Rowland's attention? The War is long over, and there is perhaps a grotesque tragedy in Roderick's being reclaimed by his fiancée and mother, who have never understood his artistic adventure. They will belatedly transform his memory into a sacred icon of heroism, almost fit to rest alongside his brother and compatriots.

Will Roderick actually be buried next to his brother, though? There is no mention of the final disposal of his body in the last paragraph of the novel. Repatriation of the corpse would technically have been possible at this period, through the use of embalming, an air-tight metal coffin, or by packing the body in a cask of alcohol. These were methods to which bereaved families resorted during the Civil War for the distressing business of having their loved ones transported back home from remote battlegrounds.[33] Though the text does not spell it out, some such choice presumably faced the Hudson family in the case of Roderick's brother, who was 'brought home from Vicksburg' (*RH* 194), a Mississippi town where lie 17,000 Union soldiers in a military cemetery. The Swiss Alps are even further from Massachusetts, but Mary and Mrs Hudson do have the body to hand, and Rowland to help them, should they insist on burying Roderick in his native soil. Alternatively, they could bury him in a Protestant cemetery in Switzerland, as Daisy Miller is buried in Rome; this would be the simplest solution, provided that Mary and Mrs Hudson are prepared to leave Roderick behind in a grave that they might never revisit. If they were to leave him in Europe, would this be a rejection or an acknowledgement of his artistic vocation? If they brought him back to America, would they do so in order to honour him as his brother was surely honoured during the great national crisis ten years earlier, or out of some meaner motive? We can only speculate about such matters, based on our understanding of the characters. Yet these are not trivial questions, since they concern our final evaluation of Roderick's story and the significance of his death in relation to American national narratives and other topical debates, such as around aestheticism.

The text's silence about the disposal of the corpse spares its characters and the reader the undignified spectacle of violated and decomposing body-matter. The ending covers up the dead body so as to preserve some of the mystery of the scapegoating process, as outlined by Girard. As we will see in the next chapter, Roderick's body is not the only one to disappear in James's fiction. The vanishing corpse is a characteristic Jamesian device, central to his larger narrative effects and not at all innocent.

2
Corpses and the Corpus

Readers of James's novels and tales get to see very few corpses and only rarely witness a moment of death. In only a handful of cases is the moment of a character's death directly reported by the narrator. Mrs Marden in 'Sir Edmund Orme' and Morgan Moreen in 'The Pupil' (1891), Ralph Limbert in 'The Next Time' (1895), George Stransom in 'The Altar of the Dead,' and Miles in 'The Turn of the Screw' all fall dead on the spot in the closing lines. The heart suddenly fails. In a few more works, such as *Roderick Hudson* and *The Princess Casamassima*, the narrative gives us a fairly direct view of the principal corpse. But even when the fiction does deliver the shock of an apparently direct encounter with death – the narrative seeming to bend the reader's head to gaze into a character's lifeless face – this moment is constrained. Our access to the spectacle of death is policed by James's characteristically urbane prose style and fairly rigorous control over point of view. In many cases, the narrative elaborately denies us sight of the corpse, or even of a ritually substitute body such as the grave, and instead encourages us to peer through multiple layers of suggestion. This effect climaxes in *The Wings of the Dove*, where the whole text becomes suffused with a death so long anticipated and so pointedly unwitnessed by the reader.

For Ronnie Bailie, James's fiction systematically and unconsciously represses the bodily, and this repression drives James's creativity.[1] Though Bailie's argument is limited to a psychoanalytic reading, his central observation about the general absence of the body from the surface of James's fiction is relatively uncontentious. Hugh Stevens claims that *Roderick Hudson* revolves around the display of Roderick as a male body available for eroticisation and wounding,[2] but surely his body is only visible relative to the invisibility of other characters' bodies and not to the nudeness of his sculptures. The representation of the body in this novel and throughout James's fiction is consistently pushed back from the private bodily real of naked flesh, fluid, and organ to the clothed bodies seen in public space. The intimate, personal body is displaced from direct perception by the narrator to various levels of implied perception; we gather that the characters do move around in a real world like our own, only the materiality of this world is heavily filtered so as not to present too literal and materialistic an account of human experience. Many readers find the filtering excessive, especially in James's later work, where the characters can seem disembodied. Yet physical appearances, whether of facial feature, gesture, or dress, remain crucial in James's novels and tales to the end of his career: such appearances, even if infrequent, are used as signifiers of characters' social position, personal history, and inner life, as subtle expressions of communication and power-dynamics between characters, and to produce a reality effect.

The body and its various processes are also present in James's writing metaphorically. Eve Kosovsky Sedgwick, for example, finds sexualised images of bowel exploration in the New York Edition Prefaces.[3] Less contentiously, James's letters contain numerous explicit reports of James's medical symptoms and, especially later in his life, passionately tactile addresses to young male friends. In comparison with these letters, James's fiction is clearly much more reticent in its representations of bodies, whether living or dead.

Unlike Bailie, however, I do not interpret this absence as necessarily an unconscious gap. One obvious alternative explanation is censorship. In her recent discussion of James's late style and the topicality of divorce scandals in *The Golden Bowl* (1904), Barbara Leckie argues that James's fiction actively uses the boundaries set by censorship to create new meanings and collusions with his readers.[4] While genteel nineteenth-century mores prohibited exhibition of the body, James's novels and tales do not simply obey this law; their author is not a passive victim of censorship or uncritical exponent of dominant ideology. Rather, James's representations of the body, conducted often through characteristic use of unspecificity and lacunae, can be seen as part of a creative, critical rewriting of conventions and meanings.

Certainly the reticence of James's fiction about the physical body is a mark of difference between his brand of literary realism and that of French realists and naturalists. In Flaubert's exemplary realist description of Emma's death from poisoning in *Madame Bovary*, material details are essential to the deliberately brutal stripping away of her humanity: 'the whole of her tongue protruded from her mouth,' 'her eyes were beginning to disappear in a viscous pallor, as if covered by a spiderweb,' 'a rush of black liquid poured from her mouth, as if she were vomiting,' and so on.[5] Responding to the rising status of medical discourse, such heightened physical details of Emma's death-throes and the decay of her corpse strive to demonstrate the grim actuality of dying, death's demolition of idealistic illusions, and the representability of the corpse in realist fiction. What is at stake in analysing the representations of corpses in James's fictions is certainly not mere verisimilitude, but rather the significance of the representations – the power they may exert – within their particular literary, social, and cultural moments. As *Madame Bovary* demonstrates, the corpse becomes a key site of discursive contest during a period of increasing medicalisation, secularisation, and scientific materialism.

This chapter explores three interrelated tropes, or complex figures of desire and transcendence, for Jamesian corpses: necrophilia, abjection, and vanishing. Each of these reflects James's position in literary and cultural history. Initially my discussion concerns the dead bodies of characters within James's narratives, but these are not the only corpses to be considered. The term 'corpus' designates the textual body of a writer's work. In James's fiction, it is often this textual body, rather than the body of flesh and blood, that is fought over; the most obvious example is 'The Aspern Papers.' What is the relationship between James's representations of the corpse and his representations of the corpus? In effect, this is a question about the way that dead bodies and dead texts within James's fiction might anticipate James's own literary afterlife – expressing the author's hopes and fears for his posterity. In this sequence of corpses, there is also James's own body, which was cremated and then interned in the family plot at Cambridge, Massachusetts, but also preserved in the form of a death mask. What figures of the corpse are constructed by James's own death scene and the final disposal of his body, and how do these recall the figures in his fiction?

Deathbed

James's fiction tends to avoid deathbed scenes. As Garrett Stewart shows, these were central to the novel's maturation as a literary form in the nineteenth century. The deathbed scene developed as a way to manage a moment of crisis in the form's enterprise of showing the meaning of human lives. The novelist must find a way to represent the experiential void of death. Dickens's language, for example, tends to point to the transitional moment of death's arrival, rather than try to describe this moment directly. Many of his most famous deathbed scenes, such as little Paul Dombey's, provide a last chance to affirm the consolation of moral order and emotional sweetness even in a world of injustice and suffering.[6] Here the deathbed scene is central to the moral function of fiction, whereby an author disposes of his characters through the dispensation of punishments and rewards. This function can be related in turn to mid-Victorian fears about the possibly immoral nature of fiction and to the loss of Christian faith. James's avoidance of deathbed scenes is thus in part a realist move away from both Dickensian sentimentalism and Christian morality.

Roderick Hudson provides an early example of how James's fiction avoids the deathbed scene. After Roderick goes missing during the storm, the search party, led by Rowland, cannot set off until the next morning. After several hours searching the mountains, Rowland hears a sound, looks up hoping to see Roderick, but sees only Singleton. He is on the opposite side of the valley and has seen something lying at the foot of Rowland's side, out of Rowland's sight, as if nestled in his genital region, which Singleton can look across at directly. Rowland must watch Singleton seeing what he cannot, must ask ' "What do you see?" ' (*RH* 509). Singleton declines to tell, forcing Rowland to climb down and beating him to the body:

> Half-way down [Rowland] saw something that made him dizzy; he saw what Singleton had seen. In the gorge below them a vague white mass lay tumbled upon the stones. He let himself go, blindly, fiercely. Singleton had reached the rocky bottom of the ravine before him, and had bounded forward and fallen upon his knees. Rowland overtook him and his own legs collapsed. The thing that yesterday was his friend lay before him as the chance of

the last breath had left it, and out of it Roderick's face stared upward, open-eyed, at the sky. (*RH* 509)

Roderick becomes a 'thing' and a 'vague white mass' beyond Rowland's power to comprehend. Roderick could have been found alive and then died in Rowland's arms; instead, all of the commiseration and reconciliation that might have been exchanged are thwarted by the impossibility of dialogue. Before he even reaches the body, Rowland is chastised by Singleton's having got there before him.

Rowland despatches Singleton to fetch help and waits beside the body in a seven-hour vigil, which is passed over relatively quickly. The episode then evolves further away from a deathbed scene towards the classical convention of the dispute over the corpse. The body is carried down from the mountain on a 'rude bier' in a 'little procession,' to be received by a 'pitying, awe-stricken crowd,' before whom Mary, 'with the magnificent movement of one whose rights were supreme,' flings herself upon the body (*RH* 511). At this moment, Rowland is dispossessed of the corpse. He is turned back by Mary's cry of triumphant bereavement on to lifelong, private meditation on his subjugated rights. Rowland thus becomes one of several Jamesian heroes who end up being haunted by the lack of either private consummation or public recognition of their emotional adventures – like those bystanders at the grave, Marcher in 'The Beast in the Jungle' and Winterbourne in 'Daisy Miller.'

Rowland's displacement as mourner is an imposition of gender and sexual norms. As a man, he cannot produce before the crowd an emotional display to match Mary's. He has had his chance already for spontaneous emotion, before Singleton and then during his private vigil. In the company of men that carries Roderick's body on a makeshift stretcher down the mountainside, Rowland's concern is to preserve whatever dignity he can for his friend. How, then, should he mount a fresh display of grief to rival Mary's after such an interval? Rowland's surrender of the corpse can be read as a sacrifice to convention in exchange for a return to the quiet rationality of moral order with which he is temperamentally more at home, together with secure, private possession of intimate memories. By continuing his futile devotion to Mary, Rowland simultaneously escapes marriage and continues to be near Roderick.

The lack of a deathbed scene in *Roderick Hudson* is a function of the novel's fairly rigorous restriction of point of view to Rowland. His exclusion from what Singleton can see from the opposite side of the valley makes the reader particularly aware of the restrictions on what can and cannot be narrated within this scheme. Focalisation enables a controlled release of death. At the same time, the decision not to narrate a death from the point of view of the person dying is a practical one, for how in that case could the narration continue after the moment of death? The narration could switch to the consciousness of another character, or to authorial mode, but such a switch brings its own technical problems, particularly for the smooth narrative flow that characterises James's style.[7] Instead, James's fictions use point of view to control access to the moment of death and to the corpse so as to control the reader's sense of the meaning of the death and to engineer subtle effects of closure.

Necrophilia

Restricted point of view alone does not explain why the narrative does not report more about Roderick's corpse during Rowland's vigil. He has the opportunity to examine his friend's body directly, to be physically intimate with it in a way that he could never enjoy while Roderick was alive. Any such examination or intimacy is carefully excluded from the narrative. The paragraph between Singleton's departure and return focusses on Rowland's regrets and imagination of the circumstances of the fall. The closest we get to a description of what goes on physically during the seven hours is the suggestive statement that Rowland 'would have lain down there in Roderick's place' (*RH* 510). This statement falls short of revealing full-blown necrophilic desire for the physical corpse, either in gothic mode or as part of a realist study of sexual perversion.

As Lisa Downing argues, the idea of necrophilia emerged during the nineteenth century as both an aesthetic and a sexological category.[8] A host of French writers drew on the legacy of de Sade, the visibility of death in urban experience, and theories of cultural degeneration to explore the connections between death and desire. These explorations could be Romantic, gothic, realist, naturalist, or symbolist. Only by the end of the nineteenth century did necrophilia become named and thereby fixed as a sexual perversion within the control of medicine and the law. For Downing, narrow definitions of necrophilia as taboo acts of sexual intercourse, in particular as male penetration of dead women's bodies, obscure the wider function of necrophilia as a cultural fantasy and as a model of the complexities of desire. Writers such as Baudelaire, she suggests, use tropes of necrophilia as a representational strategy to make conscious 'the human fantasy relationship with death,' a relationship both 'desirous and idealizing.'[9]

Throughout his career, James's critical assessments of French writers enabled him to position himself within the Anglo-American literary field: now allying himself with their aesthetic and intellectual ambitions, now distancing himself from their morbid excesses. Correspondingly, James's fiction flirts with necrophilia rather than exploring it for its own sake. For example, James's novels and tales adopt the gothic mode on occasions, and thereby perforce entertain its necrophilic associations. The ending of 'The Altar of the Dead' shifts into gothic mode by staging death in a candlelit church as the climax of a romance plot. The final phrases of the tale, as so often with James's fiction, expertly manoeuvre the reader into a particular responsive corner, in this case centred on a moment of horror. The anonymous female companion of the protagonist, George Stransom, is left holding his corpse. Before the shrine of candles lit in memory of his dead acquaintances, he says there is space for one more: his own.

> 'Ah, no more – no more!' she wailed as if with a quick, new horror of it, under her breath.
>
> 'Yes, one more,' he repeated simply; 'just one!' And with this his head dropped on her shoulder; she felt that in his weakness he had fainted. But alone with him in the dusky church a great dread was on her of what might still happen, for his face had the whiteness of death.[10]

The 'quick, new horror' is a first shudder of anticipation, but the final line leaves the nightmare 'still' to happen. The description of Stansom's face is a moment of both present physical horror and unspecified future terror. Only moments before, Stransom's companion surrenders to him about a matter that had kept them apart. Now, holding him for the first time, she finds herself suddenly caught in an obligation of fidelity to his memory – a burden made literal in what is left in her hands.

This moment of dread and physical shock is introduced so as to provide a satisfying sense of ending. More fully gothic tales, such as Poe's 'Ligeia' (1838), inhabit horror and terror more consistently throughout their narrative length. 'Ligeia' is a defining contribution to the gothic mode that is so central to the literary representation of necrophilia. By comparison, 'The Altar of the Dead,' which is among James's most gothic tales, adapts the existing conventions of the mode far more than it contributes to defining them. Necrophilia enters this tale only as a subtle suggestion within the rich, multi-faceted frisson engineered by the ending.

'The Altar of the Dead' is overtly concerned with the cult of the dead, but this constitutes a relatively dephysicalised zone against which the ending works its shock by the brief eruption of physicality. The simple whiteness of Stransom's face counterbalances the elaborate mourning carried out by Stransom and the woman during the tale. In so far as necrophilia is defined as a narrowly carnal interest in the corpse, it will be relatively excluded and repressed in James's fictions, given the extent of their reticence about the body and sexuality. Necrophilia as a concept will have more direct applicability to his fictions if it is allowed to expand into the excesses of grief: a madness attending the crisis of a long romantic strain; a crazy moment of power accessed when the romance plot crashes off the rails; a desire to sacrifice oneself in place of the dead beloved; the start of an obsession with the memory of the dead; or even envy of the dead person as if they are experiencing something as yet inaccessible to the living.

Each of these could be read into Rowland's vigil, though the text does not explicitly invite this. The very inertness of Roderick's corpse enables subtle suggestions to emerge in the ending of *Roderick Hudson*: his body becomes available for pushing and pulling around; his corpse becomes incapable of initiating, resisting, or responding to sensuous attention but is not yet entirely unsexed. These elementary differences in the status of his body and the interpersonal relations it might sustain provide a basis for hints of transgression and wonder that enrich the ending. The currents of desire that we have felt running ambiguously from Rowland to Roderick cannot immediately switch off; the sudden stop to Roderick's life leaves an unsettling remainder, especially because the narrative reports Mary's embrace of the corpse but not any details of Rowland's vigil.

Fiedler labels James a 'necrophiliac' without explaining the possible shades of meaning of this term. For Fiedler, what defines James's distinctive place in American fiction is his addition of 'necrophiliac titillation' to female archetypes drawn from Hawthorne's fiction. Inspired by the death of his cousin, Minny Temple, James identifies 'the immaculate virgin with the girl dying or dead' and therefore it is 'from the dead that James's truest, richest inspiration comes, from a fascination with and a love for the dead, for death itself.'[11] Though this comment supports my own argument about the importance of death in James's novels and tales, its reductive formulation neglects a wide range of cultural and critical contexts for reading James's fiction in other ways. Fiedler's exclusive focus on James's dead women, such as Daisy Miller, belies the preponderance of male characters in James's fictional death-roll and downplays the variety of social and cultural factors other than gender that might pattern a reading of James's use of death and of his representation of the relationship between death and desire. James's necrophilia surely extends to the possible eroticisation of dying male characters and of dying children; these cannot be excluded in principle as the basis for suggestions of transgressive desire. Fiedler's focus on dead women points to Bronfen's central thesis in *Over Her Dead Body*, that the death of a beautiful woman becomes a spectacle of otherness found again and again in Western literature. However, Bronfen's discussion of 'The Altar of the Dead' does not simply use necrophilia as a label, but instead seeks to complicate the relationships between death, desire, memory, loss, self, and other in James's writing.[12] Indeed, Bronfen recognises that this tale regenders the positions of spectator and corpse implied in her thesis, since here it is a woman who gazes upon the body of a dead man.

An explicitly carnal sense of necrophilia might be brought to the surface of *Roderick Hudson* by psychoanalytic or queer readings. On the other hand, there are further tropes organising James's representations of corpses that defuse the association with necrophilia, in so far as they combine together to form a rich polysemy. If the corpse is desired, it is also disgusting, demands purification, or must even be removed altogether and replaced by spiritualised symbols.

Abjection

Roderick's corpse regains a grace that he had lost while he was alive.

> He had fallen from a great height, but he was singularly little disfigured. The rain had spent its torrents upon him, and his

clothes and hair were as wet as if the billows of the ocean had flung him upon the strand. An attempt to move him would show some hideous fracture, some horrible physical dishonor; but what Rowland saw on first looking at him was only a strangely serene expression of life. The eyes were dead, but in a short time, when Rowland had closed them, the whole face seemed to awake. The rain had washed away all blood; it was as if Violence, having done her work, had stolen away in shame. Roderick's face might have shamed her; it looked admirably handsome.

    'He was a beautiful man!' said Singleton. (*RH* 509–10)

The purification implied here is an authorial act, since the plot would have been served with no loss of realism if Roderick had slipped and fallen *after* the rain had stopped. The washing clean has the air of a conciliatory gesture, as if apologising for violence even while endorsing its necessity. At the very moment of the discovery of the corpse, the assertion of Roderick's unbroken beauty moves the narration beyond the actuality of death to some higher meaning. The reader and the characters are spared any visible signs of violence; when the bier is taken up by the bearers to be carried down the mountain, there is no further mention of the 'hideous fracture' and 'horrible physical dishonor.' These phrases perhaps signal mere nakedness as much as any specific damage to the body. They gesture towards gothic horror, as if allowing limited recognition of psychic overload at the very point of repressing it. The narrative's reticence about the actuality of the corpse characterises Rowland's point of view – his embarrassment and sorrow – but also reveals James's manoeuvring of the reader into a particular state of mind at the ending. It is also an indication of what Bailie sees as the virtual taboo in James's fiction against direct representation of the bodily.

    If blood suggests vitality, female fertility, and having dared to live, then whiteness suggests sterility, frigidity, a failure of courage, and an obsession with purity. In a different symbolic register, whiteness also suggests physiological realism, though this could be accentuated by suggestion of other colours, such as blue. By contrast, when blood is explicitly visible – hot red liquid – in some of James's earliest fictions, the description is fundamentally conventional and of merely simulated interest. A clear example is provided by an early scene in *Watch and Ward*, a markedly less subtle and controlled novel than *Roderick Hudson*.

The hero, Roger Lawrence, hears a shot during the night and discovers the corpse of a man whom he had met for the first time the
previous day:

> In the middle of the floor lay a man, in his trousers and shirt, his
> head bathed in blood, his hand grasping the pistol from which he
> had just sent a bullet through his brain. Beside him stood a little
> girl in her night-dress, her long hair on her shoulders, shrieking
> and wringing her hands. Stooping over the prostrate body, Roger
> recognized, in spite of his bedabbled visage, the person who had
> addressed him in the parlor of the hotel.[13]

The last sentence suggests a defence against the invasive power of
the spectacle of the corpse; Roger inspects the body without physically
touching it and loses no time to assure himself of its identity.
'Bedabbled visage' is tellingly poetical. The next paragraph describes
the scene a second time over, this time from the point of view of the
dead man's daughter, told to Roger by the landlady who has taken
care of the girl overnight. This mixing of points of view is perhaps
meant to suggest the confusion and social buzz of such an event's
aftermath, but it also allows the narrative to keep the bloody corpse
at a distance. The girl 'found her father on the floor, bleeding from
the face.'[14] This is indirect speech, attributed to the landlady reporting
the daughter's account. Does 'bleeding from the face,' surely a drastic
understatement of the physical actuality of the wound, characterise
the hero, the landlady, the child, or authorial reticence?

White, red – or black: 'her eyes had attached themselves to the
small bed. There was something on it – something black.' When
Schinkel and the Princess break down Hyacinth's door at the end of
The Princess Casamassima, the narrative does not gaze steadily at
Hyacinth's corpse, nor greedily drink in the spectacle, but instead
snatches furtive glimpses at it:

> The door collapsed: they were in the light; they were in a small
> room, which looked full of things. The light was that of a single
> candle on the mantel; it was so poor that for a moment she made
> out nothing definite. Before that moment was over, however, her
> eyes had attached themselves to the small bed. There was something
> on it – something black, something ambiguous, something

outstretched. Schinkel held her back, but only for an instant; she saw everything, and with the very act she flung herself beside the bed, upon her knees. Hyacinth lay there as if he were asleep, but there was a horrible thing, a mess of blood, on the bed, in his side, in his heart. His arm hung limp beside him, downwards, off the narrow couch; his face was white and his eyes were closed. So much Schinkel saw, but only for an instant; a convulsive movement of the Princess, bending over the body while a strange low cry came from her lips, covered it up. (*PC* 552)

The phrase 'her eyes had attached themselves' establishes the scene as a visual test. Before Schinkel or the Princess can do anything about it, the spectacle on the bed immediately captures their gaze. The point of view seems to flow back and forth between the two characters. 'Black,' echoed by 'back' in the next line, colours the body to match the surrounding darkness of the room; the warm, living blood has dried and become dehumanised, almost excremental matter. The repeated 'something,' designed to suggest a moment when the Princess has seen some but might yet be saved from seeing all, contrasts with the more specific sequence of references to Hyacinth's body that follows. Yet these are no more than gestures towards naturalistic anatomisation: very indirect allusions to the full-on spectacle of the corpse exemplified by *Madame Bovary*. The Flaubert association is offset by others, such as the trailing arm's similarity to Chatterton's in Henry Wallis's painting (1856) or to Christ's in Michelangelo's *Pietà*.[15] In the description of Hyacinth's body, whiteness, contrasting with blackness, is used to evoke a mixture of spiritualised purity, physiological realism, and quasi-gothic horror. The corpse does not confront death, the characters, or the reader with eyes staring out of the night; instead it awaits collection with the closed eyes of a child sleeping by the light of a candle – that is, evoking a sense of innocence and hope alongside the sense of horror. The mention of Hyacinth's heart, separated by the gentle 'on the bed, in his side' from the damage implied (scarcely enforced) by 'a horrible thing, a mess of blood,' suggests that this vital organ has become open to the world to an unprecedented extent, its powers of affection, generosity, and courage symbolically revealed at their apotheosis, not smashed to pieces and hideously disfigured.

Hyacinth's landlady enters the room, causing the Princess to step away from the body. There is no mention of blood staining the Princess's dress; even though 'something black' implies that the blood has dried, the Princess seems to recoil as from something capable of contaminating her. Hyacinth's name does not appear in the last half-page of the novel. From the last mention of his name in 'Hyacinth lay there as if he were asleep,' he descends into 'he,' 'his,' and 'the body' for the space of the remaining handful of lines. At the same time as this remainder is filled with tenderness and sorrow for Hyacinth, he starts to become in them something no longer human: his body is some kind of base matter and his spirit has gone elsewhere. Using some of Julia Kristeva's concept of the abject, we could say that in the closing paragraph Hyacinth's corpse moves towards becoming a radically unacceptable otherness, virtually an excrement that defiles. The corpse, after all, is one of Kristeva's primary examples of abjection.[16]

Kristeva's study is psychoanalytic and feminist. Her central idea, that the experience of abjection is a breakdown of subjectivity, draws on biblical ideas of abomination but finds its major examples in the experience of the modern subject in the twentieth century, illustrated especially by the work of Céline. James's fiction sufficiently anticipates aspects of modern subjectivity to allow an application of Kristeva's concept of abjection not to be entirely anachronistic. 'Not me. Not that. But not nothing, either. A "something" that I do not recognize as a thing. A weight of meaninglessness, about which there is nothing insignificant, and which crushes me.' '[A]n Other has settled in place and stead of what will be "me." Not at all an other with whom I identify and incorporate, but an Other who precedes and possesses me.'[17] These phrases have most force when taken to describe an unmediated encounter with death, or such fearful representations of it as holocaust photography. They clearly overestimate the level of visceral impact of which the description of Hyacinth's corpse is capable. Yet Kristeva's phrases suggestively articulate some of the swooning subjectivity in face of the corpse aimed at in the ending of *The Princess Casamassima*.

Roderick's body, too, starts to become base matter – as indicated by the phrase 'senseless vestige' (*RH* 511) – but this suggestion is fairly slight in comparison with the staging of Hyacinth's corpse as a spectacle worthy of filling the ending in its own right. This difference makes

Hyacinth's death more abject, in Kristeva's sense, than Roderick's. The washing of Roderick's corpse by the rain counterbalances an implied disgust with the 'horrible physical dishonor' that must be hidden. Shame enters the matrix of feelings, including pity and anguish, suggested in the 'vigil' passage describing Rowland's response to the discovery of Roderick's body – hence the phrase 'as if Violence, having done her work, had stolen away in shame.' Though the Alps provide grandeur for Roderick's death, a sense of dishonour enters the landscape, which becomes wasteland during Rowland's search. He finds empty chalets with 'low, foul doors' and 'a hideous *crétin*, who grinned at Rowland over his goiter' (*RH* 508). The rock, dumb and unsculpted, down which Roderick has fallen, becomes a 'blank and stony face [...] with no care now but to drink the sunshine' (*RH* 510). Yet we feel it must be looking, as if a vast audience on all sides is witnessing the scene. These suggestions do not add up, however, to the breakdown of the classical, liberal subject implied in Kristeva's concept of abjection, both because our vision of Roderick's corpse is less spectacular than our vision of Hyacinth's, and because the earlier novel works with a slightly less modern understanding of the individual subject.

A secondary example of the abject body in James's fiction is the wound. A wound 'does not *signify* death,' suggests Kristeva; it '*show[s] me* what I permanently thrust aside in order to live.'[18] Faced by the sight of a wound, we cannot negotiate with it to make it mean what we would like or to make it stand symbolically for death itself. The sight of a wound assaults us, teaches us directly one lesson alone and all on its own terms. We cannot read from the gaping wound the secrets of death; like the corpse, the open wound sends us into a swoon where we experience an evacuation of our self-possession.

Roderick Hudson is not left wounded and alive by his fall. That he might survive, paralysed or hideously disfigured, seems unthinkable in a Jamesian universe, so carefully does it avoid direct physical violence and instead explore psychological violence. Very few of James's characters live to carry substantial physical wounds. The two fingers missing from the hand of Spencer Brydon's alter-ego in 'The Jolly Corner' (1908) stand as a miniature emblem of an excluded volume of real amputations and disfigurements that occurred during the Civil War. (Wartime issues of *Atlantic Monthly* carried advertisements for prosthetic limbs.[19])

Woundedness is a major trope in James's writing, but always removed from that direct encounter with physicality that connects the wound with the corpse as a site of abjection. Thus Susan M. Griffin can claim that James's fiction and autobiography represent scars as 'texts' revealing the construction of masculine interiority from the outside position of unwounded women and civilians. 'James does not spend much time detailing the look of wounds,'[20] she explains, because pain is necessarily internalised and inaccessible to the viewer, and thus the viewer can only be interested in what scars represent. This argument works best for James's writing later in his career, when the scars carried by veterans of the Civil War indeed signify a past trauma. The use of language as a response to epistemological frustration belongs to a time after the wound has begun to seal up as a psychic and material scar that the wounded man will live to bear. At this point, the viewer's sense of self no longer has anything to fear from the abject look of the wound; it has become the site of a wholly internalised, subjective experience of pain and is no longer a potentially mortal rent in the fabric of the wounded man's body and of the spectator's universe.

By contrast, Rowland's fear of the 'horrible physical dishonor' to Roderick's corpse occurs at a moment when the violence done to the body would still have the power to assault him should he look. Roderick's wounds are fresh and have not begun to signify. James's narrative does not look at them because to do so would be to expose the limits of its representational system: the narrative surface would have to rupture to allow the entry of some other language, such as that of medical anatomy or the gothic, capable of signifying where James's authorial voice, up to this point of the narrative, cannot. The constraints on this voice are not only aesthetic, but also ethical, since the reticence about Roderick's corpse suggests both genteel respect for bodily privacy and James's concerns for biographical privacy reflected in tales such as 'The Aspern Papers.'

The 'look' of a wound opens into questions about the power of medical discourse, transgressive desire, social and literary conventions, *and death*. Instead of reporting an abject encounter with the wound, James's fiction explores woundedness, for example through the portrayal of characters, such as Rowland Mallet and Catherine Sloper, whose lives become a matter of stoical endurance. The fresh disfigurements of the bodily corpse are compressed into an originary scene rarely attended and never reported in detail. For Ronnie Bailie, this amounts to a wholly unconscious repression that generates meta-phorical images of bodily mutilation throughout James's fiction. Against this view, we can propose that James's redirection of attention away from the body as the site of death's intrusion into the world is part of a conscious, creative writing about death in other ways: responding to both genteel, nineteenth-century forms of censorship and to the rise of secular, scientific materialism.

Vanishing

None of James's novels and tales reports a suicide or murder scene directly. These deaths are particularly interesting because of their associations with dishonour and scandal, with climaxes of self-determination and desperate action in the face of personal crisis. By positioning the death offstage, beyond the narrated scenes of action and perception, James's narratives allow their dead characters to vanish without the shame of becoming a visible corpse.

For Philippe Ariès, James's aversion to reporting the corpse directly in his fiction might exemplify what he calls 'invisible death.'[21] This is a phase in the cultural history of death, becoming dominant in the twentieth century but with roots in the nineteenth. The dying person, the family, and medical professionals collude to keep the approach of death secret; death is frequently hidden from society by taking place in hospital; the word 'death' becomes taboo; and the bereaved become social exiles until they have completed the shameful task of mourning. Of these characteristics, the one that emerges earliest is the dissimulation of approaching death, which Ariès illustrates by examples from the fiction of James's contemporaries, Tolstoy and Twain.[22] The desire to protect the dying person by concealing the seriousness of his or her condition is a modification of a sensibility characteristic of the previous, Romantic phase in Western cultural attitudes towards death. As affectivity became centred in the privacy of the nuclear family, death became a crisis requiring the development of consolatory mourning rituals and a cult of the dead. In the nine-teenth century, the death of the self became less important than the 'death of the other,' which was exalted into a beautiful, sublime moment of communion between the dying man and his loved ones.[23] James's fiction moves away from the Dickensian deathbed scenes that exemplify this moment, while continuing to represent death, for the most part, as more a matter of the significant other than of the self.

By not showing us the death-moment, and in most cases not the corpse, either, James's fiction reclaims the dead body as something mysterious. This is in part a response to medicalisation and secularisation. Only rarely do we gain access to sick rooms in James's fiction, where we might witness a deathbed scene. We are suddenly presented with Daisy Miller's grave, surrounded by her namesake flowers. In 'The Beast in the Jungle,' Marcher is turned away from May's house during her final days of life and in the cemetery the names carved on her headstone seem to watch him 'like a pair of eyes that didn't know him.'[24] In *The Wings of the Dove*, where there is not even a grave-side scene, Milly Theale seems to be limited to no such particular location, but becomes omnipresent in the world of those she leaves behind. Each of these three women disappears in a narrative vanishing trick, by virtue of the lack of direct reporting of a deathbed scene. As Bronfen points out, Minny Temple's death in America while James was visiting England provides a template for this characteristic narrative device.[25] Creating a sense of mystery around the corpse enhances its sacrificial quality. The vanishing of Daisy, May, and Milly entails transubstantiations recalling the Christian Eucharist and Ascension: their spirit becomes matter or their physical body becomes etherealised. Non-reporting of the death-moment and the corpse defers the finality of death as a material event subject to a scientific and secular worldview. In *The Wings of the Dove* especially, this device enables the narrative to evoke a religious quality of feeling.

As with necrophilia and abjection, vanishing needs to be understood as opening on to other literary tropes and cultural contexts, and as blending into the rich suggestiveness of James's endings rather than dominating them under a single figure. Whereas *abjection* registers the assault of the corpse's materiality upon heart and mind at a specific time and place, and *necrophilia* implies that the attachment between the living and the corpse persists beyond the moment, *vanishing* names a power of imagination and writing to transform time, place, and the materiality of the corpse altogether.

These three concepts are interconnected; they are complex, entangled responses to bereavement, mortality, and the representation of death. To experience necrophilic desire for a dead body is closely related to experiencing abjection before it, and both might motivate a desire to hide the corpse away. In his foreword to Abraham and Torok's discussion of the Wolf Man (one of Freud's patients), Derrida – in his customarily complex style – explores some such contradictory and convoluted territory.[26] He develops the idea of the crypt as a buried secret that radically undermines common-sense ideas about place. Rather than assimilating his trauma and bereavement into the self (a process known as introjection), the Wolf Man represses them whole and undigested as a foreign body (incorporation). It is as if he has swallowed a locked safe in an act of 'vomiting' into a pocket inside himself.[27] His most precious secret is a sense of exclusion, of being an outcast. His *innermost* self is yet *outside* the crypt, which is itself an outer space sealed up and stored within his heart.[28] For Derrida this bizarre process is, among other things, a way to make the dead vanish. The crypt destabilises the inside/outside distinction so that the departed is 'nowhere to be found, *atopique* [no-place].'[29] This process of incorporation stands to healthy introjection much as melancholy stands to healthy mourning – a distinction we will find relevant for reading *The Wings of the Dove* in the next chapter. Though James's response to Minny Temple's death may have been unusual, no one is suggesting that he was another Wolf Man. Even so, the lack of visible corpses in his novels and tales allows psychoanalytic readings to get a foothold, as illustrated by Bailie's study.

In *Roderick Hudson*, as we have seen, the corpse is transformed into something less immediately material and more potentially spiritual or ideal. The text remains silent about the final disposal of Roderick's body and effectively refuses to bury him. He vanishes from the material world; like Milly, he has no grave. Instead of visiting a cemetery, Rowland visits Mary; she becomes the physical presence through whom, along with Roderick's sculptures, Rowland maintains the suggestion of contact with his dead friend. She is the keeper of her fiancé's flame.

James's fiction offers many examples of such guardians and heirs. In 'The Altar of the Dead,' Stransom guards the memories of his friends, each represented by a lighted candle, while his anonymous companion guards the memory of her beloved, Acton Hague. James's novels and tales also show the memory of the dead being preserved in material objects, especially letters and artworks. His last tales, such as 'Crapy Cornelia,' are suffused with a sense of the dead surrounding the characters. The vanished dead return in photographs, fashions, and artefacts from bygone eras; through renewed acquaintances with former associates; and through memories triggered by meetings with a younger generation. For Spencer Brydon, returning to the house of his youth in 'The Jolly Corner,' the feel of 'the old silver-plated knobs of the several mahogany doors [...] suggested the pressure of the palms of the dead.'[30] When the presence of the dead floods out beyond the confines of ritually sanctioned containers, such as the grave, every object and aspect of the world has the potential to act as a surrogate corpse. Morbid nostalgia and the supernatural are two overt modes of such a process.

Roderick Hudson inhabits a younger man's view of the world. There is no play on letters or documents as Roderick's artistic remains, but in addition to Mary and his sculptures there is a third material vessel into which Roderick's corpse might be said to vanish, namely the novel itself. It becomes his memorial. Whenever a character dies, his or her story to some extent becomes metaphorically a grave. Often, as in *Roderick Hudson*, this is a relatively weak suggestion, expressed in the conventional phrase that a dead character *disappears into the narrative*. By contrast, in some of James's fictions, particularly those concerned with writers and posthumous reputations, the identification of text with a character's memorial goes beyond this weak sense to become an explicit idea within the narrative. In 'The Aspern Papers,' for example, the climactic nocturnal episode where Juliana Bordereau catches the biographer at her desk is clearly suggestive of a grave-robbing scene; his desire for the papers has a necrophilic quality.[31] Of all the objects that can carry the memory of the dead, written documents are in James's novels and tales among the most potent and sacred. They stand in place of bodies of flesh and blood that have departed the world. This privileging reflects James's increasing self-consciousness about the potential value of his own writings for literary history.

The term 'corpus' implies a unified textual body: an alternative body that a writer constructs during his or her lifetime and that can survive into posterity, where readers can reanimate it through the act of reading. For Richard Salmon,

> James considered the publication of private texts to be a violation
> of the author himself. The literary text, and its physical containers,

retain the capacity to exude the 'personality' of the artist, even after death. It is this organic relationship between author and text which is specified by the term 'literary remains': the textual corpus is conceived as a residual extension of the authorial body.[32]

As we will see in Chapter 4, in his final decade James actively anticipated his death by burning personal papers, writing his autobiography, and creating the New York Edition. These are meta-level operations on the Jamesian corpus whereby the author modifies an evolving textual alter-ego. Hence Tim Armstrong connects James's revisions for the New York Edition with his simultaneous adherence to a Fletcherist diet – that is, reshaping his literary body through a process of revision and selection while he reshapes his physical body through obsessive chewing and dietary restrictions.[33]

Letters and other documents appearing within James's fiction, of which there are many, can also be read as figuring his corpus. James's novels and tales frequently represent textual remains and battles fought over them, and these narratives implicitly anticipate the possibilities of James's own literary afterlife. They often tell of texts lost or destroyed. In 'The Aspern Papers,' Tita Bordereau reveals to the biographer that she has burned the letters ' "one by one, in the kitchen." '[34] In 'The Death of the Lion' (1894), the manuscript of Neil Paraday's last, great work will never be recovered after it is left on a train.[35] In *The American*, Newman burns the paper that he had hoped would humiliate the Bellegardes.[36] In *The Wings of the Dove*, Kate burns Milly's letter in front of Merton, who is thereafter haunted by it.[37]

In each case, a text dies, so to speak; it becomes a corpse beyond the reach of future readers to reanimate. Aspern's letters evade the clutches of the unscrupulous biographer once and for all; Tita cremates them so that they can never be exhumed. The loss of Paraday's masterwork foreshadows his final absolute obscurity; if the lionisers had left him alone he might have completed the work and won a place in literary history, but instead he will receive belated recognition that will soon pass. Newman burns the paper as a renunciation of vengeance, but also because he has lost faith in its capacity to exact that revenge; the paper has become a dead letter that he cannot cash in. The scene where he and Mrs Tristram watch the paper burn is a funeral service to his hopes. ' "Is it quite consumed?" she asked, glancing at the fire. Newman assured her that there was nothing left of it.' A few lines later 'Newman instinctively turned to see if the little paper was in fact consumed; but there was nothing left of it.'[38] The repeated phrase draws attention to the perfection of the document's physical destruction. As for its continuance in Newman's heart, that is another matter.

This is how Milly's letter goes up in smoke:

> She had already turned to the fire, nearer to which she had moved, and with a quick gesture had jerked the thing into the flame. He started – but only half – as to undo her action: his arrest was as prompt as the latter had been decisive. He only watched, with her, the paper burn; after which their eyes again met. 'You'll have it all,' Kate said, 'from New York.' (*WD* 2: 386–7)

The letter is destroyed in a moment that is one of the novel's blanks. We do not see the envelope blackening and catching light, as we might in close-up in a filmic adaptation of this scene; we do not share the rapt gaze of either Kate or Merton. In other words, not just Milly herself but also the letter which is her surrogate presence in the world performs a vanishing trick, whereby the material is transformed into something immaterial. The burning of the letter leaves the reader, like Merton, with an intensified sense of Milly's presence in some other, magical space, corresponding to her emphatic absence from the material here-and-now. When Merton first receives the letter, on Christmas Eve, instead of being given a description of the letter as a physical object, we are told that he turns out the light, lies on the sofa without undressing, and has a sleepless night (*WD* 2: 352). Here the letter is already transformed from its material form as a paper document into the nocturnal restlessness in mind and flesh of a man who has honourably given up his bed. And after Kate burns the letter it becomes something altogether protean in Merton's mind: 'he took it out of its sacred corner and its soft wrappings'; it is 'a priceless pearl,' 'something sentient and throbbing' (*WD* 2: 396).

The burning of Milly's letter here begins to figure her posthumous transformation, which we will explore further in Chapter 3. James famously burned many of his personal papers at Lamb House, rather than let them fall into the hands of unscrupulous biographers. Can these burnings of documents, both within the fiction and in life, be understood as dress-rehearsals for James's own cremation? What became of the author's body? In the sequence of Jamesian corpses – characters' dead bodies, dead texts within the narrative, James's corpus, and his own corpse – how does each anticipate or evoke the others? This is a rich field of potential meanings of which we cannot assume James was unaware, as we can see by considering his death mask.

James's life/death mask

The front cover shows what Houghton Library's catalogue records as James's plaster life mask, made by his nephew, William.[39] At the time of writing, this designation is problematic because of conflicting evidence, which has not yet been resolved. A letter written by William's mother, Alice Howe Gibbens James (Henry's sister-in-law, who played an important part in caring for him in his final days), to her other son, Harry, describes the making of a *death* mask by an anonymous sculptor.

> Though I said 'no flowers, by request' in my notice in the *Times* & *Telegraph* quantities of flowers have come. A most magnificent offering from the Am[erican] Accademy [*sic*] & wreaths from the Embassy, from the Ranee,[40] Soc[iety] of Dramatists & countless more. And there Henry lies in the front room among his books and laurel wreaths with the most unearthly beauty in his face. It is so *young* – his vanished youth has come back with an expression of wisdom & of grandeur which it breaks my heart not to have you see. Mr. Sargent said it must be kept & sent a man as soon as I agreed (which you may believe I instantly did, to take a cast). This was very very kind for Mr S. is much pressed just now with his own affairs. He said he knew an Austrian who could do this better than any man he had ever seen. He came yesterday, & after he had finished told me it was the most perfectly beautiful cas[t] he had ever taken. He made almost no disarray & I am sure you will all be thankful.[41]

If a life mask already existed, it seems strange that Alice should make no mention of it here unless she did not know about it. If there were two masks, one taken during life by William without Alice's knowledge and subsequently bequeathed to Houghton and another taken after death as Alice describes, what has become of the latter? *Does the front cover show the face of a dead man or a living?*

Alice creates an image of James lying in state. Arranged around him are bouquets received in tribute, wreaths honouring him as a poet, and (nameless) books representing his beloved literature. Her observation of peace returning to James's face after his death-struggle is an understandable, commonplace response on the part of the bereaved, but this can now also be tested against the Houghton mask, supposing that might be the one Alice is describing. Despite the eye patches and the limitations of photography, we might agree with Alice that the Houghton mask successfully captures some sense of serenity, if not 'wisdom & grandeur,' 'unearthly beauty,' and 'youth.'

Sargent, a fellow American expatriate, had known James for many years and had painted his portrait in 1913. The two men were neighbours in Chelsea, with Sargent's Tite Street studios round the corner from James's flat on Cheyne Walk. According to Sargent's biographer, he was 'much pressed' in early 1916 by the supervision of the packing up of a monumental set of murals for Boston library, on which he had been working for 26 years, for shipping across the Atlantic.[42] Sargent was at the heart of the London art scene, so it is not surprising that he could recommend someone to take James's death mask; three years earlier he had recommended to James the sculptor Derwent Wood.[43] At that time, James had submitted himself to the taking of amazingly candid photographs by a studio photographer as preparatory studies for his bust.[44] Those photographs do show a man apparently more elderly and anxious than in the mask.

The most striking aspect of the Houghton mask is undoubtedly the patches – presumably some form of padding and gauze – over the eyes. These are very unusual in a death mask, as the plaster is usually applied directly over the closed eyelids so as to reveal, in the finished sculpture, their every expressive wrinkle and contour. Nietzsche's death mask has a similar masked-over area, but upon his mouth: Zarathustra is gagged, as it were, or rather the place whence his radical voice would emerge is nullified. Victor Hugo's death mask shows him fully bearded – clay solution or oil was used to prevent facial hair sticking in the plaster[45] – so the covering of Nietzsche's mouth presumably hides a distortion of the mouth in death, which might perhaps be read as a sign of the philosopher's madness in his final years. If, by contrast, the Houghton mask of James was taken during life, the patches are still unusual. In life-castings only the airways are protected, so as to create the best possible likeness of the rest of the face. The process of being cast is bound to be uncomfortable, but why bother to go through it at all if the result will be spoilt to such a degree by protecting your eyes?

The masking of James's eyes implies a possible distortion hidden behind the padding and gauze. If the patches are intended to disguise some deformation underneath, they nevertheless become the most prominent part of the mask; blocking us from seeing the most intimate signs of James's personality, they seem to be a foreign imposition upon the face. The distortion reminds us of the importance of visual perception in James's writing. Sight for this author is an active function of the modern intelligence; the great crises in his novels and tales – personal, moral, and aesthetic – typically occur via this sense. In the Houghton mask James's sight is rendered frail and wounded, as if wrapped in bandages. The disfigurement is multiply, irrationally suggestive: of Gloucester, Tiresias, and Milton, of cosmetic surgery, alien growth, and prosthetic implants.

The lips seem ready to part in speech or to curl into a smile; breath seems ready to pass through them and the still nostrils even yet. The mask evokes the particular moment in the past when it was taken, but it also has a degree of uncanniness as a memorial sculpture capable of preserving some illusion of its subject's presence. Death masks excel in conveying this sense of elusive interiority: 'the illusion that the deceased now somehow communes with their own essence,' suggests Jeremy Stubbs.[46] This illusion is dispelled when one peers at the underside of the mask and sees where the plaster has slopped into the mould.

The Houghton mask invites the viewer to reflect on James's greatness and to do so in what feels like an intimate audience. When I saw the mask in the library's reading room, it lay on one of the grey foam rests designed for fragile books. A strange material relic to a life long gone, it resembled both a head on a platter and some geological specimen. To be able to inspect James's face minutely seemed an invasion of domestic privacy to which he would normally have objected – as if I had been transported back to his bedside and his head lay before me as it had once lain on the pillow.

The bronze copy[47] nestled amidst a mane of age-browned paper curls inside a cardboard posting box. It seemed to await an invitation to appear, mounted on royal velvet, before admirers and devotees. By contrast, Houghton displays its bronze of Keats's death mask in pride of place in a room dedicated to the poet. His mask has become an icon of translucent, consumptive beauty and Romantic attitudes towards death, whereas James's seems to languish, generally neglected both in critical discussion of James's life and writing and in representations of his figure as an author. James's masks have only recently become listed on Houghton's public online catalogue. I have not found any substantial discussion about the mask in print, and I believe it has never been photographed or publicly displayed outside the library. Edel's biography makes no mention of either a life or a death mask. His version of James's life is so influential that this omission has been perpetuated. Kaplan's biography also neglects the mask(s), and David Lodge seems to have been unaware of the subject when describing James's death in some detail at the end of his recent novel[48] – even though the making of a mask, with the cold, wet plaster being applied reverentially to encase the author's face, is surely a powerful scene to evoke in fiction. By contrast, Joyce's death mask is displayed prominently, like the centrepiece of a shrine, at the James Joyce Museum, Sandycove. It contributes to the iconography of a modernist master in a way that James's mask has hitherto failed to do.

Shortly before visiting Houghton I attended a major conference on James, over which presided an image from Katherine McClellan's portfolio of publicity photographs, taken in 1905 during James's visit to America.[49] Posing as the modern, clean-shaven, professional author, James looks askance at the viewer with a faintly supercilious smile. Such photographs of James, increasingly used as front-cover illustrations to monographs, show him alive, alert, and actively engaged with the modern world. From photograph to photograph his image and expression are mobile and changing. In the Houghton mask, by contrast, he is shut away from our present. It seems to freeze the truth of his personality once and for all in a single moment, with all potential of ambiguity, play, and style immured forever inside its eerie likeness. The mask shows a face at a point of no return, beyond words and, apparently, beyond life, but so lifelike that we might almost imagine a consciousness continuing within.

Yet the mask is also distinctly unmodern; it pulls James back into the nineteenth century – an effect that might have been counteracted by a phonographic recording of his voice, should he have chosen to make one, as Joyce did.[50]

Whereas there are many photographs of James, there appears to be only this one surviving cast of his face. It was made through direct physical contact with his body rather than through the indirect mechanism of light, camera, and photosensitive paper. The power of the mask's illusion suggests that we are seeing James's face itself, but the mask is nevertheless a representation. Looking at the Houghton mask, it seems as if we can *know* James by gazing on him unawares. But does the mask's frozen immobility reveal to us James's soul and its traumas, or is the mask rather a shield protecting his inner self from the world even to the end of his life, even in death?[51]

As J. Hillis Miller argues in *Versions of Pygmalion*, mistaking a sculpture for a living being – fetishising a graven image – is a potentially dangerous error.[52] The rhetorical trope of prosopopoeia, more commonly known as personification, means literally *making a face*. Prosopopoeia is violent, in that an anthropomorphic face or other human body *part* (such as a hand) is made to displace and stand for an incomprehensible, inhuman whole.

> [Prosopopoeia] does not [...] confer a soul, an anima, on the absent, the inanimate, or dead. It ascribes, through language, a face or a mask, a voice, and a name to representatives of one or other of those three classes. Prosopopoeia projects not the wholeness of the self, body and soul together, but fragments that stand for the whole, as the face stands for the person who presents that face to the world.[53]

Creating a life or death mask materialises the process of prosopopoeia – literally enacts what is normally a rhetorical procedure. However lifelike it may be, the Houghton mask is *not* James, nor will it ever awaken, even if we gaze upon it longingly like Pygmalion upon his statue or implant upon it a magical kiss. The mask is merely a piece, and the whole that it represents is now absent, dead, and beyond our reach. Even though we might think of James as an especially cerebral writer, for whom personality was of high importance and whose fictions tend to underplay the physicality of his characters, his body and self-image did extend beyond his face. Some of the most interesting criticism of James in the last decade has derived from re-embodying his scene of writing (for example, in terms of his switch from longhand to dictation, discussed in Chapter 4). One of the alarming qualities of the Houghton mask is its evocation of beheading. Part of its illusion is to make one expect to find the rest of the body, which can only be hidden behind the surface on which the mask rests.

Displayed as the front-cover illustration to this book, the Houghton mask, whether taken during life or after death, potentially functions as a title sign: a charismatic but reductive master figure for *Jamesian death-itself*, subsuming all other arguments. Existing as a visual icon aside from James's writing, the mask might seem to have a power of explanation different in kind from that possessed by mere written texts – which in relation to James often go under suspicion of obscurity. The mask offers itself immediately, as if to cut through all verbosity.

Though appreciative of the visual arts, James deplored the encroachment of visual culture upon literary culture. For example, he preferred that his fiction not be illustrated. This changed somewhat in his final years, as he recognised the likely importance of visual media, such as photography, in the twentieth century. By the time of his death, he had already been painted, photographed, and sculpted, so it was not as if there was anything to be gained by withholding his face from history (so that his unknown physiognomy might join those of the long-dead great as a mystery to tease future generations). However, the Houghton mask is different in kind from all of these earlier images to which he had consented because of its utterly diminished sense of authorial participation. Even if this mask was made during life, we have received no reports back from James himself about its production. Instead, it appears to be a spoil whose creation and posthumous fate he could not control. If the mask is a death mask, then it marks the complete loss of his agency as an artist and is an image of grim finality.

So used are we to reading James's intelligence into his writing that it is hard to find no basis for it in the making of the Houghton mask too. A death mask had been made of James's brother, William, six years earlier – also recorded by Houghton as having been made by William James, Jr.[54] The taking of that mask was presumably an act of mourning by members of the James family and a tribute to assert the greatness of the deceased. As Ernst Benkard explains, during the nineteenth century the death mask tradition had evolved away from the votive and effigy traditions, in which the bodies of saints and royals were recreated for display to the populace, to the civic tradition, in which great citizens (starting with Sir Isaac Newton) were recognised on their deathbed as being of historic importance.[55] Presumably James's mask was made for similar motives; in this respect it can be compared with the Order of Merit, which was conferred upon him in the 1916 New Year's Honours list in anticipation of his imminent death and election to the ranks of greatness.

James's apparent obliviousness – or, at most, prior verbal consent – to the taking of a mask contrasts with the way that Marcel Proust allegedly stage-managed his deathbed scene in advance. According to Nicola Luckhurst, Proust effectively pre-marketed his death and initiated his posthumous myth by arranging that a portrait drawing be made of his corpse and that his books and manuscripts be laid out around him in a manner recalling part of Bergotte's death in *The Captive* (1923). Journalists latched on to the idea that Proust had rewritten Bergotte's death on his own deathbed so as to better record the experience of dying.[56] There is no comparable story about how James's mask or death scene were fictive performances of his own making. For example, the death of neither Dencombe in 'The Middle Years' nor Limbert in 'The Next Time,' both of which are unusual in James's fiction in showing the death-moment of a writer, is typically read as a pre-emptive writing of James's own death-moment, comparable with Proust's description of Bergotte's death.

In *The Sacred Fount*, Mrs Server and the anonymous narrator discuss a painting of a clown carrying a mask. They find it to be a portentous hermeneutic puzzle, which soon feeds into the narrator's suspicions of illicit sexual relationships among his fellow house-guests. Does the mask enable a sad young man to come alive, like an actor stepping out onto the stage, or in donning it does he undergo a kind of death of his own personality? Should the painting's title be 'the Mask of Life' or 'the Mask of Death?'[57] The notorious unreliability of the narrator in *The Sacred Fount* makes this scene difficult to use as a source of clues for reading James's possible attitudes towards his mask.

A more suggestive example occurs in 'The Jolly Corner,' where a death mask figures Alice Staverton's early sense of the hauntedness of Spencer Brydon's fine old New York home, which has been unoccupied for years. Introducing her to the house for the first time, he avers that it must be swarming with ghosts. Gazing into the rooms, she 'imagined some element dimly gathering. Simplified like the death-mask of a handsome face, it perhaps produced for her just then an effect akin to the stir of an expression in the "set" commemorative plaster' (*JC* 705). Even when serene, the faces depicted in death masks are rarely 'handsome' or simple; more often they are aged, distorted in some way, and mysteriously expressive. The mask in this image is therefore an idealised one, half way to a theatrical mask. The idea that the hardened plaster might magically move, as if alive, helps to prime the reader for the uncanny events to follow. When Spencer does meet the ghost of the man he could have been, it initially covers its face with 'white masking hands' (*JC* 724). Then, with 'a sudden stir' (*JC* 725), the apparition drops its hands to reveal a face that Spencer horribly recognises as his own and yet cannot accept. It is vivid, alive, and intensely present, as if the 'commemorative plaster' has fully awoken, grown a body of living flesh, and for one night walked abroad. 'The face, *that* face, Spencer Brydon's? [. . .] Such an identity fitted his at *no* point, made its alternative monstrous. A thousand times yes, as it came upon him nearer now – the face was the face of a stranger' (*JC* 725). Seeing himself is unbearable, and Spencer swoons. When he recovers, early next day, he describes the stranger as 'brute' and 'black' (*JC* 730) whereas Alice, who has seen the ghost in a dream, is more accepting. The early death mask image in this story is thus an important preparation for the climactic confrontation, where the face is the crucial test of identity. Alone in the night, Brydon is faced down – the ghost has 'a rage of personality before which his own collapsed' (*JC* 725–6) – but in the light of morning his friend reconfirms his authentic, own identity. Apparently the imposter has not taken Brydon's place in a secret transfer during his faint. ' "And he isn't – no, he isn't – *you!*" she murmured as he drew her to his breast' (*JC* 731). In this closing cadence there is a pleasing sense of trembling uncertainty about Brydon's recovery, something smothered by his holding on for dear life to Alice. He appears to survive, but only just. He comes close to losing face, but in the end his face does not become plaster-white with death, like Stransom's at the end of 'The Altar of the Dead.'

In so far as this story, written in 1908, offers an explanation of how James might have thought about his own mask, it highlights a potential for uncanniness within the material object. What is asleep may yet awaken, and the set plaster stir. The sight of a face may unmake a man. However, the mask image in this tale would need to connect up with a range of further such images or references elsewhere in James's writing in order to build a convincing case that James genuinely sought to prewrite the possible meanings of his own mask. Rather, this object now enters the field of Jamesian corpses and the James corpus as an underdetermined element. It is not clear how to read the mask as a text by or about James.

Neglecting (suppressing?) the mask, Edel's biography establishes as the defining moment of James's death scene something more flattering to the iconography of James as an author. What we are asked to remember are the fragmented deathbed dictations, taken after James's second stroke, and his hand's persistent movement across the counterpane during his coma, as if trying to write up until the very moment of death.[58] These are images of the Master's active resistance, down to the wire, to his loss of agency as an artist, a resistance occurring finally on an habitual, nervous level pathetically hollowed of conscious creative power. By contrast, the Houghton mask – a dumb material thing, whose features refuse to move however long we stare – seems to show the loss as an already completed process. It confounds the desire to find a continuation of James's creative pulse right up till the end of his life and even after his death. He did not make the mask; it is not a text from his hand.

I felt a comparable effect at James's grave. Kaplan's biography implies that it is not even certain whether James requested the repatriation of his ashes or if a decision was made on his behalf by Alice.[59] In any case, the grave clearly absorbs James into a family hegemony. His headstone is uniform in material composition and style with those of his parents and of his siblings, Alice and William. Patriarch and matriarch are at the centre, with the eldest son on his father's right hand. Henry is sandwiched on the left between his mother and sister – feminised. In their aesthetic and location, the James family graves are deliberately modern and modest; they eschew both the banality of popular ornamentation and the grandiosity of monuments in the neighbouring Mount Auburn Cemetery, the garden cemetery that houses the rich and famous of Boston and Cambridge. The James graves lie in a municipal cemetery and are bare of overt Christian iconography – and, as yet, of much patina of age. James describes his visit to his sister's grave in almost ecstatic terms in his 1904–5 American Journals.[60] Personally, when I visited the graves the day after seeing the Houghton mask, I found little of James's authorial presence there. It nominally contains his cremated remains and is demarcated as his final resting place, but otherwise, like the mask, is rather an empty shell. W. H. Auden's poem, 'At the Grave of Henry James' (1943) develops its wartime meditation on the role of the poet out of the 'intransigeant' blankness of the 'small taciturn stone.'[61] In response to the emptiness of the grave, Auden turns to James's writing, from which he quotes evocative phrases and the titles of some of the tales. In the same situation, I found my mind filling with thoughts about what James's writing represents in my own life, the extent of his continuing presence as a cultural figure, his intentional strategies for controlling his posthumous reputation, and his will to literary immortality. In the cold light of day, James's grave marks absence; for me, he is present there less than he is in Venice, Rye, and his writing.

Part of the relative blankness of James's grave derives from the thought that his body was cremated. At the time of James's death, cremation was an overtly modern and untraditional method of disposal in both Britain and America. After Lincoln's embalmed body was processed around the cities of the North at the end of the Civil War, the American funeral industry established itself as a new profession, with embalming its central area of expertise and the central practice in the emerging American way of death.[62] Cremationist pioneers in Britain and America during the 1870s argued that cremation was a form of both sanitary and social reform: it was more physically pure and more culturally genteel. Cremation was allied to secularism, but also to interest in Eastern religion and philosophy and to a shift in cultural attitudes to the body, whereby the individual spirit might be released into an afterlife without the need of a Christian, bodily resurrection.[63] Cremationism can thus be understood as a kind of modernism.

By being cremated, James was again following his elder brother, William.[64] Cremation also meant that James could be repatriated with relative ease (unlike Roderick at the end of *Roderick Hudson*). As we have seen, James's fiction suggests a further motive, in that cremation appears to dematerialise the body. When letters and other documents (textual bodies) are thrown into the fire in James's novels and tales, they are not reduced to ashes – a feeble reduction of material presence in the world – but are instead completely consumed and thereby vanish to a different plane altogether. From there, what or whom they represent may embark on a career of haunting. Death by fire becomes a way to create a subtle potential for mystery: we shall never know what was in those documents, nor will we ever get our hands on those bones. The mystery of James's corpse is enhanced rather than undermined by the materiality of the plaster and bronze masks. Though they are heavy and sculptural, an illusion of presence flickers over them, as if preserving a perpetual moment before James became a corpse. They powerfully resemble but are not his body, which has eluded us.

Whether it was taken during life or after death, the Houghton mask invokes a deathbed scene so often missing from James's novels and tales. It materialises his own body that otherwise vanishes between the scenes caught on camera and the grave in Cambridge. For Alice's letter, the death mask also brings a return of James's 'vanished youth.' The Houghton mask transforms the potential abjection of James's corpse into something less terrible and more transcendental. But this is also a potentially gothic object, capable of inspiring and by itself incapable of resisting transgressive, necrophilic desires.

If James's grave and mask primarily testify to his absence, this cannot, of course, be said of other things that he has left behind. James is represented by his correspondence, diaries, and notebooks, his published works, his will, his painted, sculpted, and photographed image, Lamb House, and the plaque in Westminster Abbey. And there are many more places and things that would testify to his life but that have been lost, such as the house in Washington Square, the burnt papers, the bombed Garden Room at Lamb House, and the manuscripts and typescripts of virtually all the published fiction. This multiplicity of items bearing James's name, standing in for him in the world or enhancing the mystery of his absence and mostly doing so in a more interesting way than the grave and the Houghton mask, dilutes their power to tell of his death and its secure location in the past. Grave and mask are vested with authenticity by virtue of their very form rather than by any authorial act attributable to James. To date they have remained obscure artefacts, seemingly unable to speak to or interest the present. They have left the field for

James's writing. James's letters, by contrast, have sustained intense biographical, critical, and scholarly interest. In the absence of the manuscripts or typescripts of the published fiction, the letters are the holy relics of James studies. *His* hand moved across *this* page. With only a small proportion of James's ten thousand-plus letters yet published, his corpus is still very much alive and growing in this respect, via the ongoing *Complete Letters of Henry James* project.[65]

While life and death masks testify in a uniquely material way to death, in James's case this testimony has scarcely received a hearing. Keats's mask is central to the iconography of this poet because death thematically dominates and cruelly cuts short his writing and because there are so few other visual representations of him. James has left us a lifetime's work and numerous images of his appearance, and death has not generally been recognised as a primary concern of his fiction. Though the Houghton mask will perhaps become more eloquent as it becomes better known, it seems unlikely that it could ever speak with James's own loquacious intelligence. It remains to be seen how it will affect prevailing ideas of James's prodigious creativity and will to literary immortality. Viewing James's mask might be an occasion for recognising what is past and finite – his life and death – but this moment is easily displaced by a sense of James's lingering authorial presence through his writing. This effect is partly a generic quality of all memorials to the dead: they bring to mind the life and legacy of the deceased and expose the mind's inability to conceive of death as utter void. They reveal our aversion to confronting our own mortality and instinctive turning back towards life. When viewing the Houghton mask, such effects are filtered by our personal experience of reading James's work. It is surely the narratives of death and afterlife, both in James's own words and in those of his biographers and critics, that are most liable to be reconsidered when the mask becomes better known. It is an unsettling addition to the iconography of James as an author.

3
The Wings of the Dove and the Morbid

What, for a novelist or a novel reader, is a proper degree of interest in mortality? Is *The Wings of the Dove*, with its protracted and convoluted story of Milly Theale's death, an unhealthy novel – one that only morbid readers would choose as their favourite among James's works? By what techniques does this novel aim to fascinate readers in its heroine's demise?

Death is so pervasive in *The Wings of the Dove* that almost anything you can say about the novel can also be developed into saying something about how it represents death. However, whereas Shoshana Felman can identify fairly readily the ways in which death enframes 'The Turn of the Screw,' death is pointedly underspecified in *The Wings of the Dove*. The novel's representations of death are more complex, more obscure, and less popular than those in the tale, even though written only a few years later. The novel tends to avoid overt references to its contemporary setting, so that the connections between aspects of turn-of-the-century modernity and how the novel represents Milly's death are difficult to discern. Her death is filtered through both a dense, elliptic style and an array of responses to cultural continuity and change at the start of the twentieth century.

Because death is so deliberately unnamed for most of *The Wings of the Dove*, it seems to flood out across the novel and to become accessible as an almost existential awareness and a morbid fascination with the idea of sickness and dying. *The Wings of the Dove* inhabits a very different philosophical worldview from that of *Roderick Hudson* (though the revisions to the latter in the New York Edition bring the two novels somewhat closer stylistically). In *Roderick Hudson*, death comes suddenly, as if with a blow delivered from outside human experience; in *The Wings of the Dove*, violence has been internalised. Whereas Roderick falls from a cliff and dies instantly, Milly does not leap from the Alp where Susan Stringham discovers her early on, but instead makes a gradual descent towards her death as if following steps into Hades. Whereas Roderick seems to participate in his death only partially – his suicidal motives are cloudy – Milly and her friends actively explore the approach of her death, even though this eventuality is for the most part never named. Whereas Roderick seems to crumple with insufficient resistance to external pressures, prompting James in his New York Edition Preface to bemoan 'the rate at which he falls to pieces' (*RH* xiv), Milly apparently fights to the end, so that in the Preface to *The Wings of the Dove* 'the last thing in the world [the idea for the novel] proposed to itself was to be the record predominantly of a collapse' (*WD* 1: vii). The shame of Roderick's disintegration becomes in the character of Milly a proud resistance: 'my offered victim [. . .] had been given me from far back as contesting every inch of the road, as catching at every object the grasp of which might make for delay, as clutching these things to the last moment of her strength' (*WD* 1: vii). Nevertheless, Milly's death is as surely the generative centre of *The Wings of the Dove* as Roderick's is of the earlier novel. At the end, Milly turns to the wall as if, finally, embracing death.

Roderick's fall cauterises the woundedness of the characters in *Roderick Hudson*; it figures and seals them once and for all. Milly's woundedness, by contrast, circulates on and on as an open secret; it is virtually a medium of exchange between the characters and between the text and the reader. The narrative seems to be one great wound, fascinated with itself and never condensing into a single, definite form, though the novel implies that consumption – the privileged metaphor for illness as a sign of artistic sensitivity in the nineteenth century[1] – is the primary diagnosis of Milly's unspecified ailment compared with other diagnoses, such as neurasthenia and cancer. *The Wings of the Dove* has been much studied as a novel about medicalisation and gender. Diana Price Herndl suggests that James's experiences of his sister's illness and relationship with doctors made vivid to him a cultural shift in discourses on illness around the turn of the century. Milly Theale is a transitional figure between the victimised innocents of earlier, sentimental fiction, whose illness represents self-sacrifice and forgiveness, and wilful invalids of twentieth-century fiction, who use illness manipulatively.[2] Athena Vrettos notes that the use of different points of view in *The Wings of the Dove* and the omission of a deathbed scene do not allow a final judgement between competing interpretations of Milly's illness. Instead, the reader is suspended between 'sympathetic participation and clinical detachment.'[3] Hugh Stevens points out that James's Preface hints at but ultimately elides substantial questions of ethics and aesthetics for a male author setting out to represent a sick woman.[4] The novel steers carefully between vulgarity, sentimentalism, and sanitation; it blends and transforms these rather than avoiding them altogether.

What I miss from the focus on medicalisation in these accounts of *The Wings of the Dove* is a recognition that Milly is dying, not just ill, and *that* is what makes the novel so fascinating. The narrative strongly suggests that Milly's health is inexorably deteriorating at the same time as it carefully shrouds her ailment in uncertainty. News that Milly dies precedes the reader's experience of the novel – whether from word of mouth, cross-references in critical works on other texts by James, back-cover blurbs, editors' introductions, or James's Preface. In practice there can be few first-time readers who avoid all of these. Indeed, the assumption shared by these advance notices is that prior knowledge that Milly is to die forms an important part of the pleasures offered by the novel and by no means pre-empts its climactic effects. The narrative constructs Milly from her first appearance, dressed in mourning for her whole family and perched on the edge of a cliff amid the Romantic scenery of the Alps, as a character through whom the reader will be able to enjoy the pathos, tragedy, and (in)justice of the death of a modern-day princess. Even if the allusions to Milly's consumptive nature (her restlessness, pallor, bravado, and lovesickness[5]) are no longer as current as they were in 1902, the expectation that Milly will eventually somehow die is fundamental to the interest of plot, character, and style throughout the novel. Medicalisation contributes to the narrative's construction of Milly as a character bound to die – what Girard might call a ' "sacrificeable" victim' – but her prognosis and the character of Sir Luke Strett are then relatively demedicalised. Milly's struggle for life is represented as a social, aesthetic, and spiritual progress; she does not fight against a medical condition with the aid of treatments but rather seems engaged in a battle of nerve, cunning, and affection.

The primary creative impulse behind *The Wings of a Dove* is a fascination with death and dying, not as a medical or religious phenomenon but as a personal, social, and aesthetic construction. The novel goes out of its way to avoid directly representing Milly's illness and death so that it can instead explore what the idea of dying might do for her and her friends, in advance and posthumously. I will argue that the reader becomes implicated in this strange process because the novel's style demands such a high level of active interpretation and attention to subtle signs. The reader of *The Wings of a Dove* thus participates in what can be termed an *elaborate performance of morbidity*. Around 1900, 'morbidity' was central to discourses of decadence, degeneration, and modernity. James's novel tacitly defies these prevailing uses of the term so as to develop death and dying as a complex and expansive zone of interest for a modern fiction of high seriousness.

Degeneration

John Stokes has argued that 'morbid' was a crucial term in the 1890s to discredit and oppress discursive challenges to dominant moralities, especially relating to definitions of proper masculinity. From its origins as a medical term for the diseased parts of an organism, it became a label to be wielded against artists and homosexuals so as to lump them with lunatics, criminals, and other anti-social identities.[6] This usage was part of the discourse of cultural degeneration, famously brought to a pitch in the mid-nineties by Max Nordau's book.[7] According to William Greenslade, 'morbid' individuals were figured as defects in the British body politic, detracting from the nation's imperial fitness. From the late nineteenth century until the First World War, popular journalists and other writers constructed a polarisation of masculinity: on the one hand the hard, athletic, and healthy, on the other the soft, artistic, and morbid.[8] Darwinian psychiatry associated the morbid with introspection, obsessive ideas, and asocial behaviour – symptoms that were the result of the individual's degenerate heredity. Against this definition of the 'morbid,' artists sought to reappropriate the term, for example by using it comically. By the turn of the century it had lost some of its force as a pejorative label, though the underlying discourse of degeneration that it exemplified continued to be influential. In the late nineteenth century the morbid was associated with fin-de-siècle fears and negative aspects of modernity, and this became more difficult to sustain with the start of the new century. What had been a label to condemn decadent literature became a marketing term for decadence as a modern fashion.

James's use of 'morbid' reflects much of this history. It is a key term of potential judgement in his vocabulary. Highly subject to irony and complex narrative effects, the term is used as a stalking horse in his fiction to sensitise the reader to subtleties of perception and judgement. As Jeremy Tambling points out, it was not only men who could be labelled morbid; female morbidity took the form of hysteria or, as in the case of Olive Chancellor, masculinisation and feminism.[9] 'Morbid' is used to convey Basil Ransom's condemnation of Olive's excessive seriousness and deviant rejection of marriage, shortly after their first meeting.

> But this pale girl, with her light-green eyes, her pointed features and nervous manner, was visibly morbid; it was as plain as day that she was morbid. Poor Ransom announced this fact to himself as if he had made a great discovery; but in reality he had never been so 'Boeotian' as at that moment. It proved nothing of any importance, with regard to Miss Chancellor, to say that she was morbid; any sufficient account of her would lie very much to the rear of that. Why was she morbid, and why was her morbidness typical? Ransom might have exulted if he had gone back far enough to explain that mystery.[10]

Merely to apply the label of morbidity here proves an utterly deficient form of explanation. The repetition of 'morbid,' which becomes comic, suggests a lack of conviction lurking within Ransom's brandishing of the term to himself as an unproblematic means of judgement. The phrase 'Ransom announced this fact to himself' designates the preceding 'it was as plain as day that she was morbid' as reported interior monologue, whereas the following sentences seem to switch to the narrator's judgement upon Basil's shortcomings. But the distinction between narratorial omniscience and provincial ignorance is not so clear-cut. The qualifications introduced in the sentence beginning 'It proved nothing of any importance' suggest complex social and ideological tensions, not just within the world of the novel but also in the contemporary world of its readers. Why might Basil, the narrator, James, other characters in the novel, or different kinds of reader need to *prove* anything about Olive – and to whom? The narrator proposes 'Why was she morbid, and why was her morbidness typical?' as more challenging questions to answer, but the novel does not adopt them for its keynote. As Basil's earlier, showy designation of himself to Olive as '"Boeotian"'[11] indicates, provincialism has no straightforward implications of inferiority in a novel that satirises the Athenian pretensions of Bostonian intellectual culture. The values behind Ransom's judgemental use of 'morbid' begin to be put up for questioning, but are not immediately baffled.

James's critics do not always use the term in so subtle a manner. In popular usage, 'morbid' no longer functions as such a recognisable, pseudo-medical label for specific, deviant identities and behaviours, as it did in the 1890s. The major historical contests over the 'morbid,' in which James participated, have to a large extent been subsumed within continuing critical usage of this term as a relatively ill-defined and somewhat archaic pejorative for unhealthy introspection and interest in mortality.

For example, in his forceful discussion of James's relationship to symbolism and decadence, John Auchard clearly associates morbidity with perversion, egotism, and degeneracy. Among James's ghostly tales, 'Maud Evelyn,' 'The Way It Came' ('The Friends of the Friends'), and 'The Altar of the Dead,' all written during the 1890s, are especially vulnerable to accusations of morbidity-without-reserve; they reveal a degree of continuity with decadent literature. *The Wings of the Dove*, by contrast, lacks the 'more sure morbidity'[12] of such tales and constitutes a mature and authentic approach to spirituality. Auchard is correct to suggest that James had an ambivalent relationship with the French decadents, such as Baudelaire, as he did with the French naturalists and realists. His career-long series of critical writings on French writers is one of the main stakes whereby James negotiates his position within Anglo-French–American cultural relations. He was consistently wary of being too closely associated with these writers whom, in many respects, he evidently admired. Morbidity was indeed one of the topics through which James carefully defined his position, but his writings – as illustrated by the extract from *The Bostonians* above – contest rather than accept this term as a given. Without specifically defining 'morbidity,' Auchard implies that it denotes a narrowing and wasting away of life in an unhealthy fascination with death and decay; it is pseudo-spiritual, solipsistic, and doomed to failure. The key question posed by 'The Turn of the Screw' and other ghostly tales by James is: 'Is life that is lived for silent, ghostly forces [. . .] life at all, or is it foolish, fictive, comic, morbid?'[13] The way this question is set up, morbidity is equated with laughable delusion and an utter sham of life; it is already on the side of the damned rather than the name of the ground to be contested.[14]

To accept a definition of the 'morbid' as a taint of perversity recapitulates the line in mid-twentieth century criticism of James that finds his later work to constitute a falling off from the realist density of reference and virile, moral wholesomeness of his earlier work. Behind such judgements as F. R. Leavis's that *The Portrait of a Lady* is James's fullest expression of vitality – showing 'the abundant, full-blooded life of well-nourished organisms'[15] – lie assumptions about what constitutes a healthy, as opposed to morbid, conception of 'life.' These assumptions flatten the later fiction's construction of value *in* decomposition and its troubled questioning of easy separations of 'life' from death.

James's New York Edition Preface to 'The Altar of the Dead' defends its protagonist's sensitivity to the general neglect of the dead in busy, overpopulated London. In doing so, it challenges the easy use of 'morbid' as a way of colluding with such neglect. 'Brutal, more and more, to wondering eyes, the great fact that the poor dead, all about one, were nowhere so dead as there [London]; where to be caught in any rueful glance at them was to be branded at once as "morbid." '[16] 'The Altar of the Dead' by no means simply endorses Stransom's way of honouring the dead. Nevertheless, this comment implies that James hopes his tale will encourage readers to question the relationship between the dead and the living and expectations of how fiction should represent death and mourning. If not that illustrated by Stransom, what is a proper interest in one's own or another's death – socially, ethically, or medically? For an artist especially, when, if ever, might the interest become immoral, pathological, philistine, sensationalist, or counterproductive? These are questions implicitly raised by James's most 'morbid' fiction and by this remark in the Preface to 'The Altar of the Dead.'

The usage of 'morbid' by Auchard, Stokes, Greenslade, and Tambling illustrates the movement of this term in critical currency away from its specific relationship to death. As Michel Foucault explains in *The Birth of the Clinic*, the morbid was a category arising from profound epistemological change around 1800 in medical perceptions of disease.[17] Previously disease had been thought to invade the organism from outside; now it was understood as an intrinsic aspect of the organism's very substance and organisation. Living organisms constantly carry within themselves the basis of their death; life itself is pathological. The unfolding of death from within becomes fully visible only in the autopsy; until then, medical examination detects a series of signs veiled by the individual's still living flesh. Whereas in the Middle Ages and the Renaissance individual deaths merged into the dance macabre of fate and fortune, the nineteenth century raises the individual's death to the level of singularity. Death starts to belong to the individual and to be that which ultimately defines the modern subject, giving him a kind of liberation from homogeneity through his construction by the power-knowledge systems of the emerging medical profession.

> [I]t is in that perception of death that the individual finds himself, escaping from a monotonous, average life; in the slow, half-subterranean, but already visible approach of death, the dull, common life becomes an individuality at last; a black border isolates it and gives it the style of its own truth. Hence the importance of the Morbid. The *macabre* implied a homogeneous perception of death, once its threshold had been crossed. The *morbid* authorizes a subtle perception of the way in which life finds in death its most differentiated figure. The morbid is the *rarified* form of life, exhausted, working itself into the void of death; but also in another sense, that in death it takes on its peculiar volume, irreducible to conformities and customs, to received necessities; a *singular* volume defined by its absolute rarity.[18]

For Foucault, the morbid is above all a means of individuation by living towards death. There is nothing to be gained after death from this individuation except by the doctor carrying out the autopsy or perhaps by the bereaved; the individual must enjoy it in advance, within life, as a mode of 'subterranean' anticipation and self-consciousness. To have a pathology is a secret luxury, a privilege legitimised and regulated by medicalisation.

This definition of morbidity, with its emphasis on rarity value, heightened sense of subtle differentiation, and laborious approach to death, is particularly suggestive of *The Wings of the Dove*. Originally a relationship to the medical gaze, morbidity diffuses beyond literal encounters with doctors to become an ongoing relationship to one's own death – an internalisation of personal pathological capacity. Milly's meeting with Sir Luke Strett is a *token* application for authorisation to think of herself as uniquely capable of dying. She goes to him with this capacity in mind and he enhances her sense of it, not by specifying any particular pathology, nor by depriving her of her right to become ill, but by recognising her individual freedom and creativity with genteel reticence. The novel shows Milly's delicate and ambivalent celebration of her personal capacity to die, and how her interest in this process finds a responsive audience in her acquaintances.

Among James's novels and tales, *The Wings of the Dove* is the most sustained exploration of morbidity in Foucault's sense of the term. There is only one use of 'morbid' in the whole novel, and this is used to signal the trivialisation of the term as a topical buzzword. The first chapter of Book Fourth shows Milly's attempt to get her bearings within the London social scene, narrated from her point of view. Aware of her difference from the confident and handsome Kate Croy, Milly finds herself at the dinner table acting out Lord Mark's stereotype of overly self-conscious Americans so as to maintain the light-hearted urbanity of the occasion and her fragile feeling of belonging.

> The burdens they took on – the things, positively, they made an affair of! This easy and after all friendly jibe at her race was really for her, on her new friend's part, the note of personal recognition so far as she required it; and she gave him a prompt and conscious example of morbid anxiety by insisting that her desire to be, herself, 'lovely' all round was justly founded on the lovely way Mrs. Lowder had met her. (*WD* 1: 153)

It is not clear here if 'morbid' is Milly's own term for herself, or whether this term is being applied to her by the narrator, or by Lord Mark. In any case, the term is implicitly critiqued – much as if it were in scare quotes, as ' "lovely" ' is – in so far as the context presents 'morbid anxiety' not as an inherent condition but as a performance given under social pressure. The reader witnesses the performance from the inside, where Lord Mark is felt as an external power over discourse.

This instance of 'morbid' indicates what is going on in the narrative as a whole; the novel is a performative exploration of morbidity from the inside, otherwise careful not to name its principal subject.

Preoccupation with one's own or another's individual death marks a move in James's fiction away from its early realism. Such preoccupation challenges the ethical and aesthetic imperative to engage anti-solipsistically with the consensual world. Consider, for example, how morbid femininity is handled in *Washington Square*. Dr Sloper diagnoses his own death without flinching and uses the opportunity to continue his patronising contempt for his daughter.

> 'I shall need very good nursing. It will make no difference, for I shall not recover; but I wish everything to be done, to the smallest detail, as if I should. I hate an ill-conducted sick-room; and you will be so good as to nurse me on the hypothesis that I shall get well.'[19]

Catherine performs this task assiduously. After being scorned by her father one last time, in his will, Catherine becomes a stony stoic, who chooses spinsterhood over marriage. This is partly out of conscious choice but also, we fear, a repetition of her father's bitterness, to which he has reduced her. 'There was something dead in her life, and her duty was to try and fill the void. Catherine recognised this duty to the utmost; she had a great disapproval of brooding and moping' (*WS* 173). The last phrase especially suggests a scrupulous avoidance of self-pity. This quality is clinched by the cadence of the novel's closing sentence: 'Catherine, meanwhile, in the parlour, picking up her morsel of fancy-work, had seated herself with it again – for life, as it were' (*WS* 189).

Whereas frustrated sexuality, introspection, and awareness of mortality are suppressed and concentrated through the character of Catherine, they unfurl and diffuse at leisure through the character of Milly. *The Wings of the Dove* investigates morbidity experientially, whereas *Washington Square* uses an implied critical notion of the dangers of 'brooding and moping' to regulate the reader's experience of the ending. Though the ending of the earlier work strongly evokes the pathos of Catherine's fate, criticism of morbid self-absorption is relatively easy to decipher in the realist tenor of *Washington Square* as a whole. No such assessment is possible in *The Wings of the Dove*.

As well as bringing bereavement to James's own life, the years between the two novels (1881–1902) saw literary and cultural movements overtake the realism of which *Washington Square* is a high-water mark. Aestheticism, symbolism, decadence, and naturalism all provide new contexts and new means for representing Milly as interestingly, valuably morbid. That *The Wings of the Dove* chooses not to advertise itself as a work about morbidity is understandable, in so far as by 1902 the term had already peaked in its currency as a site of discursive contest. By not littering the text with the word – just as it systematically refrains from naming Milly's illness and from reporting the scene of her death – *The Wings of the Dove* gets on with addressing that neglect of the dead bemoaned in the Preface to 'The Altar of the Dead.'

Not all readers are impressed by the subtle, mannered, and protracted representation of death in *The Wings of the Dove*. Arguments such as Auchard's have to make the case that this novel maintains a critical perspective on morbidity, precisely because this is not obvious. Writing in 1891, Wilde attacks the use of 'morbid' as a pejorative label for artists.

> For what is morbidity but a mood of emotion or a mode of thought that one cannot express. The public are all morbid because the public can never find expression for anything. The artist is never morbid. He expresses everything. He stands outside his subject and through its medium produces incomparable and artistic effects. To call an artist morbid because he deals with morbidity as his subject-matter is as silly as if one called Shakespeare mad because he wrote King Lear.[20]

In its reticence and disavowal of objectivity, *The Wings of the Dove* does not fit this defence of the artist's detached relationship to morbidity. James's novel refuses to be explicit about so much of its subject matter that it tempts readers to lose patience. Its carefully developed, suggestive blanks, such as Merton's final visit to Milly's sick-room, are crucial to the novel's overall effect, but risk appearing to constitute a failure of expression – a failure of which, according to Wilde, the artist is never guilty. Moreover, the text does not establish an explicit authorial position aside from the points of view of the characters. The narrative contains no position of authorial mastery over its subject; as Vrettos notes, such a position is instead immanent within the novel's contrasting of points of view. The New York

Edition Preface to *The Wings of the Dove* does defend the novel's choice and treatment of its subject, but not by erecting a straight-forward category distinction between artist and subject. That would be to betray the memory of Minny Temple (who is cited by the Preface as a major inspiration for the novel and is generally accepted as such by biographers and critics) and the art of fiction.

Thus Wilde's defence will not work in this case. James's novel *is* vulnerable to charges of morbidity – that is, to certain kinds of reduc-tive, value-laden thinking about the representation of mortality. Rather than rebutting this thinking directly, the narrative strategy of *The Wings of the Dove* consists in fascinating the reader in death by stealth. This strategy remains potentially transgressive even when, long after 1900, 'morbid' loses its role as a buzzword. The ideas of moral hygiene that this term expresses remain current, as indicated by Auchard's usage. Foucault's definition helps us to reappropriate morbidity as a contested zone and as a name for the interest of death in *The Wings of the Dove*.

Seeing death

There is no part of *The Wings of the Dove* that is not infected with the interest of Milly's approaching death, but the character of Kate in Book First presents an approximation to ideas of health and vitality. These recede, along with her point of view, as the novel goes on. Ideas of death, centred on Milly, eclipse ideas of life, centred on Kate.

James's Preface proposes that the central subject of the novel is a 'young person conscious of a great capacity for life, but early stricken and doomed, condemned to die under short respite, while also enam-oured of the world' (*WD* 1: v). In this scheme, Kate and Merton are reduced to foils, to means to an end, to the interesting conditions in which Milly's story plays out. This is not necessarily how we read the novel. Psychosomatic readings of *The Wings of the Dove*, such as Vrettos's, suggest a shift in sympathy away from Milly as she becomes implicated in power-games. Also, Kate more obviously represents modern, enfranchised, working women than Milly. However much today's readers might like the novel to favour Kate, its ending declines to follow her into the future. There is no doubt that the narrative as a whole spends the balance of its efforts on weighing the reader's sympathies towards Milly and what she represents. Nevertheless, the novel does construct Kate's character to the point where she constitutes at least an alternative centre of sympathy, and it is the entire new century that is her implied field of action.

The Wings of the Dove does not neutrally balance contrasting points of view. The exploration of subjectivities through the novel's use of focalisation engineers a specific, narrowed range of sympathies towards its central triangle of characters. The most striking example of the inequitable distribution of points of view is the occlusion of Kate's. The refusal to return to her point of view after Book First creates the effect of her displacement in Merton's affections by Milly. Kate's decline as the centre of interest is in inverse proportion to Milly's rise in interest; and what we are interested in more than in Kate is Milly's decline towards death. The occlusion is initially slight, since Merton's point of view in Book Second seems so close to Kate's. Among the technical achievements of the novel is its representation of the gradual divorce of their points of view, which at the start seem so intimately shared. On a first reading of the novel, the reader cannot know whether or not Kate's point of view will reappear following its disappearance after Book First. One of the drives of the ending is to make such a reappearance seem unthinkable; there cannot be a Book Eleventh from Kate's point of view, because it would be irredeemably impoverished, definitively overshadowed, anticlimactic, and numerically surplus.

As in James's Preface to *Roderick Hudson*, the Preface to *The Wings of the Dove* masks some of the ideological effect of the use of point of view by faulting the novel's execution. In this case, the 'makeshift middle' renders the second half 'false and deformed' (*WD* 1: xviii). The Preface in fact mistakenly suggests that the point of view returns to Kate. 'It is in Kate's consciousness that at the stage in question the drama is brought to a head, and the occasion on which, in the splendid saloon of poor Milly's hired palace, she takes the measure of her friend's festal evening' (*WD* 1: xvii). This presumably refers to Book Eighth, Chapter III, which is clearly narrated from Merton's point of view; it is in his eyes that Milly's white dress and pearls turn the sartorial tables on Kate.

Despite the claims of the Preface, the interest of Kate's character asserts a substantial challenge to the interest focussed on Milly. The complex satisfaction of the ending relies on a sense of impasse: not just cognitive undecidability, but affective ambivalence, brought to a final pitch. We are drawn to Kate, even as we recognise that she has done wrong. The ending has a doubleness – will she or won't she (take the money, walk out)? – that invites readers to make a judgement based on the gathered history of their responses to the entirety of the preceding narrative. The satisfaction of this moment relies on the judgement appearing neither trivial nor straightforward, but brimming with the effort of discernment and responsiveness towards the characters' needs and desires that have defined the experience of reading the novel all along.

The Wings of the Dove opens with Kate, dressed all in mourning black, looking at her reflection in a mirror. The sight of herself provides reassurance that she can fight to save the family name. She recognises that her appearance is an asset, and this appraisal is different in kind from mere vanity. 'She stared into the tarnished glass too hard indeed to be staring at her beauty alone' (*WD* 1: 5). The most obvious parallel with this gaze into the mirror is the pivotal scene, much discussed in critical accounts, where Milly is introduced by Lord Mark to the Bronzino portrait (Book Fifth, Chapter II). Both scenes present a subjective and primarily visual moment of awareness of mortality. The representation of Milly's encounter with the painting is lengthier and altogether more morbid. It consists of a complex series of perceptions and articulations, rich in social, philosophical, aesthetic, romantic, and psychic dimensions. These are all brought under the idea of death and thereby make death more complex in a way that does not occur in Kate's scene.

Kate is alone with the mirror. She sees her reflection in an apparently direct revelation of self. The medium of the mirror – a technology operating as if automatically and bypassing human agency – enables a revelation of heightened accuracy and immediacy, free of social and aesthetic interference. In the midst of mourning her mother's death and father's disgrace, she sees herself as alive. She comes away from the moment with increased determination to make the most of her opportunities, though the subsequent meeting with her father soon challenges this initial optimism. By contrast, Milly encounters the painting within a dialogue with Lord Mark. She sees herself through a complex medium (portrait painting) that is embedded in history, human agency, and discourse. She imagines herself as already dead. She reacts to the painting with appalled admiration; she comes away in tears and wanting to see a doctor.

When Milly sees the woman in the portrait as unmistakeably 'dead, dead, dead' (*WD* 1: 221), this recognition releases feelings of excitement and dread. Jonathan Freedman goes so far as to claim that this scene is a 'paranoid scenario' and the beginning of 'a process that can only climax in [Milly's] re-creation of herself as a beautiful, fully aestheticized corpse.'[21] We might see a greater degree than Freedman allows of resistance on Milly's part to her identification with the beautiful image of a dead woman. Even so, this resistance is clearly different in kind from the affirmation of vitality with which Kate responds to her reflection. The Bronzino scene articulates morbidity as an intense encounter, bringing death to the verge of conscious awareness, representability, reification, and desire. At this point in the novel, Milly's death seems to become something simultaneously sought and yet occluded. She seems to internalise death as an obsession, specialisation, quest, and secret distinction (rather like Marcher in 'The Beast in the Jungle'). Appalling, the idea of her death yet becomes something harboured, hidden, and nurtured; separate from herself, but also within herself – rather like the crypt that Derrida describes in his Foreword to the study of the Wolf Man. By comparison, Kate's frank observation of herself in mourning in the novel's opening paragraph seems like a model of relatively healthy mourning and getting on with the business of life. Morbidity – not just a sickness within the living organism, but living-towards-death – has become in this scene more interesting and authentic than the idea of health, which is eclipsed by the idea of a 'life' from which Milly has somehow been separated even while she is still alive.

As Hugh Stevens points out in a discussion of sexuality in *The Wings of the Dove*, Kate's mirror scene is a 'classic trope' confirming a traditional alignment of women's power with 'beauty, charm and grace.'[22] Stevens sees Kate as ultimately confounded by her inability to escape patriarchal power, operating through Lionel Croy and Merton Densher.[23] But in the final chapters Kate seems to be defeated by *being alive* while Milly is dead, as much as by the limitations of 'beauty, charm and grace' that she sees in the mirror. The ideas of death that awaken in Milly as she stands before the Bronzino painting develop a power that seems to overshadow, not just the ideas that awaken in Kate as she stands before the mirror, but her very life. Though *The Wings of the Dove* works with the idea of illness, which Stevens rightly analyses in terms of social, sexual, and political dynamics, it works even more with an horizon beyond illness, namely death.

Rooms and tombs

Space becomes tomblike in *The Wings of the Dove*. The domestic interiors and urban parks and squares in which the action occurs become claustrophobic with the sense of Milly's death and Kate's frustrated purpose. The novel as a whole becomes a funereal chamber in which the reader lingers.

As Lustig demonstrates in *Henry James and the Ghostly*, rooms are fundamental to the creation in James's fiction of liminal and threshold effects, including supernatural suggestion.[24] 'The Jolly Corner,' for example, intensifies the significance of boundaries between interior spaces, so that a humble door can appear to stand between this world and the mysteries of the next. Philip Page makes an analogous argument about *The Princess Casamassima*: the use of room, door, and threshold imagery throughout the novel prepares the reader to imagine that Hyacinth, in his suicide, steps out of life into the unknown of death as if across the ultimate threshold. The imaginative investment the reader has made during the novel propels her to follow Hyacinth in spirit.[25] How, then, do rooms in *The Wings of the Dove* contribute to its performative exploration of morbidity?

When we meet Milly in the open air of the Alps, Susan Stringham identifies the vast expanse of space below with 'the kingdoms of the earth' and decides that Milly's destiny will turn away from the possibility of suicide to 'some more complicated passage' (*WD* 1: 124–5). Virtually all of the other action of the novel takes place either in interiors or in urban spaces, such as Hyde Park and the Piazza San Marco, that feel like outdoor rooms. But we famously do not enter Milly's death-chamber. Imbued with emotions and promises that we imagine to have been exchanged within it, this room haunts the final chapters, where Kate and Merton acknowledge the effects of Milly's death upon their lives. Nor do we enter the room where Kate's father lies crying and terrified, as if in fear of dying, in the penultimate chapter. Our missing of this room reinforces our missing of Milly's. All of the spaces to which the narrative has admitted the reader become retrospectively tainted with the possibility of death associated with the room unvisited. By the close of the novel, the narrative's sense of worldly time and space become dominated by the morbid interest of Milly's death in that room in Venice.

Kate moves through rooms that she does not own. They are shabby-genteel or confront her with a tantalising splendour. In such rooms, her life-challenges play out. For example, her meeting over tea with Merton early in Volume II takes place in an upstairs room at Maud Lowder's house: 'one of the smaller apartments of state, a room arranged as a boudoir, but visibly unused – it defied familiarity – and furnished in the ugliest of blues' (*WD* 2: 18–19). Such descriptions reinforce our sense of the lovers' frustration over the lack of a venue for intimacy and also of the economic motives behind their befriending of Milly. The relentlessness of Kate's containment within such rooms – even the various rendezvous in Hyde Park give little sense of escape – implies that she is confronting her destiny in those scenes narrated in the novel, for there is nowhere else where she will have the chance to make her life happen. The relationship between Kate and the rooms she inhabits verges on claustrophobia, but is distinguished from it by her resolve and pluck. These qualities come under increasing pressure in the final chapters as the whole of 'life,' whether inside a house or in the open air, becomes like a closed room, haunted by the memory of Milly.

The final image of Kate, poised to leave Merton's room, echoes her circumstances at the end of the novel's first chapter, where her father ushers her out on to the draughty communal landing. Her movement through different rooms during the course of the novel has both moved her away from the opening scene and returned her there repeatedly. At the novel's end, the door fails to slam with the conviction of her choice. Such a difficulty in imagining Kate leaving is a mark of the dominance that Milly's character has acquired over the narrative. *Remembering what has happened* in the novel – summoning how its entire length bears upon achieving satisfaction from the ending – has become so closely associated for the reader with *remembering Milly* (who has not entered the narrative directly since the end of the first chapter of Book Ninth, some one hundred and fifty pages in the New York Edition) that forgetting, and imagining Kate leaving, seems out of reach.

The primary effect of the ending is to engineer a suspension of the reader, both haunted by Milly's memory and on the cusp of a return to Kate's point of view. The novel's closure is a tableau in which Kate and Merton, engaged in one last negotiation, are frozen in a perpetually incalculable encounter. The last sentences expertly position the reader at an interpretative zenith.

> He heard her out in stillness, watching her face but not moving. Then he only said: 'I'll marry you, mind you, in an hour.'
> 'As we were?'
> 'As we were.'
> But she turned to the door, and her headshake was now the end.
> 'We shall never be again as we were!'
> THE END (*WD* 2: 405)

Some critics find a powerful finality in Kate's last words.[26] The ending does drive towards the conviction that there can be nothing more to say between Kate and Merton of any purpose. But neither the characters nor the reader are released by this moment into a future; both remain within the orbit of the past.

Consider again the detailed wording of the last lines. The affirmation '"We shall never..."' seconds 'was now the end' by repeating the claim of finality. But it also contradicts this claim; Kate's headshake might have been the end *then*, but 'now' has already moved on, minutely but sufficiently to deprive 'was now the end' of some of its authority. The act of speech leaves the conversation open, as if Merton might yet reply or Kate add something more – though we cannot know what either of these utterances might be. The final exclamation mark trembles with a desire to end, and the reader is left with this desire on her hands. 'THE END' spells out a finality that leaves us still moving in response. The reader is left struggling, with a particular pleasure, to make the ending 'THE END.' Reading these words releases us only into an eerie narrative after-glow.

James's refusal to sever the threesome categorically is part methodological habit and part theatrical artifice. The momentum of the ending encourages the reader to make a choice between deciding whether Kate walks out (with or without the money) or whether she stays to attempt to salvage the wreck of her relationship with Merton. But the novel's dense style, which has all along required a labour of attention, exerts a counter-movement, detaining the reader at the point where the looming end pushes towards a final, decisive choice.

Far from enabling acceleration towards escape velocity, the final pages maintain a demand for concentration. This effect could be described as a peculiar kind of suspense, from which the reader is not fully released even at the end.

As it proceeds, the novel becomes a space, like a haunted house whose parts we cannot see all at the same time, filled with anticipation and memory, hope and dread, echoes and cross-references, and all gathered under the largely unspoken sign of Milly's death. We wait for the exit from the narrative that her death would provide, but her deathbed-scene is withheld and Kate's final choice remains unspecified. The reader lingers on the threshold of the room/tomb of the novel, caught under its morbid spell. The reader has shared the narrative's fascination with imagining death and cannot immediately return to the light of day – to 'life.'

Style, the cult of the dead, and mourning

The reader of *The Wings of the Dove* performs a kind of death by entering the narrative illusion and vicariously sharing in Milly's demise. By meeting the arduous demands of the novel's style, the reader becomes implicated in the burden of mourning Milly and is initiated into a cult of appreciation.

There are substantial differences in the ways that *The Wings of the Dove* and *Roderick Hudson* enact sacrificial thinking. These can be summed up by saying that sacrifice is generalised in *The Wings of the Dove*. The idea of sacrifice is diffused through the relationships between its characters, and also into the relationship between the novel and its readers. The ending of *The Wings of the Dove* suggests a welter of different candidates for and modes of sacrifice, compared with the relatively overt scapegoating of Roderick. Though only Milly physically dies, all of the main characters are implicated in her death to such an extent that sacrifice and the sacred seem to saturate their world. Wherever they turn, they find them in some form or another. This is tested most by Kate, the major character most resistant to the sacrificial thinking radiating from Milly's death. She cannot have everything but must forfeit love, money, or integrity; and whatever she chooses to forego Milly will have pre-empted her by setting an unsurpassable model of sacrifice. In so far as the reader has become involved with the narrative, some of the difficulty of shrugging off the thinking of the novel also applies to the reader, who becomes implicated in the novel's sacrifices.

One of the ways in which *The Wings of the Dove* enacts sacrificial thinking more thoroughly than *Roderick Hudson* is through the demands on the reader of the more 'difficult' style. *The Wings of the Dove* requires a much higher level of stamina and concentration from the reader, and this challenge can be understood as an intrinsic part of the novel's representation of death. The degree of attention demanded by the style, supported by the detective-fiction aspect of the plot (will Kate and Merton get away with their murderous scheme?), involves the reader in a process of becoming fascinated with Milly's demise. 'She waited' are the novel's opening words, and we wait for Milly's death for hundreds of pages. In the meantime, the novel actively constructs the frustration of our desire for her death as a zone of complex interest and value in its own right. 'Of course, as every novelist knows, it is difficulty that inspires,' suggests James's Preface (*WD* 1: xviii) – inspires both the novelist in creating his characters and situations and the reader in actively responding to what the novel has to offer. *The Wings of the Dove* excels in detaining and entangling the reader in its possible meanings, by virtue of both its dense style and its subject matter. It seeks to initiate its readers into a cult of inspiring difficulty, of appreciation and attentiveness.

Downplaying the difficulty of James's late style is understandable as a publisher's strategy in back-cover blurbs and critical introductions to popular editions. Nevertheless, the stylistic challenge posed to readers of *The Wings of the Dove* is fundamental to the novel's overall effect; this challenge is a primary characteristic of the novel, not an incidental misunderstanding about it. It is impossible to disprove that there might be some readers, not just hardcore Jamesians, who would find no difficulty in reading *The Wings of the Dove*. However, it is possible to point out the kinds of stylistic features that have given rise to the novel's reputation for difficulty – such as its frequent use of personal pronouns in place of proper names, so that it is unclear which character is meant, or the carrying over of abstract concepts from a previous sentence to become the subject as 'it.' Going back to reread in an attempt to clarify meaning generates a peculiar rhythm, as it does in many of James's later texts. There is a notable lack of concrete referentiality, so that descriptions of material objects or indications of physical sensation leap out, producing an intensity of effect that would not occur if there was more descriptive writing with obvious reference to the material world. The overall effect, for me, is that my absorption in the narrative illusion is often interrupted by a lack of fluency in reading. The illusion is not entirely destroyed, but brought into tension with self-consciousness about the difficulty of reading.

Such effects may be common across much of James's later writing, but they have specific implications in the case of *The Wings of the Dove*. The tension between illusion and self-consciousness becomes an aspect of the representation of Milly's death, because the attempt to stay inside the narrative illusion and to grasp the meaning of the novel's sentences becomes a *tribute* to Milly's struggle for life and the significance of her death. Waves of immersion in the narrative, where I seem to be 'inside' the story and it seems real, alternate with periods of floundering, when each phrase is a struggle and I clutch – like Milly 'contesting every inch of the road' – at the wreckage of my concentration.

The difficulty of James's style is indicative of the construction of a modernist high culture that in turn enables such difficulty – whether in a novel by James, Proust, Joyce, or other comparable pioneers of modernist narrative – to seem valuable. The difficulty of *The Wings of the Dove* constructs both Milly's death and the novel itself as worthy of an exceptional level of appreciation. The novel contributes to this task alongside James's other writing and within a literary marketplace increasingly differentiated, from the turn of the twentieth century, between an expanding mass market of fiction and journalism and a minority high-brow market consisting of a literary avant-garde and academic literary criticism. We need not revert to myths of James as an élite formalist detached from social and political change to recognise that his late style is, in part, a response to his perceptions of his market position as an author at the turn of the century. Disappointed by his foray into the theatre, James never entirely surrenders his hopes of commanding a mass readership but recognises his effective status as a minority writer.[27] His late style is a strategy for creating a niche market position, in which all-out attempts to attain a mass readership are sacrificed in favour of pragmatic strategies for securing a small but devoted and influential readership and a reputation for exclusivity.

One way to express the process by which *The Wings of the Dove* seeks to define a select readership is in terms of a cult of the dead.

Like Merton Densher, whose point of view dominates the final three Books, the reader of James's novel becomes involved in a process of deciphering and attributing value to something underspecified, something potentially mysterious, elusive, ineffable, and sacred. This process is akin to initiation into a cult of the dead.

For Ariès, this term describes a cultural shift occurring early in the nineteenth century. The afterlife becomes the scene, not of hell, but of spiritual reunion between loved ones. Public cemeteries become sites for elaborate private memorials. In France, the Revolutionary government secularises the disposal of the dead and, in planning for the development of spacious and hygienic suburban cemeteries rather than the old, cramped churchyards, use the grave and the occasion of personal bereavement as a means to foster a powerful, cult-like attachment to ancestors, land, and nation. The cult of the dead can thus be entered into by Christians, spiritualists, non-believers, and freethinkers.[28] By the end of the nineteenth century, mourning rituals and paraphernalia become highly developed, so that the cult of the dead is an established cultural phenomenon capable of being critiqued. 'The Altar of the Dead,' with its suburban cemetery setting and protagonist obsessed with keeping the flame burning for his dead friends and fiancée, is James's most extreme representation of a secular cult of the dead. Merton's private homage to Milly's memory is clear enough as a further example.

The religious and emotional power of the cult of the dead centred on Milly rubs off on James's novel. By ending before Merton turns into another Stransom and by not showing Milly's grave, the novel evokes the pathos, awe, mystery, and seriousness of a private experience of bereavement and leaves the reader in the midst of this experience, with these emotions unresolved. For Walter Benjamin, this is a way that art maintains a vestigial 'aura' in the age of mechanical reproduction. New media such as photography, film, and lithography undermine the aura of original artworks and strip away the ritual function they previously served. Portraiture, with its unique representation of the face of the dead beloved, provides a last semblance of magic. 'The cult of remembrance of loved ones, absent or dead, offers a last refuge for the cult value of the picture.'[29] *The Wings of the Dove* similarly appeals to the cult of remembrance, even if with some irony and realist detachment, so as to enhance its own aura.

Cult was also the label attached by Maxwell Geismer to mid-twentieth century champions of James's fiction, such as Leavis and Trilling.[30] The meaning of 'cult' here is clearly some way removed from the sense in which it now applies to so-called New Religious Movements, but even so Geismer's charge remains one with some substance, given James's marginal position in English and American literature, the growth of a scattered community of James scholars, and his reputation, however undeserved, for difficulty, élitism, and snobbery. To specialise in James, even as an undergraduate student, is to take on some of this reputation among one's peers, and this can almost have the effect of a social stigma.

The idea that *The Wings of the Dove* constructs a cult of the dead is thus a rich and ambivalent one. The representation of a cult of Milly within the novel is, of course, a different kind of thing altogether from a cult of James outside the narrative. Nevertheless, the projection of Merton's intimate devotion to Milly's memory beyond the narrative and into the relationship between reader, text, and author is a central quality of the after-glow that the novel's dense style and relatively open ending seek to construct. The fragility of this illusion is part of the charm.

Writing about the nature of illusion in James's fiction, Denis Flannery proposes that, by pitting against each other a variety of modes of representation, such as the fairy tale and realist novel, *The Wings of the Dove* creates the illusion that it lies outside all such modes. It thus resists the usual process by which the story becomes reified as a mere book. This effect attaches particularly to Milly, who seems to move into an extra-narrative dimension, analogous to that of the narrator: 'by linking her "unwritten life" with his, James promotes the illusion of her existence as far outside the novel's confines as possible.' However, 'not even the most naive reader is going to consciously assign Milly a place in the historical extra-textual world,' and the illusion that she does make this transition, from character to historical person, is therefore 'far less intense in a second or third reading.' Even so, suggests Flannery, such illusory effects are 'none the less achieved and none the less engaging and important.'[31]

The Wings of the Dove seeks to maintain its hold over the reader up to the final lines and beyond. The depth of engagement demanded by the novel's style fuses with the narrative pleasures of tracing a rich and beautiful woman's demise to create a burden of remembrance that is not easily shrugged off. James's novel seeks to implicate its readers in the processes of cult-like remembrance and appreciation and to make them feel responsible for mourning Milly.

The Wings of the Dove mourns more than just a fictional character. It also mourns the real historical person of Minny Temple as well as its author's dreams, in the wake of his failure in the theatre and his increasing difficulty in obtaining serialisation for his fiction, for a novelist's art of both high refinement and mass influence.

Merton's point of view filters the reader's sympathetic mourning response to Milly's death; in the last Book, his grief becomes a model of mourning. While Kate Croy, Maud Lowder, Susan Stringham, Lord Mark, and Sir Luke Strett will all mourn Milly in their own way, Merton's grief becomes the pervasive atmosphere of the ending. Yet his style of mourning is hardly unproblematic, as it is defined by betrayal.

For a while, Merton is haunted by the sex he has with Kate in his room in Venice. She visits his room between Books Eighth and Ninth, whereas he visits Milly's between Books Ninth and Tenth. Though censorship of direct representations of sexuality in English print culture goes some way to explaining the lack of direct reporting of these scenes, their formal similarities are deliberate. Both scenes occur in the door-like space of the intervening blank page between Books. Merton's memory of each peak experience of intimacy constitutes his privacy, which he jealously guards by denying anyone else access to his room or thoughts. When he closes his door to leave, the memories are kept inside; when he returns, he finds them still there. The visit from Kate is carnal and Book Ninth opens with a localised account of its effects upon Densher. By contrast, we gather that the visit to Milly is spiritual and its effects are not reported directly but instead defuse throughout Book Tenth. In remembering Kate, Merton is the almost helpless subject of a forceful 'hallucination' (*WD* 2: 236) whereas in remembering Milly he is a tender, baffled mystic straining in devotion to something ineffable. This is a specific transformation of his masculinity. The meeting with Kate is an attempt to resolve his long-standing feelings, climaxing in Venice, of being demasculinised by the enforced company of women and of being controlled by Kate. Now, having asserted his masculine ego's sexual prerogative, he seems to adopt a post-coital celibacy – 'for life, as it were,' to borrow the phrase from *Washington Square*. He exchanges a fallen woman for a virgin. Having satisfied his curiosity to cut the hymenal pages of Kate's 'uncut volume of the highest, the rarest quality' (*WD* 2: 222), he tires with the prospect of domestic familiarity and regresses to a fantasy of lifelong courtship of an unobtainable woman: to the uncut page of Milly's lost letter. Hence the final scene of the novel is a kind of divorce, even though there has been no actual marriage.

Merton's visit to the Brompton Oratory implies his desire to desexualise Milly's memory, disassociate his two experiences of intimacy in Venice, and be absolved of his guilt in bringing about Milly's death. James was among a generation of writers who felt the draw of Catholicism around 1900 as a response to aesthetic as much as religious needs. He never converted. Merton's entry into the Oratory exposes him to criticism as much as it proposes a model for mourning Milly. Thus Merton's obsession with her lost letter can be read as a sign of profound psychological damage – of melancholia.[32] In its pathological relationship to healthy mourning, melancholia resembles morbidity as a medical construction enabling the definition of normative behaviour. Freud, for example, characterises melancholia in terms of obsessive thought patterns and self-absorption; it is closely related to narcissism, in that the loss of the beloved is transformed into a loss of a part of the ego.[33] Merton's sense of responsibility towards Milly's memory recalls James's objection to the neglect of the dead in London in the Preface to 'The Altar of the Dead' and is given much space at the end of the novel. Yet his point of view is not a comfortable one for the reader to share in the closing stages, as we become aware of how much he has lost, how his life is ruined, and how he has been ethically compromised.

In the final pages, Merton hands Kate the power of choice (to marry him or take the money) in a competitive gesture of renunciation that aims to prove he is more pure than her. We want to know what Kate will do in response, and this desire takes us away from wholly identifying with Merton's point of view. Indeed, the novel all along makes the reader work to establish a position of understanding from which to judge the characters and their actions. It encourages us to take responsibility for our own interpretation rather than expect to find one given to us, defined for example by a particular character's point of view or by an intrusive narrator. For Gert Buelens, this process is characteristic of Jamesian narrative, which 'demands of the reader not just an emotional responsiveness, but also an ethical assumption of responsibility for the history that is enacted.'[34] Power, ethics, and history are constructed in part through language and representation, and James's writing strives to make its readers aware of their role in this process.

The responsibility of the reader of *The Wings of the Dove* is to feel, with Merton, the pathos and fascination of Milly's death and simultaneously to deconstruct its fictionality, romance, and pseudo-spiritual quality. The novel's appeal for responsiveness from the reader is tempered by a realist refusal to allow consolation or easy judgement. The reader is invited to perform Milly's journey towards death and Merton's mourning along with these characters, to investigate morbidity experientially, and to take responsibility for this experience.

The ethical nature of the reading proposed here differs from that of explicitly moralistic approaches that imply an absolutist ethical framework for judging the characters' actions – for example, that Kate's lies automatically deserve moral censure. A similar judgement can be the outcome of reading *The Wings of the Dove* in terms of religious allegory, as Dorothea Krook illustrates in her classic study of James. The novel parallels the religious

> in the use, to begin with, of the Dove as a central image; but even more in the conception of the tragic conflict as a clash between the powers of light and darkness – between the power of the world, figured in Lancaster Gate, to undermine and destroy the noble and the good, and the power of the good, figured in the person of Milly Theale, to abase the proud by answering it with forgiveness, loving-kindness and sacrificial death.[35]

Krook's grand, abstract oppositions of light and darkness, goodness and worldliness, and nobility and pride imply that the novel, for all its complexity, ultimately arrives at a simple conclusion where the characters can be categorically judged. By redeploying the structure of Christian thinking less problematically than the novel itself does, this reading narrows the novel towards melodrama – an approach later developed persuasively by Brooks.[36] Evil is an already anachronistic rhetorical register by the time James was writing, 'a matter of texts and letters' inherited, according to Robert Weisbuch, from the Bible, Dante, Milton, Hawthorne, and the Puritan tradition.[37] To suppose that the idea of evil might on its own offer a sufficient means of detailed ethical, let alone cultural or aesthetic, analysis of James's representations of death is to melodramatise by insisting too quickly on judgements about right and wrong. While *The Wings of the Dove* flirts with melodrama and sensation, it strives to construct a world of complexity, subtlety, ambiguity, and fluidity that exceeds those modes. Unfortunately, perhaps, Kate's lies do not automatically damn her; the novel shows action and responsibility to be pragmatically situated within a web of need, perception, representation, and social relationships. Ethics in the novel blend with politics, erotics, and semiotics, without these elements becoming entirely indistinguishable.

The desire to label Kate wrong or evil bespeaks the desire to assert a healthy moral realism and the corresponding morbidity of moral relativism. As Robert Pippin suggests, the idea of evil is a stake in debates about the continuing survival of ethical awareness in a modern, secular world.[38] The recognition that Kate at the end of the novel is ethically compromised is not an escape into a separate ethical realm, but a heightening of awareness of the conditions of modernity, in which ethics are entangled with power, representation, and desire. There is no clean, uniquely ethical space in this novel, just as there is no position outside culture, language, and subjectivity, in which the representation of Milly's death might be hygienically performed.

The prevailing critical meaning of the term 'morbid' – today as much as when Auchard was writing and in the 1890s – is pejorative. The ethical basis for this usage, stemming from its medical meaning as defined by Foucault, is a desire to police the interest of death for writer and reader in the name of moral and social hygiene. Through its style, use of point of view, reticence about Milly's demise, and carefully open ending, *The Wings of the Dove* seeks to implicate the reader in its protracted representation of death and mourning and thereby to complicate the reader's sense of a proper interest in death beyond medicalisation, sensationalism, melodrama, or religious allegory. The end of the novel leaves the reader *still* attached to the interest of Milly's death.

James's novel is not yet existentialist, but nor does it work primarily with 1890s discourses of morbidity as decadence and degeneration. *The Wings of the Dove* seeks to wean its readers off the neglect of the dead and the desire not to be 'branded at once as "morbid." ' It appeals to the vestigial aura of fiction's capacity to memorialise the beloved dead and thus accrues readerly appreciation for itself and its author as exemplars of a modern art of rare refinement and ethical responsibility.

4
Afterlives

Roderick Hudson's marble sculptures will physically outlast him, however good or bad they may be as works of art. Though we know relatively little about them, they presumably aim to succeed within the tradition of classical and Renaissance sculpture, whose enduring stone forms, omnipresent in the great Italian cities, are the very model of the so-called immortal masterpiece. Writers, by contrast, know from the start that any enduring fame their productions may win will depend upon reputation and reproduction, for their words are not set in stone. At the end of James's career, troubling questions about literary posterity are made urgent by the commercial failure of the New York Edition of his works, the task of writing his autobiography, and the legal niceties of settling his estate. *The Wings of the Dove* anticipates, but is not yet driven by, the career endgame. In this novel, the posthumous potential of James's art becomes a grave and fabulously complex matter, awaiting construction with a sense of both fresh opportunity and rising urgency. Responses to personal experiences of bereavement since the 1880s find expression in the forging of a new style in the face of ongoing difficulty in establishing a mass audience for his fiction at the start of the new century.

The Wings of the Dove grapples with questions about what survives, how, and at what price, most obviously through the triangular relationship between its three main characters. Different kinds of survival and casualty, of response and outcome in the face of an unavoidable endgame, define this relationship. The strongest contrast is between

Kate and Merton, who physically survive, and Milly, who seems to survive in the hold of her memory and money over her friends. The novel plays out a terminal scenario that entails the conclusive exercising of power in specific manoeuvres. When it comes down to the line, the relative positions of those involved are clinched, once and for all. Irreversible divisions are made between survivors and casualties. The narratives that define what counts as survival have to get themselves heard, because there will not be a later period when these things can be renegotiated. As well as reprieve – continuing to live after the moment when you could have died – survival is also about mastery. Milly seems to have outplayed Kate. Like a parasitical ghost, she lives off Merton's devotion to her memory. Her lost letter assumes an authoritative status in his mind as if commenting on life from beyond the grave.

These are some of the shades of meaning of 'survival' that Derrida teases out in 'Living on: Borderlines.'[1] Derrida proposes that a narrative text can enact a suspension of the binary difference between life and death by a process of interruption. His examples are a novel by the philosopher Maurice Blanchot and a poem by Percy Bysshe Shelley, but he could also have cited *The Wings of the Dove*, with its deliberate omission of Milly's climactic deathbed scene and sustained withholding of news of her death. At the end of the novel, Milly is divided from Merton and Kate by the line between death and life, but the difference between these terms has been eroded so that all three characters, each in their own way, become examples of the living dead.

Fraught with James's suspicions about modernity and elegiac desire to champion the past, *The Wings of the Dove* creates subtle intimations of afterlife. These suggestions are important aspects of the novel's overall affect, but they are not easy to spell out. The novel derives much of its power from the reader's recognition that Milly, finally, is dead, but the meaning of this term is no longer quite what it was. The novel transforms ideas about death into ideas of a strange, fragile, and yet potent afterlife. This shift reflects both the rich cultural matrix of the turn of the twentieth century and the strategies of a writer beginning to anticipate the end of his career. I explore Jamesian afterlives in terms of three inter-related contemporary contexts: new communication technologies, quasi-magical notions of consciousness, and publicity culture.

Communicating with the future

To the technophobe, new equipment and associated techniques spell death to a previously held way of life. At its most extreme, retraining is an entry into a kind of afterlife – into the experience of living as a stranger in the future. The complaint that technology dehumanises is a familiar one and provides the ground for a celebration in cyborg theory of the breakdown of binary distinctions between human and machine.[2] *The Wings of the Dove*, superficially devoid of reference to machines or new media, nevertheless anticipates the technologisation and mediatisation of society, culture, individual experience, and discourse in the twentieth century. The novel was composed during the first few years of James's adjustment to the help of a typist, and through subtly affecting the novel's composition the typewriter becomes an inherent part of the complex representation of Milly's death. At the same time, the typewriter is a filter for James's internalisation of and creative response to far-reaching impacts of new technologies and media at the start of the new century – that is, for an aspect of James's sense of modernity. Today the typewriter is a machine of the past, displaced by computers in all but the most impoverished or old-fashioned of offices, but in 1900 it was a symbol of the future. Composing Milly's death via a typewriter thus subtly introduces ideas of afterlife into the novel.

It is not yet clear whether or not technology will become a major concept for reading James. Critics have begun to recognise the social, aesthetic, and subjective impacts of telegraphy, the typewriter, and photography as part of James's nuanced responsiveness to modernity. For Mark Seltzer in *Bodies and Machines*, a major part of the work performed by James's late style is to disguise the presence of the typewriter at the scene of writing.[3] He argues that the extent to which individuals and culture at the end of the nineteenth century have become machine-like is offset in James's fiction by regressive appeals to a market culture that has been largely superseded in its influence. Though Seltzer does not discuss *The Wings of the Dove*, this novel plays into the hands of his argument in so far as it is saturated by economic metaphors, such as the description of Maud Lowder as the 'Britannia of the Market Place' (*WD* 1: 30). Following Seltzer's argument, the novel's monetary imagery disguises a more fundamental problem for James at this time, namely the machine-likeness of society, culture, and individual consciousness. The typewriter is pivotal because it materialises the gendering of new communication technologies within James's compositional process itself. Compared with the old market culture, machine culture constructs its subjects as embodied beings, interfacing with new technologies in specific ways. The privilege of appearing to remain a liberal, self-possessed, and disembodied individual is mostly gendered male. Hence James does not work at the typewriter himself – a task performed for him mostly by women – and he describes the experience of dictation in terms that preserve his sovereign creativity and personal relationship with his muse.[4] In other words, James covers up his own *becoming-cyborg*.[5] His dictated fictions – including *The Wings of the Dove* – inscribe this hidden work of self-preservation.

For Friedrich Kittler in *Discourse Networks 1800/1900*, the end of the nineteenth century marked a paradigm shift in the global conditions for producing, distributing, and consuming discourses. This shift is illustrated by James's switch to dictation.[6] By 1900, literature professionalises itself in the face of rival visual and aural media, such as cinema and the phonograph. Writing becomes a form of information-processing, and the typewriter is its distinctive machine. The author becomes an expert encoder of a stream of signs, which the reader must learn to decode. For modernist writers, the limits of encoding imposed by the medium of print become a new frontier, and the resulting literature requires new kinds of responsiveness from its readers. These changes to discourse, observed at large in Kittler's complex argument, are surely borne out by James's late style. *The Wings of the Dove* is densely encoded, has a strong sense of secrecy, and at times seems to be exhaustively detailed. The difficulty of the novel's style risks appearing to be illegible and demands that the reader effectively train themselves in something akin to a new language. The awareness of other media, such as photography, is not overt in this novel in the way it is in, say, 'Crapy Cornelia,' where photographs play an explicit role in the narrative. In the New York Edition, the addition of photographic frontispieces retrospectively modernises *The Wings of the Dove*, published seven years earlier. Even in the 1902 text, however, it is possible to read the presence of photography in the cultural field as making itself felt as an *anxiety* about the capacity of the written word to represent and hold the memory of the dead. Thus Kittler, extending the point made in Benjamin's famous essay, suggests that photo-albums, with their appearance of capturing the dead accurately via an automatic process, broke the monopoly that literature had previously enjoyed. 'Our realm of the dead has withdrawn from the books in which it resided for so long.'[7]

How, then, can the novelist represent death with refinement and power when fiction has become a peculiar kind of information-processing? How can the typewriter help to honour the memory of the dead?

The presence of the typewriter at the scene of writing can to some extent be felt in the strange sound quality of *The Wings of the Dove*. Its sentences, despite being originally spoken to a typist, do not sound in the reader's mind like anything that could easily be read aloud.[8] The novel neither looks nor sounds obviously like machine output, yet part of the difficulty of the style is the gap between the fluctuating concentration span of a human reader (no matter how expert, or how sequestered her environment) and the sustained, relentless demands for concentration made by the text. This is a version of the complaint commonly levelled against machine interfaces, namely that the machine sets an undeviating pace, to match which the subject must make herself machine-like. At the same time as the novel is difficult to read, the sound quality is doubtless part of the way that the text nevertheless gets itself read. In the final stages of *The Wings of the Dove*, the mystery of Milly's illness and the mystery of whether the conspiratorial lovers will get away with their scheme merge into the mystery of Merton's sanctification of Milly's memory. His conscientious straining to hear the 'faint far wail' of her lost letter (*WD* 2: 396) is a primary model for the aural effect of the novel's style. In other words, sound quality is part of the novel's construction of a cult-like relationship between reader and text, resembling that between Merton and Milly's memory. Narrative enchantment is performed in part through the sound quality of the novel's distinctive style.

This is a question of power relationships between author, text, and reader. A topical form of this question in the late nineteenth century was mesmerism. As Daniel Pick argues in his study of Svengali, fin-de-siècle discourses around mesmerism crystallised chronic and emerging concerns about the moral dangers of demagoguery and crowd psychology, about the power of advertising, music, and celebrity, and about cultural degeneration.[9] James participated in such discourses, for example by satirising mesmerism in *The Bostonians*. Part of the realism of his earlier fiction, such as *Roderick Hudson*, is its postulation of a mature, liberal reader, persuadable but fundamentally freer than the reader constructed by the later fiction, where the power relations between author, text, and reader are thoroughly entangled. *The Wings of the Dove* offers a critique of the enchanting power of fiction, but one that is immanent within an extensive, subtle, and diffuse *performance* of mesmeric power, both in the narrative structure and in the aural and semantic aspects of the novel's style.

Discourses around mesmerism in the late nineteenth century in turn reflect what Jonathan Crary describes as a culture of attention. In *Suspensions of Perception*, Crary shows how discourses of attention combine with technologies of attention to construct the modern subject within a culture of spectacle and consumer capitalism. Crary has in mind ideas such as Helmholtz's theory of the physiology of vision, devices such as Edison's kinetoscope, and socio-aesthetic configurations such as the vogue for theatrical exhibitions of hypnotism.[10] While appearing to liberate the viewer, inventions such as cinema (and, more recently, television and the personal computer) actually function as panoptic architectures for social and economic organisation. 'They are methods for the management of attention that use partitioning and sedentarization, rendering bodies controllable and useful simultaneously, even as they simulate the illusion of choices and "interactivity." '[11] This statement is again suggestive of James's late style, in so far as that, too, demands a high level of attention, typically within private, sedentary conditions. With its careful use of ambiguity, the late style gives the reader the sense of being an active interpreter with a peculiar freedom to construct the meaning of the text. Crary illustrates his argument with visual images from the late nineteenth century, but James's novel shows how Crary's argument might be extended to reading fiction of the period, too. *The Wings of the Dove* is not a mass medium, like cinema, broadcasting, or the Internet. Instead of constructing its readers as being useful to consumer capitalism, James's novel constructs its attentive readers for the privatised purposes of memorialisation – what I have compared with the nineteenth-century cult of the dead.

James's New York Edition Preface to *The Wings of the Dove* repositions the idea of attention as far away as possible from instrumentality.

> Attention of perusal [...] is what I at every point, as well as here, absolutely invoke and take for granted [...]. The enjoyment of a work of art, the acceptance of an irresistible illusion, constituting, to my sense, our highest experience of 'luxury,' the luxury is not greatest, by my consequent measure, when the work asks for as little attention as possible. (*WD* 1: xx–xxi)

James's urbane argument here aims to flatter the reader by presenting the requirements of attention as a 'luxury,' in the spirit of the idea of fortunate difficulty that recurs in the Prefaces. The reader should apparently be grateful that *The Wings of the Dove* is so hard to read. Elsewhere, a less confident idea of attention figures in James's critical sense of cultural change around the turn of the century. On 11 December 1902, James writes to W. D. Howells, his long-time friend, realist ally, and associate from *Atlantic Monthly*:

> The *faculty of attention* has utterly vanished from the general anglo-saxon mind, extinguished at its source by the big blatant *Bayadère*[12] of Journalism, of the newspaper and the *picture* (above all) magazine; who keeps screaming 'Look at *me, I* am the thing, and I only, the thing that will keep you in relation with me *all the time* without your having to attend *one minute* of the time.' (*L* 4: 250)

Condemning journalism and illustration, James determines to deploy contrasting strategies and devices, namely those novelistic practices that constitute a common ground between him and Howells. The newspaper and illustrated magazine require no attention and yet monopolise the reader. James's fiction will compete with such power by reasserting the importance of attention to the select few of those still capable of responding. In *The Wings of the Dove*, demands upon the reader's attention are foregrounded so as to engage the reader in a form of *service*: towards the representation of Milly's death and towards literary attentiveness for its own sake. This service is analogous to that which Merton bears towards Milly's memory.

The extremity of the novel's style – derived in part from the use of the typewriter in the compositional process and suggestive of Kittler's idea of high modernist literature as an expert language of encoding – constructs the novel, Milly's death, and the attentive reader as machine-like. This machine-likeness is modern rather than industrial: that of producers and consumers of discourse rather than of workers in cotton mills. Though *The Wings of the Dove* is elegiac and sides against Kate as a woman of the new century, the novel is also experimental, in both its style and its representation of Milly's death. The typewriter was not an absolute novelty by 1902 – Mark Twain was one of a handful of journalist pioneers who 'threw away their pens' in the 1880s[13] – but it was an overt sign of modernity for James when he introduced it into his workroom in the provincial town of Rye. The typewriter in this context is a symbolic manifestation of the future, absorbed into the very heart of James's compositional process prior to his eye-opening visit to America and rebirth as a cultural critic and autobiographer in his final decade.

Writing fiction via a typist in 1902 is like writing both in the future and on time borrowed from the past. To dictate Milly's death – representing also his cousin, Minny Temple's death and the death of James's dream for an art of high refinement and mass popularity – to a listening typist is to have already an attentive audience who will outlive the older author, carry on the memory of the dead, and testify to the value of the novelist's art. (In 1901 James had just hired Mary Weld, and *The Wings of the Dove* perhaps reflects the author's hope that he had found in this woman a more amenable listener than his previous employee, William MacAlpine.[14]) To compose Milly's death via a typewriter is to equip her memory in advance with some protective aura of a future that will consist in more such machines and machine-like communicative relations. Although the modernity of the typewriter was to last no more than a century, in 1900 this device occupied the horizon of the future sufficiently to begin transforming Milly's death into a kind of afterlife. Without turning his hand to science fiction, James could go no further in this direction.

The text's construction of the reader's attention modernises a mesmeric relation between performer and audience. Written on the cusp of emergence into a new century, *The Wings of the Dove* represents simultaneously a death of the old and a survival into modernity.

Out-thinking death: 'Is There a Life after Death?'

From new technologies to the occult is a small step. As many critics have observed, the development of the two seem to go hand in hand in the late nineteenth century, with spiritualist séances, for example, making use of inventions such as the telephone and telegraph to represent communications between the living and the dead.[15] In his exploration of the emergence of telepathy at the intersection of territories including marginal science, the fin-de-siècle gothic, colonial experience, and tele-technology, Roger Luckhurst suggests that the 1890s were a period in which the nature of consciousness and its boundaries were particularly open for rethinking.[16] Unlike his brother, William, James kept his distance from psychical research; but his fiction from 1890 onwards is full of potentially occult scenarios, carefully poised between the literal and the metaphorical. For Luckhurst, telepathy is a means to read James's late novels, including *The Wings of the Dove*, as 'romances of occult relation.'[17] This relation extends not only between characters, but also between the living and the dead, and between author, medium-like typist, and reader.

The idea that artistic consciousness might, like a form of telepathy, constitute a means for thought to cross the boundary between life and death is mooted in James's essay, 'Is There a Life after Death?' Sharon Cameron suggests that this essay is a report on the experiment in techniques of immortalisation carried out eight years earlier in *The Wings of the Dove*. 'If you think enough, the essay would imply, you deny death. The novel shows how.'[18] How, then, does the essay imagine the posthumous survival of consciousness, and what does it tell us about the representation of death in the novel? How does the comparison help us to read *The Wings of the Dove*, with its cult of the dead, as a romance of 'occult relation'?

The first half of 'Is There a Life after Death?' rehearses arguments against posthumous survival. Consciousness is wholly dependent on the material brain, so has no supposable vessel through which to continue after death. The dead, even those who might most be expected to attempt to communicate with the living, are without exception silent. The interest of séances is social and psychological and concerns the medium and her trance, not the demonstration of life after death. We die piecemeal during life, and this is a one-way process. The second half of the essay, however, explains why these arguments fail to determine James's personal attitude to life after death. His life *as an artist* has reached a pitch that seems to be irreversible, even by death.

[I]t is in a word the artistic consciousness and privilege in itself that thus shines as from immersion in the fountain of being. Into that fountain, to depths immeasurable, our spirit dips – to the effect of feeling itself, *quâ* imagination and aspiration, all scented with universal sources. What is that but an adventure of our personality, and how can we after it hold complete disconnection likely?[19]

The word 'privilege' in the first line of this extract alerts the reader to issues of power and social position masked by the individualist tone of the essay, signalled by the neighbouring phrase 'artistic consciousness' and the emphasis on 'personality.' This is important, because James's proposed relation with the infinite is not just irreversible ('how can we after it hold complete disconnection likely?') but also *colonising*. There seems to be no limit to the possible extent of expansion, nor any opposing force, in the prospects for posterity formulated in the essay's final lines:

I like to think it open to me to establish speculative and imaginative connections, to take up conceived presumptions and pledges, that have for me all the air of not being decently able to escape redeeming themselves. And when once such a mental relation to the question as that begins to hover and settle, who shall say over what fields of experience, past and current, and what immensities of perception and yearning, it shall *not* spread the protection of its wings? No, no, no – I reach beyond the laboratory-brain.[20]

Once one starts to expect an afterlife, these lines suggest, such an expectation ('mental relation') of itself opens out into ever greater expectations. The 'fields of experience' to which James expects, somehow, to gain posthumous access are ostensibly limited by the phrase 'past and current,' but *future* is implied by 'shall' and 'yearning.'

Metaphors related to the dove are crucial to the strange formulation of these closing lines. Mundane doveness ('hover and settle') becomes magnified into transcendental Doveness ('immensities of perception,' 'protection of its wings'). Shortly before these final lines, the essay discounts the 'superficial' similarity between its formulation of faith in an afterlife and Christian orthodoxy.[21] This is not a matter for which we can take James's word. The title of *The Wings of the Dove* alludes most obviously to two verses in the Psalms;[22] but dove imagery is fairly consistent throughout the Old Testament in equating the dove with defence against evil through meekness and purity. In the New Testament, this defence becomes more formally glorified through the identification of the dove with the Holy Spirit and also becomes associated with righteous vengeance. James's novel modifies its readers' perceptions of the power of dove-related imagery by sensitising them to its appropriation by those on earth. Initially it is Kate who compares her friend with a dove, but Milly hungrily adopts this image and immediately applies it to measuring her social success and to planning her behaviour (*WD* 2: 283–4). The entanglement of love and power at the heart of the book here takes a decisive step. In biblical terms, Milly is hardly meek and powerless, since she is so rich, and the novel therefore implies a critique of Milly's appropriation of the image of the dove. At the same time, the novel and its author have a wider stake in the access to power figured by this image. For example, calling the Piazza San Marco pigeons 'doves' makes them seem to be Milly's spies during Kate and Merton's conspiratorial meeting.

> It was as if, being in possession [of 'solitude and secrecy' in the midst of the Piazza], they could say what they liked; and it was also as if, in consequence of that, each had an apprehension of what the other wanted to say. It was most of all for them, moreover, as if this very quantity, seated on their lips in the bright historic air, where the only sign for their ears was the flutter of the doves, begot in the heart of each a fear. (*WD* 2: 193)

Grammatically it is of each other's unspoken thoughts ('quantity') that Kate and Merton are afraid, and the doves provide a contrasting innocence and brightness of movement in the public space around them. But the convolutedness of the sentence makes the doves' movement seem to be more immediately the source of fear. By omitting just one comma we have: 'the flutter of the doves begot in the heart of each a fear.' By virtue of her identification with the dove, Milly's presence reaches out through the novel wherever bird imagery is used: perching, hovering, taking flight, alighting, and so on. In the final lines of 'Is There a Life after Death?' James assumes some such telepathic power for himself: the anticipation of massive, expansive power after his death, based on his power of thought in life.

To return to the essay, 'decently' (in 'not being decently able to escape' in the second extract quoted in p. 119) also strikes a keynote of the closing lines. Its gentlemanly tone masks not genteel ineffectuality – life after death as an opportunity merely to re-experience and refashion a personal past – but overt rapaciousness: life after death as an opportunity to possess 'fields of experience' and 'immensities of perception and yearning' as yet unlimited. The essay repeatedly claims that what matters about life after death is the survival of personality. This seems to be a way of proposing modest external limits to posthumous consciousness, within which internal deepening might quite properly carry on unlimited. These limits are not, however, merited by the formulation of the final lines, which point to imperialistic ambition. This ambition is veiled by the term 'artistic consciousness,' with its suggestion of a distinctive, isolated, personal faculty untainted by artistic *practice* – that is, by a lifetime spent producing privileged objects expressly designed to penetrate and possess the consciousness of readers.

At the time James wrote 'Is There a Life after Death?' the commercial failure of the New York Edition had just hit home, and it is therefore understandable that he should try to imagine how his consciousness might survive independently of his productions. As Christopher Stuart points out, James was deeply depressed over the Edition, since what was intended to be his monument appeared to be forgotten moments after its erection. *The Wings of the Dove* belongs to an earlier, optimistic era of James's thought about death, one still inspired, suggests Stuart, by the novel's potential to become an immortal masterpiece.[23] The novel's thinking about death and afterlife are not simply superseded by the essay's, however. The consciousness that 'Is There a Life after Death?' imagines surviving posthumously is the one created through and irreversibly containing such peak artistic experiences as the writing of *The Wings of the Dove*. For Stuart, by the end of his life James 'had given up monument building forever,'[24] but surely *The Wings of the Dove* never worked with a merely monumental idea of the novel-as-masterpiece. Its style seeks to engage readers in what feels like an intimate conversation, a fluid and cunning dialogue between author, text, and readers across complex temporal and cultural spaces. Bakhtin describes a dialogic quality of fiction where the text addresses not only immediate social addressees contemporaneous with the writing of the novel, but also an ideal '*superaddressee*,' one whose 'absolutely just responsive understanding is presumed, either in some metaphysical distance or in distant historical time.'[25] This formulation suggests some of the cult-like qualities of *The Wings of the Dove* discussed in the previous chapter. Writing did not lose its romance for James in his final years; it remained a source of power, futurity, and connection with the world even after he had relinquished the idea of writing as monument-building that preoccupied him for a few years during his final decade.

The Napoleonic mode of James's deathbed dictation is often cited as the culminating expression of an imperial characteristic that stretches back over the later stages of his career. Adeline Tintner, for example, finds it triumphant in James's autobiographies, which she reads as a new form of monological fiction, where all boundaries have collapsed between characters, narrator, and author. They are gathered up into 'the growth and development of the single consciousness of the writer' – into what, borrowing from James, she calls a 'usurping consciousness.'[26] Sharon Cameron traces the imperial mode further back to find it operating in the representation of Milly's thinking about death. She argues that thinking is so radically strange in *The Wings of the Dove* that it becomes impossible for the reader to recognise it *as* thinking. The principal object of thought in the novel is death, which is precisely that which cannot be thought about (being outside life). Therefore, for Cameron, what passes for thought in the novel is actually 'a magical or hallucinated transfer of power from death to thought.'[27] If thinking is unthinkable, then thinking is like death and thereby attains some of death's power.

The reader is implicated in this process of making thought as powerful as death. Cameron finds that *The Sacred Fount*, with its extreme use of focalisation and possibly insane narrator, victimises its readers through 'the tyranny of thinking.'[28] As we have seen, *The Wings of the Dove* has more subtle ways than 'tyranny' of manoeuvring its readers into a position subject to the power of thought. For Cameron *The Wings of the Dove* shows how to out-think death. Surely the novel also shows how to out-think the living. The vitality centred on Kate seems to be eclipsed by the novel's fascination with thinking about Milly's death, and some of this process extends over the reader, who is detained by the ending as if entombed with the characters and their mourning for Milly.

The quasi-magical and colonising qualities of James's thought are also illustrated by his relationship to his final amanuensis, Theodora

Bosanquet, as Pamela Thurschwell has shown. Many years after James's death, Bosanquet began to use techniques of automatic writing to take dictation from his spirit and so continue her earlier secretarial role. Rather than reduce this practice to 'a simplistic Freudian psycho-dynamics' of repressed desire, Thurschwell proposes an intersubjective conception of writing that 'might encompass talking to the dead or to or through a machine.'[29] In his use of dictation and his rewriting of family letters in the autobiographies, James's writing during his lifetime had already become intersubjective. For Thurschwell this quality reflects a late nineteenth-century concern with communication, expressed by writers like Oscar Wilde and Sigmund Freud. Their interest is inspired on the one hand by technologies, such as the telegraph, and on the other by quasi-magical discourses, such as the séance. James's own rethinking of communication extends to a 'fantasy of total communication, from mind to mind without interference.'[30] In other words, his later fiction uses 'magical thinking' – which Freud defines as a fantasy of the 'omnipotence of thoughts'[31] – as 'a powerful tool to expand the potential effects of consciousness and the possi-bilities for intimate ties and identifications.'[32]

Within *The Wings of the Dove*, the boundaries between characters are notoriously fluid and permeable. This effect climaxes in Merton's obsession with Milly's memory, figured in the image of the overarching wings of the dove. The novel seeks to construct a comparably intimate relationship – as between the living and the dead – between itself and its readers. As explained previously, it does this by demanding an unusual degree of attention, by enlisting the reader in the task of mourning Milly, and by detaining the reader at the ending.

If these effects are examples of magical thinking, then one name for the type of magic involved is necromancy. In magic with the dead, the living and the dead enter into a relationship where agency is ambiguous and becomes intersubjective. Are the living using the dead by summoning and commanding them? Or are the dead using the living by possessing and speaking through them? And what agency should we attribute to the texts and technologies that mediate this relationship and its subjectivities?

So in summary, Merton's intimacy with Milly's memory and the reader's intimacy with the text during the act of reading are both necromantic scenarios. The endgame of *The Wings of the Dove* imagines a cult of the dead, centred on Milly. The sustained difficulty and aural quality of the style initiate the reader into a cult-like apprecia-tiveness that is projected beyond the narrative and into the reader's relationship with the novel and its author. This effect is telepathic and necromantic, and also mildly futuristic by virtue of the type-writer's role in the novel's composition.

Biographobia and the reader as legatee

The idea of living on in the hearts of lovers, friends, and family is a commonplace consolation, even though these individuals will themselves inevitably die. Enduring memorialisation requires a stable social mechanism. An artwork can physically outlast a human body, but it will be 'immortal' only so long as it continues to receive the attentions of an audience. Thus Pierre Bourdieu defines afterlife as a collective product and social prize – 'eternal life is one of the most sought-after social privileges'[33] – and for Bauman, too, 'immortality is ultimately a *social relation*.'[34] Individuals compete through a variety of available strategies, including authorship, for the privilege of being remembered. Sociologically, personal immortality is a function of a group's perpetuation of itself beyond the lifetime of its current members – that is to say, a social product bestowed upon selected individuals, rather than a creation of personal genius.

What external steps beyond his writings did James take to obtain the social privilege of posthumous literary recognition? To what extent did he apparently rely instead on what I have been outlining so far: crafting his novels and tales (especially *The Wings of the Dove*) as narrative enchantments possessing an internal, quasi-magical power to foster a cult-like appreciation by future readers?

James's literary activities in the final decade of his life are shaped by a concern with his legacy and with setting in place measures to encourage his posthumous fame while protecting his privacy. He constructs the New York Edition, writes his autobiographies, burns personal papers, and makes testamentary requests to his family via letters and a will. Through such actions, he went some way to becoming what Ian Hamilton terms 'his own keeper of the flame.'[35] Michael Millgate, on the other hand, points out that James's will is actually less careful about his literary estate than the wills of many other writers, and than his long-term campaign against biography in his fiction might lead us to expect. Perhaps James ultimately recognised the impossibility of securing himself absolutely against the bogeyman of the posthumous biographer.[36]

Tensions between public and private simmered throughout the second half of the nineteenth century, both in James's writing and in Victorian culture more generally. The public–private distinction was first of all a gender one. According to the ideology of separate spheres, a woman's place was in the home, where she could exercise moral influence over her husband. The 'angel in the house,' a wife was her husband's second conscience, protecting him from the temptations of public life, whether in business or politics.[37] James's fiction, of course, rarely sets foot in this male world. His novels and tales consistently focus instead on private, domestic life, which they seek to expand into a ground rich in ethical, political, and social meaning. Anticipating the late twentieth-century slogan that the private is the political, James's fiction, most critics now agree, offers an immanent critique of public life and national culture.

The Tragic Muse (1890) illustrates how the public–private distinction becomes a vehicle for specifically aesthetic debates in James's fiction. Its hero, Nick Dormer, gives up a parliamentary seat so that he can pursue his painting. He thereby betrays the solemn mission passed on to him by his father on his deathbed – a memory invoked coercively by Nick's mother and by the family friend, Mr Carteret, who makes a further exhortation to Nick on his own deathbed.[38] Nick's defection from politics to art is fraught with complex and contradictory impulses which do not fully resolve even by the ending. His portrait of Julia Dallow – the woman who could ensure his success in politics – attracts the newspapers' attention when it is exhibited in a private view, but they seem no closer to marrying.[39] The other plot of the novel, concerning the rise to fame of the eponymous actress, Miriam Rooth, suggests that art cannot be dismissed as a merely private affair. She challenges gender boundaries by appearing in public, where she wields power over her audience.

By the time of *The Wings of the Dove*, however, public–private tensions in James's fiction are channelled by his bêtes noires: the new forms of biography and journalism through which James explores questions of posthumous reputation.

Merton's defection from Kate to Milly can be read as a defection from journalism (his nominal trade, which he appears scarcely to practice) to what James's fiction consistently constructs as its opposite, namely art (implied in Merton's sensitivity and respect for privacy). This defection recurs explicitly in James's tales from the 1890s onwards, for example in 'The Death of the Lion' and, as discussed later in this chapter, 'The Papers' (1903). Such defections constitute a distinctively Jamesian participation in topical debates around 'New Journalism.' This term was used casually in 1887 in an article by the new editor of the *Pall Mall Gazette*, but was then taken up by Matthew Arnold in a denunciation of the *Gazette* and its readers as 'feather-brained.'[40] 'New Journalism' thereby became a key term for debates about the relationship between literature and journalism. The populist style, content, and audience of evening dailies such as the *Gazette* make visible a challenge to the established cultural order represented by morning dailies, especially the *Times*, with its sobriety of form and substance. (This challenge recalls that of popular, illustrated serials to the literary periodicals, especially *Atlantic Monthly*, that had enabled James to emerge as a writer in mid-century America.) New Journalism introduces headlines, illustrations, and interviews and trades off sensationalism and a cult of celebrity; the roots of today's media and visual culture emerge.[41]

New Journalism named a major reconfiguration of discourse and authority, another facet of which was the relatively new form of investigative biography. The *Dictionary of National Biography* (first series 1885–1903) and *English Men of Letters* (1878–1919) are major Victorian projects that sought to memorialise figures of national importance. Both projects are respectful towards their subjects without collapsing into hagiography. For David Amigoni, the *DNB* constitutes a 'sophisticated bid for, and consolidation of, cultural power' and is designed to canonise a group of writers – both the subject and the biographer.[42] *English Men of Letters* serves a similar purpose and additionally aims to 'establish the relations of authority supervising reading' by showing how the works of key writers should be read.[43] Both projects were part of a process by which literary criticism was professionalised within the Universities. The management of the national canon, suggests Ian Small, was one of the powers and social functions of an emerging new academy.[44] A developing community of professional academics began to challenge the old network of prestigious individual writers, who worked primarily in belle-lettristic mode. A key instance of this was John Churton Collins's notorious attack on Edmund Gosse for his lack of scholarship in 1886, only a few years before the founding of the School of English at Oxford.[45]

Biography thus became an important ground for the contesting of cultural authority around 1900 through the disputing of the lives of key literary figures. Laurel Brake distinguishes between celebratory biography written by, or on behalf of, the widow and scandalous biography written by former friends of the subject, or Judas. For example, a decade after Walter Pater's death and 1895 entry in the *DNB*, he became the subject of two biographies appearing in quick succession: one of the Judas type, the other of the widow type for the *EML* series.[46] Key developments for the climate of scandal in the 1890s were the Cleveland Street affair, Oscar Wilde's trials, and the reporting of divorce court proceedings. New Journalism, investigative biography, and scandalous trials – what Richard Salmon gathers together as a 'culture of publicity' – form a crucial context for understanding James's fiction from 1890 onwards.

As James's stories show repeatedly, private letters, such as friends might have access to beyond the control of a subject's family, were *the* tool by which investigative biography could reveal an unofficial side of someone's life – hence James's burning of his own personal papers. His relation to the professionalisation of criticism was more ambivalent than to the creation of a literary canon. According to Small, James defended Gosse against Collins, both as a personal friend and as a fellow practitioner of an unscholarly form of criticism.[47] James was no Oxford man and he makes no appearance in the *DNB* as either contributor or subject. He was somewhat of an outsider in terms of his sexuality and seriousness about art, like Wilde and Pater, as well as by virtue of his nationality. Yet James was careful to keep his distance from Wilde, and the spirit of *Hawthorne* (1879), James's contribution to *English Men of Letters*, is thoroughly in keeping with its canonising, regulating spirit. (The famous passage bemoaning the paucity of features of the American scene – 'no Oxford, nor Eton, nor Harrow'[48] – was unsurprisingly taken by many American readers as a subordination of their national literature to that of Britain.) Sometimes, then, James constructed his position within the literary field by associations with respectability, while on other occasions he might court a reputation for literary daring. British writers in the 1890s and early 1900s typically constructed their position in this way in relation to a number of common topics, such as the New Woman, French fiction, coded homosexuality, and also dead writers and poets. The impact of a writer's utterances on such topics was qualified by the nature of the periodical or publisher used.[49]

'The Aspern Papers' is the most celebrated example of James's anti-biographical stories. Other tales that centrally concern the reputation of the dead are 'Greville Fane' and 'Sir Dominic Ferrand' (1892), 'The Real Right Thing' (1899), and 'The Abasement of the Northmores' (1900). In *The Spoils of Poynton* (1897), 'Covering End' (1898), and 'Flickerbridge' (1902), the dead take the form of unique ancestral homes and artworks. These texts adopt a variety of stances towards the invasion of privacy by journalists and biographers, from didacticism to more complex, ironic, self-critical awareness. James's literary realism, with its psychological and domestic focus, carries out invasions of privacy that resemble to some extent those of the journalism he decried.[50] In his stories about the defence of the reputation of the dead, the defence often consists in engineering the reader's consent to banning the characters within the narrative from making public the story to which the reader has just become privy. So in 'Greville Fane,' where the first person narrator is asked for an obituary of the eponymous female novelist, what we read instead of his flattering article is his personal recollection, that will go unpublished, of the unglamorous reality of her domestic situation.

Towards the end of his life, James's attitude towards biography seems to narrow. In a letter of 7 April 1914 to his nephew, James writes of his desire 'to frustrate as utterly as possible the post-mortem exploiter' (*L* 4: 806). This desire is made concrete in James's burning of personal papers. Millgate argues that such 'biographobia' is by no means an unusual response by twentieth-century writers to the prospect of their death.[51] The self-memorialising arc of James's twentieth-century work, especially the New York Edition and the autobiographies, together with paper-burning and the making of testamentary requests by personal letters and wills, fits a pattern matched by James's peers, such as Hardy, and by more recent writers.

The Wings of the Dove needs to be included in James's testamentary arc. The novel addresses similar concerns of self-memorialisation as the New York Edition and the autobiographies, though embedded within the original fiction itself rather than imposed in the form of revisions or a retrospective history of the self. 'The Aspern Papers' and other tales concerning the reputation of the dead can also be read as testamentary performances in their own right. These earlier fictions position *The Wings of the Dove* as intermediate, between a conscious career endgame and explicit participation in debates catalysed by New Journalism, investigative biography, and reporting of scandalous trials in the 1880s and 1890s.

The Wings of the Dove reconfigures these interconnected contexts. First, the novel is concerned about questions of privacy and memorialisation, but these are raised about a person who is not of recognisable national importance. Milly is not a statesman, nor a celebrated cultural figure such as a writer. She might have some claim to nobility and public importance by virtue of her family's wealth, but that would be in New York, which the novel declines to visit. Instead, the importance of remembering Milly and protecting her reputation comes to depend upon her private value for her group of friends. Secondly, the usual gender pattern in investigative biography is for a male biographer to try to gain power over a male subject by publishing the letters. This pattern is changed around somewhat in New Journalism when the reporter is a woman. In *The Wings of the Dove*, Kate is more active than Merton in trying to use Milly's letter to gain power over her memory, and this adds an element of demasculinisation to Merton's defection from journalism. Also, Kate burns the letter instead of publishing it, since the power of the document resides not in its potential to create scandal but to consolidate Merton's private bond with the dead woman. The gesture of course backfires. The biographical task of writing the life of another is supplanted by less concrete, more mysterious burdens of remembrance. Milly has no biographer, but Merton fetishises her letter as if it might somehow still function as a vital source of evidence for understanding her life. After being destroyed, it becomes a lost precious relic that would have testified to her existence.

Alongside a fear of biographical scandal, we can see in *The Wings of the Dove* an attempt to construct the reader as a 'keeper of the flame' – that is, as one of James's select band of legatees. Tracing James's literary influence on his peers and successors, Adeline Tintner's study of his 'legacy' and 'afterlife'[52] reveals a wide-ranging dispersal of his intellectual and aesthetic estate, from allusion to plagiarism and from literary fiction to films and advertisements, all largely unmediated by law. Her title concepts deserve more careful consideration in their own right, especially in terms of how they are constructed within James's own writings.

In Derrida's elaborate reading, Freud's *Beyond the Pleasure Principle* (1920) uses narrative strategies to reach out possessively into the future[53] – much as I have been suggesting occurs in *The Wings of the Dove*. Both texts are extended negotiations of cultural legacy. A key image for Derrida is Freud's analysis of a child's repetitive game, which Derrida reads as a father-text for the psychoanalytic movement. By not declaring that the child is in fact the author's own grandson, *Beyond the Pleasure Principle* effectively creates the basis for a Freudian reading of itself, out of its author's reach.[54] Freud explains that the game entails the child repeatedly throwing a reel wound with thread into his cot while making sounds that Freud interprets as ' "*fort*" ' (gone away) and 'a joyful "*da*" ["there"]. This, then, was the complete game – disappearance and return.'[55] Initially indicating the mother's disappearance from the house for hours each day, ' "*fort*" ' ultimately signifies death: the child's mother dies before the book is published, the First World War threatens death to Freud's sons, and he is treated for cancer of the mouth.[56] If death is the ultimate ' "*fort*," ' the post-humous ' "*da*" ' by which Freud returns is both his grandson and the psychoanalytic movement.

By contrast, James left behind neither a genetic heir nor a movement comparable to psychoanalysis. James's childlessness provides an obvious, if reductive, explanation about his interest in posthumous literary recognition. As Richard Dawkins might argue, James's writings seek to reproduce their author's ideas (or *memes*[57]) in the minds of their readers and there is added urgency to this task because James has not reproduced his genes – though, of course, he had a favourite nephew to whom he bequeathed the bulk of his estate. Compared with *Beyond the Pleasure Principle* as Derrida reads it, *The Wings of the Dove* circuitously constructs its readers as precarious legatees in the face of James's relative lack of a familial heir of his own making. The novel's textual strategies (such as use of focalisers, an overly dense style, and the open ending) erode distinctions between text, characters, author, and reader so that the reader becomes temporarily a keeper of the flame, not just for Milly, but for Minny Temple, James, and the art of fiction.

The lengths to which *The Wings of the Dove* goes to engage its readers in a cult of the dead reflect its author's mistrust of posthumous biography – a discourse nominally serving to establish enduring, communal recognition of the deserving dead. Years before James's biographobia becomes manifest in the burning of personal papers, it generates a creative interest in his fiction in securing by its own devices some of the social privilege of immortality.

Ex-novelist

Composed mostly in the twentieth century, Hardy's poetry repeatedly imagines its narrator as a ghost. After the commercial and critical failure of *Jude the Obscure* (1895), Hardy-the-novelist seems to have died and writing poetry becomes for him a kind of afterlife.[58] After the *The Wings of the Dove*, James's fictional writings include several major tales, but within the longer form of the novel there is only *The Golden Bowl*, a work that is conspicuously not death-centred. To what extent does Milly's death end the series of James's novels, so that the fictions that follow articulate a kind of post-novel afterlife? Is *The Wings of the Dove* effectively James's final writing of death in the form of the novel and, more than this, his coming to terms with the possible death of the novel in the twentieth century?

The claim that *The Wings of the Dove* marks the end of James's career as a novelist might imply that *The Golden Bowl* is not a novel, and that *The Sense of the Past* and *The Ivory Tower* (both published posthumously in 1917) and *The Other House* and *The Outcry* (1911) can all be excluded from this category too. The last two of these works are novelisations of play scenarios. Their origin shines through – to my mind to the detriment of their effectiveness as novels – in a three-act structure and restriction of action for each scene to a stage set, from which characters enter or exit left or right. The unfinished *The Sense of the Past* (which takes up an idea set aside since 1900) and *The Ivory Tower* are starting points for major novels, but whether James would have completed them if he had lived is uncertain. As in Milly's would live/could live chiasmus, James would perhaps have written these novels if he could have lived, but would he perhaps have lived if he could have written them?

Unlike these works, *The Golden Bowl* is a fully achieved novel that deserves its champions. After completing it, James embarked on his American tour, from which sprang *The American Scene* and a series of tales, and then directed his energies to the New York Edition and the autobiographies. Ross Posnock identifies these writings as James's 'second major phase,'[59] defined by a turn towards cultural criticism and away from the novel – as if that form could no longer serve his creative purposes. James's novels do not contain within themselves the sole reasons why their author turned his attention to other work, but they do offer some level of explanation in so far as they were exercises of creative energy by which James maintained his capacity as a writer. Producing a long novel, such as *The Princess Casamassima*, *The Tragic Muse*, or *The Wings of the Dove*, was a major investment of time and energy, capable of exhausting their author emotionally and artistically. After the intensively productive period of the 'major phase,' there is a rupture in the sequence of novels that had begun with *Watch and Ward* and continued for over 30 years more or less uninterrupted. This rupture is decisive, unlike James's foray into the theatre in the early 1890s. *The Golden Bowl* might be said to have caused this rupture by taking James to the limits of the novel as he could conceive the form.[60] *The Golden Bowl* is unusual in James's fiction in presenting a fertile marriage, but this novel itself does not lead on to further complete and original novels; the preceding work, *The Wings of the Dove*, gives birth to sterile offspring, as it were. This novel offers its own explanation as to why James stopped writing novel-length fiction. It is such a powerful performance of thinking about death that its author could never bring himself to surpass it afterwards (as James's Preface says of Roderick's breakthrough sculpture). *The Wings of the Dove* is an experiment in techniques of immortalisation that locks in place the connection between artistic consciousness and posthumous survival discussed in 'Is There a Life after Death?' Its representations of death, especially the construction of Milly's vanishing act and the cult-like ending, set this novel apart from its predecessors; it is the place where James's thinking about and representation of death and afterlife are most intense, sustained, and powerful.

It is tempting to read *The Wings of the Dove* as an über-text of Jamesian death. However, this novel does not overrule all of the representations of death in James's earlier fiction, which propose their own models of Jamesian death. Nor does it constitute his final, definitive writing of sacrifice and posterity, so that no further writing whatsoever is necessary. Indeed, the formulations of death and survival in *The Wings of the Dove* immediately give way to new formulations.

James does not stop writing. Any doubts that he could think comically about ideas of legacy and memorialisation, taken rather seriously in *The Wings of the Dove*, are dispelled by 'The Birthplace,' published just one year later. The newly employed warden of the official birth-place of a thinly disguised Shakespeare initially looks forward to upholding the author's posthumous reputation – a motive familiar from James's anti-biographical tales. When he realises that there is no factual basis for the site's claim to be the birthplace, he salvages his honour by performing the tour-guide's narrative of authenticity to ridiculous excess. His creative genius pulls in the crowds, who either do not notice or do not care about his irony. This tale is a special case, where the living can profit from the reputation of the dead without at the same time compromising it, since the great author has so effectively carried out a biographical vanishing trick (he has left no trail whatsoever).

'The Birthplace' satirises the pseudo-religiosity of the touristic cult of the author, who is consistently referred to by capitalised third person pronouns in the manner of God. By contrast, the principle function of the appropriation of religious dove-imagery in *The Wings of the Dove*, as discussed earlier, is to enhance the pathos and cult potential of Milly's death. The ideas of sacrifice, remembrance, and respect for the dead in the novel are rewritten most directly in 'The Birthplace' by a shift in mode; the tale is more comic than tragic, whereas the novel is more tragic than comic. 'The Birthplace' is not primarily a rewriting of *The Wings of the Dove*, but the comparison does demonstrate that the work of representing death – in the later fiction typically organised around themes of afterlife, survival, and legacy – is ongoing across James's career, is always provisional and inconclusive.

By arguing that afterlife must be personal to be meaningful, 'Is There a Life after Death?' makes anonymity a variation of death. Yet the threat of scandal and posthumous biography makes anonymity something also desirable. Many of James's stories after 1902 explore the relative values of personal prominence and personal obscurity, usually defined in relation to art and journalism, integrity and power. These stories are characterised by the mutation of, and even retreat from, notions of personality and privacy central to James's anti-biographical stance up until *The Wings of the Dove*.[61]

'The Papers' explicitly plays with ideas of death and afterlife defined in relation to publicity culture. As Richard Salmon suggests, this comic tale conjures an extreme, farcical vision of a world in which publicity culture has become 'a well-nigh universal ontological condition,' an all-enveloping medium operating as if through the ether.[62] Such a world alters traditional meanings of personhood and immortality.

Maud Blandy and Howard Bight are two aspiring journalists, who loiter around the Strand in the hope of finding an opening. As in *The Princess Casamassima*, the London streets are contrasted with interior spaces. Whereas that novel patterns the movements between these spaces under ideas of secrecy and surveillance, 'The Papers' patterns them under ideas of secrecy and celebrity. The secret is more blatantly empty and commodified in the tale. The comedy follows Maud and Howard's gradual rejection of the values of journalism. They fail to cash in on the topical value of the name of Sir A. B. C. Beadel-Muffet KCB, MP, a character who never appears directly in the narrative. He carries out the ultimate publicity coup of returning from the dead (an erroneous headline story about his suicide in a Frankfurt hotel room) to claim the capital generated by the interest in that story. Howard, who had already conceived of such a coup, suggests that Beadel-Muffet's resurrection so undermines the reliability of any future news of his death that ' "He'll never die. Only *we* shall die. He's immortal." '[63] The jest is sour and half in earnest. Beadel-Muffet's immortality consists of a complete identification with his publicised self – with the continuing circulation of his preposterous name. The story offers the contrasting fate of Maud's protégé, Mortimer Marshall. He was to gain fame by announcing revelations concerning Beadel-Muffet's death; the latter's resurrection spoils Marshall's chance for publicity and condemns him to frustrated obscurity. In the publicity-obsessed world of the tale, Marshall and Beadel-Muffet become contrasting types of the living dead.

'The Papers' rewrites concerns central to *The Wings of the Dove*. The space of mystery once constituted by private life has collapsed under the logic and power of corporate mass media. A vivid, offstage space is systematically suggested through a motif of headlines called out by newsboys, a combination of settings around the Strand, and the absence of actual scenes of newspaper production. These scenes are gendered male, as Howard has some access to them but they are completely banned to Maud, the primary focaliser. Towards the end of the story, when this ban is lifted by Maud's having an exclusive to sell, she replaces the ban of patriarchal professionalism with one generated by her own integrity. The illuminated offstage glory is tawdry, while the private life of relative obscurity that Maud and Howard move towards at the ending has lost much of the potential for sustaining mystery that privacy has in *The Wings of the Dove*. Their suggestion that they might write a 'tile' or 'ply' (*TP* 636) is self-mocking and fails to extricate them from the machinery of publicity and journalistic criticism that they have already failed to master from within. Nor does their decision to marry amount to a convincing escape from the tarnished world of journalism to a world of restored values. The closing lines announce the forthcoming marriage with a carefulness that has to mark the distinction at stake between literature and journalism.

> 'Whom will *you* marry?'
> She only, at first, for answer, kept her eyes on him. Then she turned them about the place and saw no hindrance, and then, further, bending with a tenderness in which she felt so transformed, so won to something she had never been before, that she might even, to other eyes, well have looked so, she gravely kissed him. After which, as he took her arm, they walked on together. 'That, at least,' she said, 'we'll put in the Papers.' (*TP* 638)

This affirmation of marriage gestures towards a happy-ever-after ending. Endings are always to some degree a stylistic flourish, partaking of genre conventions and also functioning as an authorial signature. The closing cadence only partially represents the complexity of the narrative as a whole. Graceful, rich, and ambiguous, James's final lines here are, in part, a formula for solving the formal problem of ending. But a substantial difficulty is perhaps signalled by the complexity of the syntax, particularly the phrase 'well have looked so' (awkwardly referring back to 'so transformed, so won'). Maud's final comment questions the successful severing of the couple's connection with the source of their anxiety. The basis on which Maud and Howard have chosen to marry, indicated by their renunciation of journalism, is presumably an embrace of an artistic refinement of taste and complexity in thought and relationships. The happy-ever-after gesture of the ending is then in danger of seeming to evoke a redemption of their relationship through a regressive innocence. We cannot swallow Maud and Howard's desire to undo their contamination by journalism – to become ex-journalists – when the tale has taken such trouble to show the pervasive power of publicity culture. This power operates as circuits of desire, exposure, and obscurity; it has always already taken possession of the characters and their relationships and cannot be excised by a single act of renunciation. Once a journalist, always a journalist.

Maud and Howard's engagement rewrites the separation of Kate and Merton in *The Wings of the Dove*. Marriage is now made possible by the joint renunciation of journalism and its worldly values. The role of Milly's death in thwarting marriage is taken by Beadel-Muffet's resurrection in enabling marriage. Whereas Kate and Merton are forced apart by the conflicting values of Milly's memory and money, Maud and Howard are brought together by recognising the triviality and unreality of Beadel-Muffet's celebrity. On the other hand, Howard seems emasculated by the ending in a way that recalls Merton's fate; Howard is positioned below Maud in the closing action, in which, 'bending,' she initiates the kiss. This twist complicates the transformation of Maud from New Woman into happy, loving wife.

'The Papers' can be read as a jeux d'esprit, rewriting an earlier, more serious work in a lighter vein. The tale sacrifices the resolution of *The Wings of the Dove* to the professional demand to keep writing, and to keep using the representation of death as a means to maintain James's position as an author. Ideas about afterlife and memorialisation, cheapened by the cult of celebrity, shift from being the most complex thing that the text reaches to comprehend to being familiar components in an effort to reach another, still emerging understanding of personal identity and representation in the coming century.

Despite Barthes's declaration of the 'death of the author'[64] and the broadening of literature courses to include a more diverse range of authors and texts, canonical authors, such as Henry James, have to a large extent retained their central position in literary studies. This book would probably not have been published otherwise. On the other hand, cinema, television, and digital media, even if they have not brought about the death of the book (which continues to sell in huge quantities), have long since deposed the novel from its nineteenth-century position of cultural pre-eminence. Though James could not have foreseen the precise form that today's popular media take, their power relative to literary fiction is anticipated in works such as 'The Papers.' The elegiac mood of *The Wings of the Dove* stems from its intimation of a post-literate future, dominated by visual forms of culture, as much as from its remembrance of Minny Temple. The novel's composition via typewriter offers only limited protection against the extent of ongoing changes to communication technologies and to the cultural landscape as a whole. Film adaptations of this novel and others by James arguably constitute a kind of afterlife in which the author ekes out his cultural capital, the value of which (probably as high now as it has ever been) is underwritten by the academy. Tintner celebrates the extent of James's enduring literary influence and iconic status, but these will need to be maintained in the cultural marketplace however it continues to develop.

Foreseeing the dwindling of literature's cultural prestige, James did not decamp to some other medium more likely to sustain his posthumous reputation. The photographic frontispieces to the New York Edition constitute only a gesture to the rise of visual media, a gesture designed in fact to reconfirm the modernity of James's prose fiction and its continuing claim to cultural authority. 'Is There a Life after Death?' avoids equating posthumous survival with the production of immortal literary masterpieces. Nevertheless, the intensity of thinking about death carried out in *The Wings of the Dove* testifies to the extent of its author's investment in the medium of printed fiction as his primary means to imagine some kind of afterlife. This novel is rendered mildly futuristic by the mediation of the typewriter and quasi-telepathic by the reach of consciousness and dialogue across time and space that it seems to enable. Writing fiction at the dawn of the new century offers no guarantees of conventional artistic immortality, given the fickle and vulgar values of the mass market, the betrayals of investigative biography, and the emergence of rival media. Literary fame can fade or turn to scandal. For all the 'magical thinking' of *The Wings of the Dove*, no amount of literary fame can actually restore a dead author to social life and a body, to his senses, loves, and power. Milly is *dead*, after all. The fragility of the cult-like after-glow of *The Wings of the Dove* reflects its author's recognition of the precariousness of posthumous reputation, and his interest *even so* in pushing the medium of printed fiction to the verge of being an elusive, idiosyncratic, and self-sustaining form of transcendence.

After 1904 James effectively abandons the novel in favour of cultural criticism, the New York Edition, and autobiography, as if these might offer a way beyond the novel, a way to survive as a creative writer. On no account can this fourth major phase be deemed a literary failure on its own terms. If we had nothing but his work after *The Golden Bowl*, James's place in literary history would still be assured, as they say. However, recognising the value of this period in his career (which for a long while went relatively neglected by critics) does not erase altogether the sense of loss created by the lack of novels in James's production after 1904. How can the author of a novel so involved as *The Wings of the Dove* truly cut his ties to the form? Once a novelist, always a novelist. Just as the ending of 'The Papers' fails to convince us that Maud and Howard can simply divorce themselves from journalism, so it is difficult to imagine James rooting up within himself the habits and desires of his former profession. The novel has surely been *the* special form whereby James has dipped into the 'fountain of being' and emerged 'all scented with universal sources.' James's rebirth into his fourth major phase is thus different in kind from his earlier artistic revivals, such as after his disaster in the theatre. He has survived again, but one more piece of him has died, this time a crucial one. His visit to America inspires an astonishing renewal of creativity, but one infused, as never before, with a terminal anxiety.

5
Demography in *The Portrait of a Lady*

None of my deaths is a statistic. This motto evokes James's authorial pride in the sophistication of his fiction, and also an assertion of human freedom and social privilege made by his novels and tales in the face of the social sciences that emerged during his lifetime.

The Portrait of a Lady is centrally concerned with the tension between types and classifications on the one hand and the singularity and aspirations of the individual on the other. In terms of the social breadth of its canvas – the range of contemporary lives and deaths that it shows – this novel is arguably James's most ambitious and densely realised work. It tries out a series of portraits of its heroine against character types defined by gender, nationality, and class. This testing process is commonly understood by critics in terms of formal properties of narrative closure; the novel's exploration of free will, responsibility, and the social construction of identity; and topical debates around the American leisure class, gender roles, and transatlantic marriages. An important contributory factor to these topical debates was the census, which introduced into public discourse new kinds of thinking about women, social structure, and nation. The census exemplified the power of statistical methods for government and social science, a power that had been growing and becoming more publicly visible throughout the century. In direct contrast to the literary project of his avowed master, Balzac, James's fiction responds to this rise of statistical thinking with an emphatic distaste for numbers and with disapproval of deterministic or systematic literary treatment of the individual in modern society. James never becomes a committed naturalist – that is, a novelist-as-social-scientist.

His heroine, the prototypical American woman, Isabel Archer, believes that she is special, and the novel's notoriously open ending, empowered by the climactic pathos of Ralph's deathbed scene, allows her character to retain a glow of indeterminacy. With its pessimism and extended play on actual and metaphorical death, the novel triumphally demonstrates its own capacity, as a form of public discourse, to make and keep its modern, representative heroine special through her darkest hours. To attempt a demographic-style survey of the characters in *The Portrait of a Lady*, and of mortality in James's fictional population as a whole, is therefore to read against the grain.

Calculation, the crowd, and the sublime

The census provides a statistical basis for topical debates around women, marriage, education, and work in which *The Portrait of a Lady* intervenes. The 1851 and 1861 figures revealed an excess of 'superfluous' unmarried women and inspired discourses of emigration and imperialism, for example in terms of British governesses exported to the colonies.[1] The census is an exemplary Victorian achievement, built on eighteenth-century actuarial work for life assurance companies, the development of a massive legal and administrative apparatus to support the 1836 Registration Act (which changed requirements for recording of demographic data), and the gradual professionalisation of statistics during the nineteenth century.[2]

The census provides a contemporary measure against which to compare James's fictional population, a measure to which historical analysis has added retrospective understanding of demographic trends. Maureen Montgomery's analysis of transatlantic marriages, for example, takes James's fiction as a primary source alongside autobiographies and newspaper articles and then contrasts these with numeric data derived from sources such as *Burke's Peerage*, probate records, and surveys of estate acreage and rental income – that is, data collected at the time but whose historical significance has become apparent only retrospectively.[3] The result is an historical narrative, illuminating for reading James's fiction, about the economic, social, and personal reasons behind the transatlantic marriage phenomenon.

James's fiction itself scrupulously avoids overtly numeric discourse. Instead, it evokes *value*, *quantity*, and *incalculability* as suggestive ideas – as if to imply that these are organic, humanist, and person-centred, whereas *numbers* are mechanical, scientific, and depersonalising. The distaste for numbers in James's fiction is sometimes part of its characteristic use of unspecificity to create effects such as erotic and supernatural suggestion, especially in the later fiction. Occasionally, actual numbers threaten to bring readers face-to-face with social and economic realities underlying his characters' predicaments. When numbers do enter the narrative, they often index vulgar commodification, for example of the financial value of a potential spouse. In *The Portrait of a Lady*, the amount of Isabel's inheritance from her uncle (seventy thousand pounds) becomes tainted in this way as it becomes retrospectively her own price tag. She sees that, for Madame Merle and Gilbert Osmond, this amount has eclipsed her own intrinsic value as an individual human being. The narrative names the number so as to savour its bitterness.

Metaphors of calculation, especially related to the idea of working on a 'sum,' pervade James's novels and tales, not just superficially but indicating a major narrative habit. For example, in 'The Next Time' the narrator ponders the riddle of why his friend, Ralph Limbert, who tries to write trash to make money, always ends up writing so finely that he fails commercially. Working with dross, Limbert produces, according to an unfathomable process, artistic gold that is worthless in the market. 'It was like an interminable sum that wouldn't come straight; nobody had the time to handle so many figures. Limbert gathered, to make his pudding, dry bones and dead husks; how then was one to formulate the law that made the dish prove a feast?'[4] The strange yoking of mathematical and culinary images suggests conceptual and emotional entanglement at a non-trivial level. The narrator's inability to understand the wizardry of Limbert's art matches the novelist's inability to understand the simpler formulae of popular successes and the impatience of a mass audience to go beyond these. This puzzle is, of course, suggestive of James's own troubled relationship with the literary marketplace.

Calculation is also a moral metaphor for the failure of the likes of Gilbert Osmond and Madame Merle to respect the autonomy of other individuals. An author may dispose of a character as part of his fictional formulae, but to do so in real life is another matter. Isabel accepts responsibility for her part in making her unhappy marriage, but finally has no doubt that her husband and Serena have wronged her by using her for their own ends. As argued at the end of Chapter 3, James's later fiction, including *The Wings of the Dove*, complicates the melodramatic character of the calculating villain, such as Kate Croy, and, in terms of its difficult style, is overtly calculated itself in its manipulation of the reader's attention. That novel makes the reader share in the calculations of the author and his characters, and moral responsibility becomes increasingly difficult to allocate in any simple manner.

The strategic preference in James's fiction for a sense of quantity over actual numbers reflects gender divisions between the masculine world of business and politics and the feminine world of leisure and domesticity. Equally, the distaste for numbers suggests patrician distaste for accountability and transparency to inspection. Being audited is an intrusion upon privacy and privilege. Transatlantic marriages betrayed financial vulnerabilities among a British aristocracy unused to either inspection or competition from outside their ranks. Conspicuous consumption – spiralling competitively into increasing commercialism and powered by nouveaux riches industrialists and financiers from both home and abroad – was a primary threat to the British landed aristocracy during the late nineteenth century. This is a backdrop to the retaliatory dramas of social exclusion, snubbing, and strategic marriage exemplified in many of James's tales.[5] James's distaste for numbers can also have an ethnic dimension. For example, in 'Professor Fargo' (1870) brute numbers appear in the form of $93.87 rent demanded by the Jewish owner of a public hall in New York, which the eponymous Irish charlatan is too impoverished to pay. The disgust expressed by James's first-person narrator – speaking from an established Anglo-Saxon ethnicity distinguishing itself from newer immigrants – extends to the spelling out of the exact amount owing *in words*.[6] The distaste for numbers in James's fiction is thus part of a high-art cultural formation that includes assumptions about gender, class, and ethnicity.

More broadly, the aversion to numbers can be read as a response to the growth of statistical, sociological, economic, managerial, and demographic discourses during the nineteenth century. Journalism might deal with these, but never literature worthy of the name. For James, these discourses are fundamentally incompatible with the art of fiction. This incompatibility extends to the representation of death. Literature must respect the death of the individual and cannot deal successfully in the abstractions of anonymous deaths among the crowd.

In James's literary criticism, Balzac is the prime example of the dangers of mere numbers for the novelist. Introducing a translation of Balzac's *Deux Jeunes Mariées* in 1902, James characterises the author of *La Comédie Humaine* as being only half an artist, because he is also half an historian. 'One asks oneself as one reads him what concern the poet has with so much arithmetic and so much criticism, so many statistics and documents, what concern the critic and the economist have with so many passions, characters and adventures.'[7] The switch from one to the other gives rise to unpardonable breaks in narrative tone, when Balzac-the-artist hands over his '*data*' to 'his twin-brother the impassioned economist and surveyor, the insatiate general inquirer and reporter' (*HB* 96). The mention of the reporter reminds us of James's aversion to new forms of journalism. James admires the realist specificity of Balzac's novels, but pities his obsession with representing the France of his time (the first half of the nineteenth century) in its entirety. Systematically organised and administered, this society is 'both inspiring enough for an immense prose epic and reducible enough for a report or a chart' (*HB* 93). Balzac resembles a caged animal captivated by the sheer scale of his self-imposed task (*HB* 99). Satisfactory neither as art nor as history, his monumental output risks amounting to a 'catastrophe' and 'tragic waste of effort' (*HB* 94). Though James opens his essay with an avowal that Balzac is the greatest of all novelists, he effectively argues for his own superiority as a purer kind of artist, less driven by material facts, less in thrall to a grand project, and more fluidly responding to the psychological and social complexities of modernity. Thus Balzac's tell-tale obsession with 'francs and centimes' is 'unfathomable' to James, who looks beyond their 'odious' existence (*HB* 98). Of course, many critics object to James's interest in the transcendence of economic conditions. Terry Eagleton, for example, reads Isabel as a social parasite whose miseries and triumphs are defined primarily by an economic basis suppressed by the narrative of *The Portrait of a Lady*.[8]

Balzac was writing in a period of optimism about statistics. In the peace after Napolean, European states produced an avalanche of public statistics that seemed to hold out the prospect of a comprehensive understanding of society. Statistics in the 1820s were thus a direct inspiration for *La Comédie Humaine*.[9] Over the next 40 years, statistics grew into a new social science, associated particularly with the name of Adolphe Quetelet, who plotted individual behaviour against the normal distribution curve and aimed to establish a system of social laws based on statistical analysis. In the 1860s, Buckle's statistical account of the history of civilisation[10] was as hot a topic of conversation as Comte's positivism and Darwin's theory of the origin of species. The anti-statistical backlash took many forms. Dickens's *Hard Times* attacked apparent indifference to the individual from utilitarian reformers, political economists, and bureaucrats, enamoured of facts and statistics. Statistical fatalism – the idea that criminals and suicides, for example, are statistically inevitable and therefore cannot help being what they are – was felt to be an offence to free will and human freedom, but also too crude scientifically. In physics the foundations of quantum theory were laid by a growing emphasis on indeterminism and probability, while statisticians themselves moved away from Quetelet's focus on the norm by choosing to explore the complexities of variation and divergence. By the 1890s, eighteenth-century ideas of a fixed human nature had been replaced in many areas of culture by ideas of normalcy and deviation – reflected, for example, in the discourse of morbidity discussed in Chapter 3. Statistical and social-scientific conceptions of the individual and group behaviour had begun to establish their influence in modern government and commerce.

Mark Seltzer takes *The American* as a text by James that particularly registers the pressure of statistical thinking. He cites the phrase 'Newman was fond of statistics' and finds in the New York Edition Preface to the novel a use of 'the idiom of the consumer survey and marketing sample (99 out of 100).'[11] James's Preface spells out this number in words, not digits, however, and the number is in any case an ideal one. 'Hundred' and 'thousand' occur many times in *The American*; they consistently show James's text assimilating the numeric and, as it were, denumericising and neutralising it. Nevertheless, Seltzer's larger argument is convincing, namely that this novel explores a double-speak about the relationship between the individual and culture. The individual is produced through becoming a type. What Seltzer calls 'statistical persons' are manufactured by the analyses undertaken in realist and naturalist fiction, by consumerism, and by surveys such as the census. Like other technologies and discourses of control and surveillance contributing to Foucault's disciplinary complex in the nineteenth century, statistics produce modern sub-jectivities by the construction of viewable, countable types of person. At the same time, social privilege attaches to having an inner life, opaque to surveillance and free of social determination. Hence in the emerging discipline of psychology the individual is conceptualised as predictable and automaton-like, but also as indeterminate and spon-taneous. For Seltzer, full literary expression of statistical thinking occurs in the stories of Stephen Crane. They are obsessed with numbers, counting, and calculation and are populated by 'statistical persons' such as gamblers, prostitutes, and war casualties – denizens of the urban underworld, 'cases' positioned at the intersection of the specific and the general, the concrete and the abstract.[12] Crane exemplifies the naturalist novelist-as-sociologist, a description that clearly cannot be applied whole-heartedly to James. Lyall Powers claims that *The Portrait of a Lady* marks the end of James's early phase and that *The Bostonians, The Princess Casamassima,* and *The Tragic Muse* constitute his most naturalist phase, but clearly there remain fundamental differences of aesthetic method and ethical stance between even these three works and those of avowed naturalists.[13]

The statistical basis of the emerging discipline of sociology is illustrated by Durkheim's 1897 study of suicide, which was *the* exemplary statistical topic of the century.[14] Durkheim negotiates a position between determinism and free will and concludes that suicide is a pathological deviation from the norm and thus a case of social morbidity. This is surely not the view that James expects the reader to take of Hyacinth's death at the end of *The Princess Casamassima.* Even if we disagree with Trilling's judgement that Hyacinth is a 'hero of civilization,' 'the very claim of the fable is naturally that he *is* special,' as James's Preface observes of Roderick. In their deaths, Hyacinth, Roderick, Ralph, and Milly are emphatically not 'statistical persons.'

A second major example of a novelist led astray, in James's view, by the lures of massive system-building, positivist reliance on docu-mentary evidence rather than personal experience, and neglect of individual psychology, is Zola. 'It was the fortune, it was in a manner the doom, of Les Rougon-Macquart [1871–93] to deal with things almost always in gregarious form, to be a picture of *numbers,* of classes, crowds, confusions, movements, industries.'[15] James admires Zola's ability to make interesting the gross, vulgar, superficial, and common, while implicitly positioning himself as a superior kind of artist, expert in the select, fine, profound, and rare that are seemingly beyond Zola's comprehension. Again, one can argue that James effectively excludes much of the political by aligning the novelist's art with the representation of the individual rather than of the crowd. *The Princess Casamassima* may be politically acute in many ways, but it does not attempt to any extent to represent crowd behaviour or understand group psychology, in both of which Zola's novels excel. James's novels are full of social situations, but rarely do they pressurise their individual characters to experience the crowd as a sense of belonging, alienation, or loss of self. Even in *The Tragic Muse*, one of James's most naturalist novels, neither Miriam Rooth on the stage nor Nick Dormer at the hustings anticipate the humiliation before the crowd that James suffered in his notorious *Guy Domville* curtain-call.

The American Scene, by contrast, actively explores the pressure of the crowd and the idea of population. Its narrator is pitched into the bustle of New York. The scale of immigration, in particular, occasions anxiety about changes to national identity. This text evokes a sense of unmeasurable excess, 'the too-defiant scale of numerosity and quantity,' and recalls Zola's 'love of the human aggregation.'[16] The visit to Ellis Island is a scene of demographic trauma, life-changing, worthy of 'a chapter by itself' (*AS* 426), yet compressed into a single paragraph. The 'million or so of immigrants' pass through 'a hundred forms and ceremonies,' while the narrator's visit of 'two or three hours' gives him 'a thousand more things to think of than he can pretend to retail' (*AS* 425–6). The blandness of these numbers marks a refusal to engage with the specifics of statistics, such as the journalist Jacob Riis had used to devastating effect a decade earlier in his campaigns against tenement overcrowding in the New York slums.[17] James's Preface defends *The American Scene* as a report of 'features of the human scene' beyond the comprehension of 'newspapers, reports, surveys and blue-books'[18] and confesses 'unashamed' ignorance of 'a thousand matters – matters already the theme of prodigious reports and statistics' (*AS* 353–4). *Quantity* is one of the central ideas of the book. The opening chapter proposes an excess of personal impressions, 'a greater quantity of vision, possibly, than might fit into decent form' (*AS* 359), and this promise is made good in the rest of the text through recurrent preference for pluralised nouns. *The American Scene* excitedly constructs the scale of cultural changes and the sheer multiplications of the alien as, on the one hand, beyond its representational limits and, on the other, within its grasp conceptually and qualitatively.

In James's fiction – the bulk of which was written before his eye-opening visit to America – the incalculable is more often a property of individual consciousness and interpersonal relationships than of the social mass. As Dickens's intrusive narrator observes in *Hard Times*, 'not all the calculators of the National Debt' can reckon the souls of Britain's factory workers; 'there is an unfathomable mystery in the meanest of them, for ever.'[19] This claim from a great popular writer reasserts for novelists at mid-century a territory and expertise that were substantially eroded by the human sciences in the following decades. A comparable spirit of resistance informs James's fiction. If his characters, such as Isabel Archer, retain a degree of unfathomability, then this quality is designed to enhance the reader's sense of the author's imaginative reach rather than to reveal deficiencies in his method of analysis. In the development of the social sciences, statistics seemed to offer the prospect of coherent explanations of behaviour where attention to individual psychology alone found only caprice. James's fiction generally denies that there are interesting mysteries about its characters at this sociological or demographic level beyond its own narrative scope; rather, the sociologist and demographer are the ones incapable of fathoming the mysteries of the human heart, in which the novelist has better claims to be expert. For example, *The Princess Casamassima* casts Hyacinth's personal dilemma, rather than the shadowy organisation that he joined, as the primary figure of excess glowing at the end with a residue of interest beyond the reader's full understanding. We marvel at the interior dimensions and complexities of individual human experience revealed by the narrative and yet retaining a sense of mystery and pathos, and care little for the precise details of the organisation behind the meetings at the Sun and Moon or of the political constituency that it may represent.

For James, creating a credible sense of the unknown complexities of human souls and social relationships is a necessary part of the novelist's art. In the New York Edition Preface to *The Golden Bowl*, he writes that 'absolutely *no* refinement of ingenuity or of precaution need be dreamed of as wasted in that most exquisite of all good causes the appeal to variety, the appeal to incalculability, the appeal to a high refinement and a handsome wholeness of effect.' The novelist's trick is to evoke the incalculable in the service of roundedness and realism, not mystification. Controlled ambiguity and uncertainty are then never 'wasted.'[20] As Banta shows, James's resistance in this novel to the idea of universal calculability also has a specific contemporary context: *The Golden Bowl* is infused with the language and logic of calculating management culture.[21] Whereas Dickens was reacting against utilitarianism and the political economists of the early Victorian period, by the end of the century the most powerful American form of systematising, rationalist thought was Frederick Winslow Taylor's theories of scientific management and efficiency. In the battle between 'two exceptionally capable executive wills,' both Charlotte and Maggie are ultimately vanquished by their own attempts to manage the ménage.[22]

In 1881 Taylorist theory had not yet emerged as a dominant narrative about the individual, society, and nation. *The Portrait of a Lady* is a highly confident work, speaking with an authoritative realist voice. As we will see, its omniscient narrator plays on statistical and demographic ideas only to leave them behind as rather superficial ways of thinking. Its ending drives to construct a form of 'unfathomable mystery' that is not remotely numeric but rather a proof of the power of fiction to represent matters of life and death and the enduring complexity of human beings.

In her famous fireside vigil, Isabel sees a 'dark, narrow alley' and 'dead wall' at the end of the 'infinite vista of a multiplied life' that she had imagined her independence to offer.[23] Instead of pressing our faces against the dead end, the ending opens a new kind of space, inserted between us and that finality and glowing with a residue of excess potential. Isabel is yet alive and, even if we assume that she returns to Rome to serve a stoical life sentence with her husband, she retains an unresolved charge of mystery. She may have been a victim, but the ending declines to affirm her as nothing but that for the rest of her life. She has been the dupe of her husband's and Madame Merle's calculations, but the sum of her life is not yet over and remains indeterminate. The ending of *The Portrait of a Lady* opens up carefully constructed vistas of incalculability, filled with a transcendent sense of quantities of suffering, time, and insight for Isabel, Caspar, and Pansy. These receding perspectives intervene between the characters and the moment of a definite final outcome. The notoriously open ending holds this effect in tension with the painful sense of reality that is its contrasting negative ground: the foreseeable difficulties that Isabel and the other characters must face.

For all the transparency of Isabel's portrait, the novel's relative lack of closure grants its heroine the privilege of retaining an inner life ultimately beyond the calculation of social, psychological, and realist analysis, beyond the reach of villains or statisticians. This kind of tribute to his heroes and heroines is characteristic of many of James's endings. For example, in the closing cadence of 'Madame de Mauves' (1874, an early version of Isabel's unhappy marriage to a dastardly European) the decent American suitor, Longmore, is left with a 'singular feeling' towards the woman he has courted: no longer love, but 'a feeling for which awe would hardly be too strong a name.'[24]

In the ending of *The Wings of the Dove*, the dead Milly becomes a figure of the sublime.[25] As formulated by Kant and Burke, the sublime is a cognitively and affectively overpowering experience, occasioned typically by outstanding examples of art and natural spectacle, from which the mind nevertheless recovers and thereby becomes stronger. Feminist critics have pointed out that this version of the sublime, typified by the Romantic poets, is masculine both in its origin and its emphasis on human mastery over the phenomenal world. Writers in the nineteenth century developed a contrasting post-Romantic, feminine idea of the sublime, in which transcendental experience is irreducibly irrational, excessive, ineffable, and abject. Sublime encounters unmake (feminise) the individual, who is left struggling to turn this experience of rapture to account.[26]

The Alps are the quintessential scenery of the Romantic sublime, yet Roderick dies amid the mountains at the foot of a 'blank and stony face' (*RH* 510), and Milly turns her back on them to come to London. Natural landscapes in James's novels and tales are certainly not the primary location of the sublime. Nor, I suggest, are explicitly religious, sexual, romantic, or even aesthetic experiences. The Jamesian sublime, post-Romantic and feminine, resides primarily in *interiorities* carefully constructed by the celebrated endings of the novels and tales. In *The Portrait of a Lady, The Wings of the Dove*, and many other works, the narrative after-glow is designed to place readers inside a powerful, lingering experience of unrepresentable excess. Although James can take credit for this effect as its author and master, he cannot collect this credit inside the narrative, where the narrator, pointedly retaining control even in the closing cadences, is nevertheless left on *this* side of the effect. The sublime is beyond the narrator, too; at best he beholds it fully and clearly whereas the reader struggles to do this, with a peculiar combination of pleasure and pain. Moreover, the narrator stands on the brink of the sublime and retains a potentially ironic distance from it, whereas the reader, separated from the narrator's voice when the words stop and there is only blank page, experiences an unfolding of the narrative's after-glow. For the reader, the Jamesian sublime is therefore an effect of art, but within the narrative illusion it is channelled through certain characters and their relationships.

The final stages of *The Wings of the Dove*, discussed in Chapter 3, create an effect of mystery and ineffability through the non-narration of Milly's death. She seems to transcend the world of the living, while Merton is left with no way to translate his overwhelming experience into conventional forms of male power. In so far as *The Wings of the Dove* is a realist novel, it prevents overly sentimental readings of Milly's death and retains an ironic distance from all of its characters. Refusing to follow her into an imaginary afterlife, the ending withholds consolation even as it glows with the potent image of the dove's wings; it is magnificently bleak with a sense of lost and wasted life.

At the end of *The Portrait of a Lady*, the sublimity of Isabel's character is filtered through Caspar's dismay at finding her gone. The paragraph added to the novel's final line by the New York Edition enhances our sense of his terror when faced by Henrietta's superficial optimism.

> 'Look here, Mr Goodwood,' she said; 'just you wait!' On which he looked up at her – but only to guess, from her face, with a revulsion, that she simply meant he was young. She stood shining at him with that cheap comfort, and it added, on the spot, thirty years to his life. She walked him away with her, however, as if she had given him now the key to patience.[27]

The force of these lines depends on us accepting the aging effect literally. The intensity of the preceding, climactic dialogue between Isabel and Caspar must have been only an illusion if her absence really is just the temporary setback to his future happiness that Henrietta cheerfully proposes. The 'thirty years' measure out a chunk of Caspar's lifespan all the more sickeningly because Isabel appears to have escaped such measures. Awful and uncertain though her future may be, at this point she seems to be sublimely outside the human scale of youth and age, desire and disappointment, that Caspar suddenly feels so heavily as a loss and as loneliness. Stupefied, he is walked away by Henrietta like a wooden mannequin into the crowd of London.

Framing life

Painted portraits evoke the idea of death because their inanimate material form often physically survives the sitter – as Milly Theale discovers in front of the Bronzino. The connection between portraiture and painting is strongly implied in the title of *The Portrait of a Lady* and is often reinforced by front cover illustrations on paperback editions. However, reflecting recent critical interest in James's relationship with photography and clearly intending to modernise James's classic brand status on booksellers' shelves, the cover of the New Riverside edition (2001) shows, not a portrait painting, but a sequence of photographs of a woman opening a parasol while walking. These images are taken from one of Eadweard Muybridge's studies of human locomotion, the massive project that he undertook in the mid-1880s with the support of the University of Philadelphia.[28] Muybridge's anonymous model has some genteel dignity compared with the majority of his subjects, which are nude, lightly draped, or animal. Nevertheless, she is viewed as an automaton, caught by a row of automatic cameras against the standard grid backdrop of Muybridge's outdoor experimental setup. The filmstrip-like presentation of the sequence, arranged in a grid formation like every other plate in the collection, anticipates cinema but has little of its glamour. The woman in this illustration is a scientific subject and what Seltzer would call a 'statistical person.' She is a specimen representing normal human motion in contrast with those plates that show abnormal, pathological motion resulting from conditions such as epilepsy and amputation. This model is surely not the woman Isabel imagines herself to be: the exceptional child and heroine of her own life story.

Francis Galton's composite photographs of facial types, developed from 1878 onwards, were similarly statistical experiments, designed to classify normal human types. James's fiction gradually acknowledges the existence of photography in the cultural field, but never allows it to eclipse painting as a portrait medium. The painted portrait is untainted by the statistical, by mechanical reproduction, and by the broader scientific and political agendas linked with photography – such as, in Galton's case, eugenics.[29]

Portraiture does not appear inside the narrative of *The Portrait of a Lady*, except perhaps in the gallery at Gardencourt, which Isabel insists on seeing, by candlelight with Ralph, on the evening of her arrival. In front of the paintings, whose genre is not specified, she asks to be shown the resident ghost (*POL* 238). Paintings, not specifically portraits, are also evoked through Osmond's collection. More generally, however, the novel 'portrays' Isabel through her own thoughts, different characters' views of her, and recurrent use of framing imagery, particularly that of doorways and entrances. The novel tests out a series of portraits of Isabel against character types familiar from fiction and circulating in culture more generally: plucky orphan, Emersonian idealist, dollar princess, dutiful wife, society lady, benign stepmother, and American woman. By the end, the novel has made Isabel's relationship with these forms, now enabling, now confining, appear to be the very stuff of her life.

Isabel is special because she resists these classifications. When she declines Lord Warburton's offer of marriage, she thinks herself to be unlike 'nineteen women out of twenty,' a figure soon confirmed independently by Ralph (*POL* 304, 343). According to him, Lord Warburton's sisters exactly resemble 'fifty thousand young women in England' (*POL* 267), a figure that matches Ralph's estimate of the acreage of their brother's estate (*POL* 266). Isabel apparently takes this number to heart, since she soon uses it to foil Lord Warburton's advances by suggesting that she is not unique among this number of her compatriots who travel abroad each year (*POL* 272). Unsurprisingly, he does not accept this claim to typicality and responds by pointing out why she is special – which, of course, Isabel thinks she is, just as she thinks Osmond is 'the first gentleman in Europe' (*POL* 634).

The Portrait of a Lady pretends to represent the American woman as *The American* and 'Daisy Miller' had previously represented the American man and girl. The initial definite article in the novel's title (used in the majority of the titles of James's novels and of many of his tales) asserts authorial ownership of the subject. This is *the* portrait of the American woman, yet it warns of the dangers of thinking in stereotypes and conventional marriage plots and sets aside any idea of statistical representativeness. Not all women are ladies. Isabel asks

Ralph to see ' "specimens" ' of English character – 'it was a word that played a considerable part in her vocabulary' (*POL* 256) – but she has no desire to pass them on for use in her friend's journalism, which is crassly commercial. When Ralph playfully apologises that there is 'not a creature in town' during their visit to London, Henrietta sarcastically scores a point for American democracy. ' "It seems to me the place is about as full as it can be. There is no one here, of course, except three or four millions of people. What is it you call them – the lower-middle class? They are only the population of London, and that is of no consequence" ' (*POL* 333–4). Ralph turns this into a complement of Henrietta. Mrs Touchett, reporting to her son the circumstances of her first meeting with Isabel in Albany, explains that Americans regard Europe as ' "a refuge for their superfluous population" ' (*POL* 233), whereas her husband later suggests the opposite (*POL* 308). These examples illustrate the playful, incidental reference to ideas about statistics, national types, and populations in the first half of the novel. The second half leaves these behind as it deepens its interest in individuals, darkens in tone, and Isabel herself becomes less of a tourist. The ending seeks to unsettle the reader's desire to see what she will become within the available range of fictional formulae and cultural stereotypes – to finish her story once and for all.

Death is kept in view throughout *The Portrait of a Lady* so as to provide the contrasting ground of Isabel's desire for 'life.' It is in the name of life that she rejects Lord Warburton's proposal; she fears she will somehow be 'separating' herself from it, a notion that she partly explains but then avoids having to explain further (*POL* 326–7). Metaphorical references to death, dying, killing, and related concepts abound in the novel. In the second half these become more serious when Ralph's death looms into view as a climax and Isabel's despair over her marriage deepens. She knows that she has 'thrown away her life' (*POL* 638), wants to 'make her peace with the world – to put her spiritual affairs in order' (*POL* 692), and during the train journey to Gardencourt has moments 'almost as good as being dead' (*POL* 767). The novel affirms instead her fundamentally positive orientation. On the train she is convinced that, however much she might long to die, 'this privilege was evidently to be denied her' and 'life would be her business for a long time to come' (*POL* 769). On his deathbed Ralph says she ' "will grow young again" ' and recover from her '"generous mistake"' (*POL* 786). After his poignant death, how ungrateful must she be not to live, keeping his memory in her heart?

In what ways does the narrative of *The Portrait of a Lady* enframe its heroine's capacity for life? What is this novel's economy of death and scheme for representing it?

Probably the best known of James's novels to undergraduate students, *The Portrait of a Lady* marks an early peak in his ambitions as a realist artist to represent the world at large. Those ambitions include the dispensing of death as a means to construct his authority. This novel is conspicuously littered with death – much more so than the shorter 'Daisy Miller' and 'The Turn of the Screw,' his other most canonical works. Confidently addressing audiences in two countries and peopling its pages with a range of characters more numerous than in any of its author's previous works, the novel is among James's most deathly, both quantitatively and qualitatively. Its use of death spans much of the range of representations of death that can be found across James's fictional output. It has a climactic death-scene (Ralph's) and the death of a second major character (his father, Daniel). Characters who have died prior to the narrative's present are actively remembered, creating both a sense of the past (Isabel's father and grandmother) and a sensation plot (around the first Mrs Osmond and M. Merle). The sense of living death, or still life – what James in 'Is There a Life after Death?' calls dying 'piecemeal' – increasingly darkens the novel as it proceeds. The revisions of the New York Edition alter the fine detail of this death-texture, but not the large outlines of the use of death in the novel. Death informs the major inheritance and marriage plots in both the 1881 and New York Edition texts. On the other hand, there are other aspects of Jamesian death that this novel addresses only marginally, such as the supernatural, suicide, and the death of an artist. None of James's novels on its own fully illustrates the entire range of his representations of death.

Ralph's death is easily the most imposing intrusion of mortality into *The Portrait of a Lady*. It can be positioned in the novel's scheme of death as follows.

The deaths of parents, spouses, and children colour the background against which Ralph's death and Isabel's progress stand out in the foreground. Like so many of James's major characters, Isabel is launched into the world by being an orphan. The absence of her parents is mirrored in other characters, such as Pansy Osmond,

Edward Rosier, and Lord Warburton, each of whom has lost one or both parents. This loss suggests by turns moral and emotional vacuum, moral and financial independence, and assumption of family responsibility. Widows and widowers, most prominently Serena Merle and Gilbert Osmond, are relaunched upon the world by the absence of their spouse. Their example faintly evokes a possible future life for Isabel as a widow. That she and the Countess Gemini both lose their children focusses the sense of futurity normally invested in children on to Pansy. At this background level, death is expository or even picturesque. Sketching the family background of characters is part of James's realist method to build up a dense picture of contemporary life, and this sometimes includes mention of offstage widows, widowers, orphans, and ancestors (for example, Henrietta's widowed sister, mother of three, who never enters the narrative directly).

Secondly, Daniel and Ralph Touchett bring death into the heart of the narrative. Their deaths are connected by the father–son relationship and by the family gathering, sickbed scene, and funeral that both characters receive at Gardencourt. Their deaths differ in that Daniel is older and dies relatively early in the story. His death, which marks the climax of Isabel's stay in England in the first third of the novel, sounds a keynote that resonates with her mourning in the opening chapters and echoes down the narrative to his son's long-awaited death. Retrospectively, Daniel's death becomes part of the background of the larger story; it has a relatively muted emotional charge and sets up Isabel for the fortune-hunting plot. Ralph's death, by contrast, is entangled in the final stages of the novel; it provides a crisis in the complex exploration of freedom and internment, marriage and celibacy, delusion and insight that makes up the core of Isabel's story. His dying is the loss of a peer, confidant, brotherly lover, and soul-mate. It is a direct catalyst to insight and action in the novel's closing pages, where Isabel feels more alone and orphaned than at the start of the narrative.

Thirdly, Isabel's doom is a kind of death, even though her destiny is also named as one of continuing life. Ralph's invalidism and Pansy's incarceration are overt pointers towards psychic trauma and extinction of vital will, which the micro-texture of the novel works out in problematic detail, in terms of life-enhancing or life-diminishing modes of thought, perceptions, and actions, at the level of character, incident, dialogue, and detailed phrasing. Discerning morbidity from vitality is a task woven into the fabric of the novel, for example in metaphors of death. Rather than signalling Isabel's recovery from the hell of her marriage to a brighter, revivified integrity, *or* dispatching her into a desert of living death from which there is no return, the ending holds these readings in a relationship of tension.

Ralph seems to die so as to save Isabel. His death from consumption functions as a sacrifice to spare Isabel's character from being associated with Minny Temple's death and to enable it to represent instead Minny's appetite for life. Ralph's death is given due prominence as the penultimate climax, informing but ultimately secondary to the ending itself. His death is partly formulaic within the conventions of the deathbed scene, but the complex texture of the novel prevents it from becoming an unexamined sacrifice. Most obviously, the ambiguity of the ending reflects back to make the reader ask what Ralph died *for*. His death disguises but cannot eradicate the idea, implicit in the comparison between Isabel and Minny, that Isabel also in some way dies inside – that maybe his death is in vain and fails to function redemptively.

James's fiction typically explores an art of living in which the deaths of others, the fear of mortality, and a failure to live as fully as possible cast shadows over the narrative climax. Among James's most common figures for conventional ideas of a failure to live, or living death, are the spinster, such as Catherine Sloper, and the older bachelor, exemplified by John Marcher. These figures express economic, legal, sexual, and Christian notions and reflect topical concerns and genre conventions; there is always some cultural scale against which relative morbidity or vitality can be gauged.

In *The Portrait of a Lady* the figure of the repressed older bachelor is largely absent. It is exemplified most fully in James's fiction following the emergence at the end of the nineteenth century of a repertoire of codes for representing eroticised male–male relationships. Prototypes appear earlier in James's fiction, working with slightly different codes and cultural sensitivities – thus Chapter 1 explores *Roderick Hudson* in terms of necrophilia and post-bellum American masculinities. Ralph Touchett's illness is situated in discourses of consumption rather than emerging gay discourse, and is relatively more life-enabling than incapacitating. This interpretation is far from clear-cut, but key pointers are the pre-eminence of the relationship with Isabel, not another man, in Ralph's life; his youthfulness and active pleasure in voyeurism compared with Mallet or Marcher; and his relative equanimity and domestic contentment.

More important as a figure of morbidity in *The Portrait of a Lady* is the unmarried or childless woman – an overtly demographic category. As Tambling points out, Isabel can be read as an example of morbid femininity, pushed towards hysteria by sexual frustration, desire for independence, and inability to express her desires within the patriarchal frameworks of dominant discourse.[30] Isabel marries and bears a child, but by neither does she become a woman fully alive in the conventional sense of conjugality and motherhood. The wedding, the honeymoon, and the child's short life are all deliberately passed over. The significance of these lacunae might be unpacked in order to construct a reading that runs against the more obvious current of the novel.[31] However, to propose that the death of Isabel's child is a psychologically realistic cause of her marital breakdown is to ignore the way that the novel deliberately sidelines this death for the purposes of making its larger points. Infant mortality rates were sufficiently high throughout the nineteenth century for the novel virtually to ignore the child's death without seriously damaging its psychological realism. Instead, ignoring the death of the child is part of the narrative's resistance to normative designations of Isabel as a failed, morbid woman. This resistance is made explicit in those readings of the novel that see it as a critical intervention by James in debates around marriage. The topicality of the novel centres on its representation of the transatlantic marriage market, but is also sensitive to wider questions of women's emancipation, such as access to education, work, and political representation. Sensitivity to gender politics empowers the evocation of Isabel's appetite for life, sense of adventure, and nubile promise in the first half of the novel, and of her frustration, claustrophobia, and loss of freedom in its second half. George Eliot's heroines, Dorothea Brooke and Gwendolen Harleth, are the major fictional precedents for Isabel in this respect.

Compared with *The Portrait of a Lady*, the ending of *Washington Square* snubs out the vitality of its protagonist much more bluntly and assigns Catherine Sloper unambiguously to the nineteenth-century category of old maid. She clutches small victories over her father, aunt, and lover but is emotionally ruined. Isabel, by contrast, appears to retain a larger hold on life at the end of her story. Largely this is because she has been endowed across the more expansive canvas of the novel with greater intelligence, charm, and opportunity than Catherine across the course of the novella. But also *The Portrait of a Lady* seeks more centrally to interrogate the institution of marriage and therefore needs a more spirited heroine who cannot be so easily cast as a victim.

As discussed in Chapter 3, the morbid names a ground of contestation and stereotypes. This is perhaps a more active ground of engagement and strategy than the representation of actual deaths and background deaths in James's fiction, though these also counter stereotypes to some extent. Here I am working with a rudimentary scheme of the range of representations of death across James's fiction, illustrated in Table 5.1. There are actual, historical, and metaphorical deaths. Characters die during the course of the narrative, are defined by the deaths of family and kin (widows, orphans, and so on), or experience a traumatic loss of the sense of self. Secondly, there is a distinction between the general narrative purposes that these three types of death serve, the most basic purposes being inheritance and marriage plots. Isabel's marriage is an example of a metaphorical death, and Ralph's death contributes to the thwarting of the romance plot between Isabel and Caspar.

Death alone does not entirely explain the subversion of marriage plots in James's fiction – in *The Portrait of a Lady* there are many ways to describe the reasons for Isabel's climactic flight from Caspar – but thwarting the reader's desire for a conventional romantic outcome regularly provides an explanation for the use of death. *The American* provides a clear example in Claire's gruesomely evoked incarceration in the Carmelite convent: a veritable dying to the world that overtly puts an end to the possibility of marriage between her and Newman. In both *Roderick Hudson* and *The Wings of the Dove*, financial and

Table 5.1 Minimum global scheme of the representation of death in James's fiction

Level	Function
Historical	Construct inheritance plot
Actual	Construct inheritance plot and thwart marriage plot
Metaphorical	Thwart marriage plot

psychological inheritance via the deaths of parents and kin establishes scenarios of conflict and desire that impel the narrative forward and shape its ending; actual deaths thwart the marriage plots; and there are blighted lives.

The term 'thwart' here is shorthand to indicate that James's fictions tend to subvert rather than adhere to marriage plots, though this is a subtle, variable, non-programmatic process. Jamesian death sometimes constructs necrophilic romance plots, such as that in *The Wings of the Dove* or 'The Altar of the Dead,' where love is cemented in the very loss of the beloved. By contrast, the balance of James's use of inheritance plots is perhaps relatively less subversive and more conventional, with regular expository use of widows and orphans, and generic use of wills. Dr Sloper's will is an example of the so-called dead hand, which reaches out of the grave to manipulate the heirs. In *The Portrait of a Lady*, Daniel Touchett's will unwittingly sets up Isabel's disastrous marriage, but by the end of the novel Ralph's guilt over his part in this inheritance plot becomes transformed into his complex spiritual legacy for Isabel.

The degree of conventionality or subversion of James's use of death varies across his fictions, depending on mode of publication, length, subject, and the stages of his career. The inventiveness of any individual fiction is not always targeted on death. For example, *The Awkward Age* (1899) is busy making radical use of a dramatic model of dialogue, and inventiveness in other areas understandably takes a back seat. This novel can stand as an example of a text where my thesis, that the representation of death is pervasive and generative throughout James's fiction, ostensibly seems at its weakest. Yet in this work there are, as usual, various widows and orphans, and Longman's memory of Lady Julia is central to his characterisation and to his relationship with Nanda and her mother. Longman's sense of the past exerts a critical position against the contemporary London scene, and Nanda's retirement to live with him in Beccles can be read as a strong criticism of the marriage market, so that her character contests a conventional view that her fall into provincial celibacy is tantamount to a living death, like Claire's incarceration at the end of *The American* or Madame Merle's exile to America at the end of *The Portrait of a Lady*. On the other hand, Longman is relatively conventional in James's repertoire of representations of death when compared with Stransom in 'The Altar of the Dead.' In fact, Longman recalls the anonymous diarist of the much earlier 'The Diary of a Man of Fifty' (1879), where the memory of the dead woman whom the diarist failed to marry sets the standard for measuring her offspring. Stransom and the diarist are more clearly characterised than Longman as having *failed to live*. This charge could be levelled against Longman, too, but would be more difficult to sustain, for two reasons: *The Awkward Age* programmatically minimises signs of authorial intervention with its dramatic model of dialogue, and the novel seems to criticise London society, to which Longman constitutes an alternative. Stransom and the diarist more readily exemplify the distinctively Jamesian figure of the repressed older bachelor, whose missing of the opportunity for passion is built up into a veritable living death.

If the motto tested by James's older bachelors is *the man who never lived*, the motto at stake in his heightened dramas of renunciation might be *no life without sacrifice. The highest form of life is the celibate artist*, to judge from the profusion in James's fiction of sensitive, aesthetically minded, financially independent orphans and a virtual ban on procreation by his major characters. The number of demonstrably fruitful marriages centre-stage in his novels and tales is extremely small. While family history often figures with some prominence, the narratives never follow a sequence of generations in the manner of a saga. James's interest in scandalous biography in tales such as 'The Aspern Papers' suggests that it is *better to be forgotten than to be mediatised*. These mottoes contrast with Poe's claim that *the most poetical subject is the death of a beautiful woman*, which Bronfen adapts as a keynote to her celebrated study of death and gender.[32] This motto does apply to some of James's narratives, such as 'Daisy Miller' and *The Wings of the Dove*, but by no means adequately suggests the range of death-scenarios developed across his fiction.

The primary motto contested by *The Portrait of a Lady*, I have been arguing, is *none of my deaths is a statistic*. How could Ralph's, so poignantly represented in the climactic deathbed scene, ever be that?

Mortality in James's population

Reflecting the maturation of statistical thinking, 'demography' emerged as a social science during the second half of the nineteenth century. The term was coined by Achille Guillard in 1855 in a study of census data and vital statistics.[33] Building on insurance studies, demography gradually developed into the techniques and theories of population studies. Populations are understood to be dynamic, self-reproducing organisms whose behaviour, potentially law-like, arises from the interaction of five principal variables: mortality, morbidity, migration, nuptiality, and fertility. In the nineteenth century, demography was largely empirical and concerned with the collection of census data, whereas in the twentieth century it became more theoretical. Today's prevailing narrative of the major demographic trends in Victorian Britain notes the increase in life expectancy due to improved sanitation and food standards; improvement in early child mortality from the 1860s and in infant mortality from 1900; and a decline in fertility from 1870. These come together to form a demographic transition in which both mortality and fertility rates become significantly lower. Demographic factors combine in this way to regulate population in a 'demographic regime,' wherein popular perceptions of improved life expectancy contribute causally to self-imposed limitation in family sizes.[34]

James's fiction does not address demographic issues overtly. At the time James wrote *The Portrait of a Lady*, demography was not a highly visible name for statistical thinking. According to the *Oxford English Dictionary* the first use of the term in English is not until 1880. This does not itself diminish the extent of resistance by James's fiction to emerging social sciences, the rise of statistical discourses, and their impact on modern subjectivity and perceptions of national identity. What I propose in the remainder of this chapter is a methodological experiment that I imagine James would recognise as emerging from the kinds of statistical thinking he knew, but would find 'unfathomable' in the sense in which he disagreed in principle with Balzac's obsession with financial figures. For James, it seems that neither the artist nor the literary critic can have any legitimate business with quantitative analysis for its own sake. This is a strategy of discursive resistance to numeric disciplines of social science, a strategy that James's critics, in common with many literary scholars and students today, tend to imitate. Personally, I side with James on the need to defend the subjective richness of fiction and humanities disciplines against the reductiveness and claims to objectivity exemplified by, say, pie charts. At the same time, I think that our current information age and technologies do open up perspectives on James's representations of death, perspectives that critics need to explore so as to make clear both their potential usefulness and their intrinsic limitations.

Demography is a model for holding James's fiction to account for mortality in its population. In a sense this is what Elisabeth Bronfen does on a larger scale in her study of death in Western literature, which she argues is consistently misrepresentative in its emphasis on the death of women. The scale of James's fictional output, though considerably less than Balzac's and not remarkable by the standards of mid-Victorian novelists such as Dickens or Trollope, seems sufficient for statistical analysis to at least get started. The population of James's novels and tales numbers hundreds of named characters and there are many more unnamed and implied characters. How many orphans, widows, and widowers are there, how many childless marriages and deaths in childbirth or infancy, how many spinsters and bachelors, how many international marriages and expatriations, how many suicides, murders, and fatal accidents, and how many deaths from disease or old age? In other words, how do mortality, morbidity, migration, nuptiality, and fertility vary in James's fictional population? The divergence of his population from the actual populations revealed by the census and by retrospective historical analysis of post-bellum America and Victorian and Edwardian Britain, and also from the population imagined in contemporary fiction and journalism, would be a measure of distinctively Jamesian representations of death. How does mortality in James's fictional population compare with that in the work of other writers? How might a demographer read James's fiction, and *The Portrait of a Lady* in particular? Initially this might be a matter of the methodology of census data collection. Then there is the question of developing theoretical models of a Jamesian 'demographic regime.'

Of course, James's fictional population is a very different kind of thing from a real-world population and cannot be assumed to behave according to comparable demographic rules. His characters are not real people. The data that might be gathered in a census of James's novels and tales does not match the kinds of data gathered in an actual census, since factors such as age, cause, and location of death are generally not recorded by the fiction, and its population moves through time and between countries. In practice there is no viable sample for statistical analysis. James's fictional population is patently *un*representative of the actual population of Britain and

America during his lifetime, since the bulk of his novels and tales treats of a relatively narrow range of social classes. Generally his characters enjoy the social privilege of being outside the demographic loop, in that whether or not they marry or reproduce does not seem to be driven by their perception of mortality and morbidity rates. James's fictional universe is far removed from Malthus's vision of populations driven to compete for scarce resources. With few exceptions, James's characters do not replenish their own population; they die without propagating. We might see this as an aspect of the queerness of James's fiction. In *The Wings of the Dove*, there is a pervasive sense of genealogical termination; the houses of Croy, Densher, and Theale are all going out of business. The regulatory principle of the 'demographic regime' of James's fictional population would not be real-world events and historical consequences so much as the author's shifting perceptions of reality and responses to his cultural context. The families portrayed in James's narratives after 1900 obey perceptions and responses specific to that period in his personal history and in cultural history, rather than the actual results of population change arising from the collective behaviour of the preceding generations portrayed in his earlier fiction.

As Laura Peters demonstrates, orphans are recurrent figures in Victorian fiction, in which they function as scapegoats for conflicts within the ideal nuclear and national family.[35] The number of orphans is a demographic aspect of James's novels and tales that his critics have noted. William Veeder offers a psychoanalytic reading of *The Portrait of a Lady* based on Freud's idea of family romance: James's repeated imagination of himself as an orphan is a defence and compensation mechanism deriving from his childhood experience in the James family.[36] Alfred Habegger sets Isabel in the context of the 'independent orphan-heroine' of numerous mid-century American women's novels.[37] Both accounts list examples of James's orphans in order to imply an important quantitative basis for analysing his fiction. However, neither substantiates the quantitative premise in the manner of an historian or demographic statistician. Implicit quantitative estimation – keeping a tally without actually counting – is rather common in James studies in so far as critics attempt to survey trends across the breadth of James's formidable output. The index to Lyndall Gordon's biography of Henry James, for example, contains two categories for his female characters, aligned to James's relationships with Minny Temple and Constance Fenimore Woolson. Catherine Sloper, Daisy Miller, Isabel Archer, and Milly Theale are among the 'ALTERNATIVE, EVOLVING, THWARTED WOMEN,' while 'DEPENDENT, MANIPULATIVE WOMEN' include Kate Croy.[38] These two index headings indicate the dominance of particular concepts of femininity in Gordon's reading. The process of indexing is retrospective but perhaps also reveals an implicit mode of understanding important to earlier stages of composition.

If we were to attempt to gather vital statistics about the population of *The Portrait of a Lady*, we would need to tabulate a set of recording categories. The novel itself offers plenty of candidates, since the narrative positions itself in relation to topical concerns and follows Isabel's progress from youthful faith in limitless freedom to mature recognition of the social construction of identity. However, James's novel clearly does not expect its readers to equate the stereotypes of childless wife, eligible bachelor, consumptive invalid, and Europeanised American with demographic variables of fertility, nuptiality, morbidity, and migration, even if they resemble these at bottom. Presumably even Henrietta Stackpole, for whom journalistic stereotypes are a stock in trade, works such categories up into a minimally literary account distinguished from the merely statistical.

The working notes for James's two unfinished novels reveal plot calculation that verges, at times, on the demographic. The following passage from the notes to *The Ivory Tower* is a typical example, showing James's manner of working out certain essential interconnections between the various elements of plot and character while leaving other elements to be decided during later stages of composition.

> I see the young husband, Gray's father, himself Graham Fielder the elder or whatever, as dying early, but probably dying in Europe, through some catastrophe to be determined, two or three years after their going there. This is better than his dying at home, for removal of everything from nearness to Mr. Betterman. Betterman has been married and has had children, a son and a daughter, this is indispensable, for diminution of the fact of paucity of children; but he has lost successively these belongings – there is nothing over strange in it; the death of his son, at 16 or 18 or thereabouts, having occurred a few years, neither too few nor too many, before my beginning, and having been the sorest fact of his life.[39]

The use of digits here ('16 or 18') is presumably shorthand by James's amanuensis. In *The Ivory Tower*, key facts of births, deaths, and marriages appear to be central to the scaffolding stage. Both the preparatory notes and the completed sections suggest that much of this demographic matter ends up as exposition, with the real plot taking off once various inheritances have been established for a set of characters representing a new generation of American youth. What the plot can bear is limited by a need to keep within the bounds of realism. James decides he needs to give Betterman offspring so as to offset a 'paucity of children' among the other characters. In a later passage of the working notes, he similarly cautions himself not to kill off an unrealistic number of parents: 'I multiply my orphans rather.'[40]

If a census were to be carried out across the whole of James's fiction, it would generate a mass of information requiring collation and analysis, presumably using computer tools such as databases. The difficulty of defining categories with which to record raw data is a classic issue in database design, and here the role of the scholar would be to guide the designer using her understanding of relevant historical contexts and literary codes – such as those discussed in earlier sections of this chapter. This could be a fruitful exercise to attempt as an extension of existing critical approaches to James.

On the other hand, computer-aided analysis cannot be expected to yield, in the foreseeable future, anything like a comprehensive tabulation of Jamesian death – whether in the form of a dedicated database, an index, or a concordance. Derrida discusses a comparable research task in his address to Joyce scholars (1984), which he delivered against the backdrop of early optimism in the emerging artificial intelligence research community about its future potential.[41] Deconstructing the 'Joycean *yes*' as both a ubiquitous signifier in *Ulysses* and a fundamental principle of dialogue between this text, its readers, and its author, Derrida imagines an *n*th generation computer programmed to construct a comprehensive typology of the *yeses* in table form. He concludes that no computer, as we can currently conceive one, could succeed in such a task. The 'Joycean *yes*' has its implicit twin, either affirming (countersigning) or laughing at the authenticity of the first *yes*, and in trying to track down all the *yeses* and their implied twins the computer would enter a kind of infinite receding perspective. Joyce's writings constitute a master-program that defeats in advance any subsequent program of analysis and interpretation of which scholars might conceive.

Jamesian *death* does not function in the specific manner of the double 'Joycean *yes*,' though there is some parallel in that any instance of *death* within James's fiction potentially implies doubles within James's own life and literary afterlife, and vice versa. This is the dynamic explored in Chapter 2. The more obvious problem that Jamesian *death* poses for computer-aided analysis arises from the proliferation of terms spawned by the fundamental impossibility of naming death itself. 'Death' can never refer to any lived experience, and so culture is endlessly inventive in responding to this referential and experiential void – finding ways to appear to represent death itself and thereby symbolically encompass it. James's fiction does so in generic and also characteristic ways. The section headings and index to this book offer terms for starting to map this process, but clearly they are far from comprehensive.

As I have begun to map out, categories of death are relatively distinct in *The Portrait of a Lady*. Even Ralph's death, milked as a sentimental climax, is discarded by the final chapter as merely the last in a series of bereavements: ultimately one-more-death serving Isabel's progress. After all, life goes on. By contrast, *The Wings of the Dove*, as suggested in Chapters 3 and 4, diffuses the sense of death into its style and structure. The narrative hides Milly's corpse as if to make death itself vanish, with the result that her memory haunts the action of the closing chapters, Merton's rooms, and the retrospective after-glow of the novel for readers. The novel seeks to make Milly's demise not one-more-death, located and given its dues through a deathbed scene, but a morbid making-deathly of the world. This effect is organic to the narrative illusion and to the dialogic relationship between text and reader. It is difficult to see how any foreseeable programmatic analysis could abstract this effect and render it into a tabular typology of its constituent parts.

Values at stake in *The Wings of the Dove* of respect for the dead, responsive mourning, and creative interest in mortality are not unique to this novel, in which they take particular form. Though personal bereavement and aging make James take death more seriously in the later stages of his career, at few points in his fiction do his artistic ambitions allow death to become entirely superficial or merely instrumental. In *The Portrait of a Lady*, the representation of death is no less complex and challenging for critical reading for being relatively explicit in the narrative, for appearing to be almost countable.

The values of James's fiction seem to protest against anything so base as counting. Don't his novels and tales implicitly pledge that their characters will not be forgotten, will never melt into the crowd or become merely a statistic? To respond to Ralph's death by merely *adding one* to a count of James's climactic deaths is surely a scandalous betrayal of all that *The Portrait of a Lady* seeks to engage the reader in feeling for its characters. How could we, after all that we have gone through in reading the novel, so disengage from the dialogical relationship set up between us and the text, so depersonalise and objectify our reading experience, and so forget the sense of humanity we have shared with the characters, as to discard the novel as just one more book?

Fiction such as James's remains a stake in ongoing negotiations between humanistic and scientific disciplines. I suspect that the kind of reader *The Portrait of a Lady* generally obtains (such as undergraduate literature students and middle-brow audiences of period adaptations on the small or large screen) is also likely to endorse this novel's humanism: *no, none of our deaths is a statistic*. The novel's sociological function is then conservative: to support a protest against the dehumanising world of modernisers, philistines, and bureaucrats. Ralph's death, in that case, is not really a death at all, but a sacrifice that keeps his proper name alive by helping to make *The Portrait of a Lady* an enduring classic. Yet there is a tension in this novel between special pleading for its characters and the novel's claims to representativeness, and this tension is crucial to its narrative effects. To reclaim James as a realist, we need to read *The Portrait of a Lady* as countenancing Ralph's death as a real loss. That implies facing up to the prospect that the novel, too, might one day enter oblivion – become a dead text, unread and long forgotten.

The Portrait of a Lady is no more the master-text of Jamesian death than any of the other works discussed in this book. Nothing written by James masters death. The iconic life/death mask, discussed in Chapter 2, might seem to transcend the entanglements of James's fiction and bring us face to face with the very essence of his personal mortality: a definitive portrait of the artist, immortalised in plaster and bronze. But this effect is an illusion; James's own death slips away from us even here. As yet the mask has little power over the reception of James's novels and tales – narratives at once so filled with death and, in many respects, so successfully constituting a literary afterlife. James's most poised endings brilliantly combine a grim recognition of finality with a powerful feeling of transcendence, released as we finish the last page and close the book. Concluding a book about death is difficult because the act of ending in itself invokes the subject. At the end of this study, the pursuit of Jamesian death, which has taken many different forms, remains unfinished and unmastered. James continues to have a presence in today's cultural field, and the study of death in his fiction potentially breathes new life into criticism. Even so, the simple necessity of ending gives us an idea of a death that we cannot avoid.

Notes

Introduction

1. The major studies are Martha Banta, *Henry James and the Occult: The Great Extension* (Bloomington: Indiana University Press, 1972) and T. J. Lustig, *Henry James and the Ghostly* (Cambridge: Cambridge University Press, 1994). For a more recent account of haunted James, see Jeremy Tambling, *Henry James* (London: Macmillan, 2000).
2. Deriving in large part from Jacques Derrida's *Specters of Marx: The State of the Debt, the Work of Mourning, and the New International*, trans. Peggy Kamuf (New York: Routledge, 1994).
3. Examples of this line of thought are John Auchard, *Silence in Henry James: The Heritage of Symbolism and Decadence* (London: Pennsylvania State University Press, 1986); Edwin Sill Fussell, *The Catholic Side of Henry James* (Cambridge: Cambridge University Press, 1993); and *James and the Sacred*, special issue of *Henry James Review* 22 (2001).
4. Henry James, *Notes of a Son and Brother* (London: Macmillan, 1914), pp. 422–79; Leon Edel, *Henry James: The Untried Years 1843–1870* (London: Hart-Davis, 1953), pp. 318–37; Lyndall Gordon, *A Private Life of Henry James: Two Women and His Art* (London: Chatto & Windus, 1998), p. 364 and at large.
5. Elisabeth Bronfen, *Over Her Dead Body: Death, Femininity and the Aesthetic* (Manchester: Manchester University Press, 1992), p. 369. James's letters are to his mother, brother, and Grace Norton between 26 March and 1 April 1870; *Henry James Letters*, ed. Leon Edel, 4 vols (London: Macmillan, 1974–80; Cambridge, MA: Belknap, 1984), vol. 1, pp. 218–32. James's letters are hereafter cited in the text as *L*.
6. Garrett Stewart, *Death Sentences: Styles of Dying in British Fiction* (Cambridge, MA: Harvard University Press, 1984), p. 4.
7. Ibid., pp. 4–5.
8. Ibid., p. 4; Stewart is citing Leon Edel, *Henry James: The Master, 1901–1916* (London: Hart-Davis, 1972), p. 546.
9. Shoshana Felman, 'Turning the Screw of Interpretation,' *Yale French Studies* 55–6 (1977), 128.
10. These positions are argued respectively by, among others, Felman, pp. 175–6; Susan Clark, 'A Note on *The Turn of the Screw*: Death from Natural Causes,' *Studies in Short Fiction* 15 (1978), 110–12; Peter G. Biedler, *Ghosts, Demons, and Henry James: The Turn of the Screw at the Turn of the Century* (Columbia: University of Missouri Press, 1989), pp. 198–219; Eric Haralson, *Henry James and Queer Modernity* (Cambridge: Cambridge University Press, 2003), pp. 79–101; and Carvel Collins, 'James' *The Turn*

of the Screw,' Explicator 13 (1954–5), 49. For an overview of criticism on James's most famous work, see Robin P. Hoople, *Distinguished Discord: Discontinuity and Pattern in the Critical Tradition of* The Turn of the Screw (Lewisburg: Bucknell University Press, 1997).

11. Henry James, 'The Turn of the Screw' in *Complete Stories 1892–1898* (New York: Library of America, 1996), p. 740.

12. Leslie Fiedler, *Love and Death in the American Novel* (New York: Criterion, 1960).

13. 'Is There a Life after Death?' in *The James Family*, by F. O. Matthiessen (New York: Knopf, 1948), p. 605.

14. Henry James, *The American* in *Novels 1871–1880* (New York: Library of America, 1983), pp. 831–3.

15. This interpretation of 'still life' comes from Robert Smith, *Derrida and Autobiography* (Cambridge: Cambridge University Press, 1995), p. 131.

16. N. A. Blain explores this point in 'Ideas of "Life" and their Moral Force in the Novels of Henry James' (unpublished dissertation, University of Strathclyde, 1981). Conversely, James's ghostly tales suggest that perhaps nobody ever reaches absolute 'death' either.

17. *The Ambassadors*, 2 vols (New York: Scribner's, 1909), vol. 1, p. 217.

18. See, for example, Jonathan Dollimore, *Death, Desire and Loss in Western Culture* (London: Penguin, 1998).

19. Arthur Schopenhauer, *The World as Will and Representation*, 2 vols, trans. E. F. J. Payne (New York: Dover, 1966), vol. 1, pp. 398–402; Henry James, *The Princess Casamassima* in *Novels 1886–1890* (New York: Library of America, 1989), pp. 287, 295, 351.

20. Studies of James and philosophy include Richard A. Hocks, *Henry James and Pragmatistic Thought: A Study in the Relationship between the Philosophy of William James and the Literary Art of Henry James* (Chapel Hill: University of North Carolina Press, 1974); Stephen Donadio, *Nietzsche, Henry James, and the Artistic Will* (New York: Oxford University Press, 1978); Henry Sussman, *The Hegelian Aftermath: Readings in Hegel, Kierkegaard, Freud, Proust, and James* (Baltimore: Johns Hopkins University Press, 1982), pp. 11–12, 230–9; Paul B. Armstrong, *The Phenomenology of Henry James* (Chapel Hill: University of North Carolina Press, 1983).

21. William Wordsworth, Preface to *Lyrical Ballads*, 1802 in *Lyrical Ballads, and Other Poems, 1797–1800*, ed. James Butler and Karen Green (Ithaca: Cornell University Press, 1992), pp. 741–60; Mark Seltzer, *Henry James and the Art of Power* (Ithaca: Cornell University Press, 1984).

22. Ibid., pp. 13, 16.

23. Ross Posnock, *The Trial of Curiosity: Henry James, William James, and the Challenge of Modernity* (New York: Oxford University Press, 1991), pp. 76–7; John Carlos Rowe, 'Henry James and Critical Theory' in *A Companion to Henry James Studies*, ed. Daniel Mark Fogel (London: Greenwood, 1993), pp. 73–93. For a further attack on Seltzer's position, see Winfried Fluck, 'Power Relations in the Novels of James: The "Liberal" and the "Radical" Version' in *Enacting History in Henry James: Narrative, Power, and Ethics*, ed. Gert Buelens (Cambridge: Cambridge University Press, 1997), pp. 16–39.

24. Leon Edel, *Henry James: The Treacherous Years 1895–1901* (London: Hart-Davis, 1969), p. 169.
25. Friedrich Kittler, *Discourse Networks 1800/1900*, trans. Michael Metteer with Chris Cullens (Stanford, CA: Stanford University Press, 1990), pp. 356–7; Mark Seltzer, *Bodies and Machines* (New York: Routledge, 1992), pp. 196–7; Pamela Thurschwell, *Literature, Technology and Magical Thinking, 1880–1920* (Cambridge: Cambridge University Press, 2001), pp. 87–114.
26. See Tom Standage, *The Victorian Internet: The Remarkable Story of the Telegraph and the Nineteenth Century's Online Pioneers* (London: Weidenfeld & Nicolson, 1998).
27. Friedrich Kittler, *Gramophone, Film, Typewriter*, trans. Geoffrey Winthrop-Young and Michael Wutz (Stanford, CA: Stanford University Press, 1999), p. 13.
28. Gordon, *A Private Life of Henry James: Two Women and His Art*, p. 364.
29. Zygmunt Bauman, *Mortality, Immortality and Other Life Strategies* (Cambridge: Polity, 1992), p. 4.

1   Violence ashamed: Sacrifice in *Roderick Hudson*

1. *Roderick Hudson* (New York: Scribner's, 1907), p. vi. Subsequent references to this edition are cited in the text as *RHNY*.
2. F. R. Leavis, *The Great Tradition: George Eliot, Henry James, Joseph Conrad* (London: Chatto & Windus, 1948), p. 130.
3. Preface to *The Princess Casamassima*, 2 vols (New York: Scribner's, 1908), vol. 1, p. xviii.
4. *Roderick Hudson* in *Novels 1871–1880* (New York: Library of America, 1983), pp. 163–511, hereafter cited as *RH*. This standard edition is close enough for my purposes to the original serialisation, 'Roderick Hudson,' *Atlantic Monthly* Jan.–Dec. 1875. Though serialisation itself will have made substantial differences to the reading experience offered by James's novel to subscribers of the *Atlantic* at the time, these differences are not crucial for my argument. I have therefore set them aside for the sake of being able to refer to a more widely available text and to focus instead on some significant differences between the first book and New York editions.
5. Richard Poirier, *The Comic Sense of Henry James: A Study of the Early Novels* (London: Chatto & Windus, 1960).
6. Ibid., p. 41.
7. Ibid., p. 42.
8. Kelly Cannon, *Henry James and Masculinity: The Man at the Margins* (Basingstoke: Macmillan, 1994), p. 44.
9. Oscar Cargill, *The Novels of Henry James* (New York: Macmillan, 1961), pp. 26–7.
10. Hugh Stevens, *Henry James and Sexuality* (Cambridge: Cambridge University Press, 1998).

11. Richard Ellmann, 'James Amongst the Aesthetes' in *Henry James and Homo-Erotic Desire*, ed. John R. Bradley (Basingstoke: Macmillan, 1999), pp. 29–30.

12. My argument here is a response to comments on *Roderick Hudson*'s role in the development of James's editorial policy for the New York Edition in Anthony J. Mazzella, 'James's Revisions' in *A Companion to Henry James Studies*, ed. Daniel Mark Fogel (London: Greenwood, 1993), p. 312.

13. Henry James, *The Other House* (London: Hart-Davis, 1948), p. 206.

14. Geoffrey Moore, Introduction to *Roderick Hudson*, by Henry James (Harmondsworth: Penguin, 1986), p. 26.

15. Kieran Dolin, *Fiction and the Law: Legal Discourse in Victorian and Modernist Literature* (Cambridge: Cambridge University Press, 1999), p. 27.

16. D. H. Lawrence, *Women in Love* (London: Heinemann, 1921), p. 465.

17. Fiedler, *Love and Death in the American Novel*, p. 395.

18. René Girard, *Violence and the Sacred*, trans. Patrick Gregory (Baltimore: Johns Hopkins University Press, 1977). For a further discussion of Girard's theory of sacrifice in relation to James's fiction, see Kevin Kohan, 'James and the Originary Scene,' *Henry James Review* 22 (2001), 229–38.

19. Girard, p. 27.

20. Ibid., p. 4.

21. Ibid., pp. 6–7.

22. James, *The Princess Casamassima* in *Novels 1886–1890*, p. 553. References to this text are hereafter cited as *PC*.

23. Lionel Trilling, '*The Princess Casamassima*' in *The Liberal Imagination: Essays on Literature and Society* (Harmondsworth: Penguin, 1970), pp. 69–101.

24. Ibid., p. 95.

25. Julia Ward Howe, 'Battle Hymn of the Republic,' *Atlantic Monthly* Feb. 1862, p. 145.

26. My discussion of *Atlantic Monthly* draws on Edward E. Chielens (ed.), *American Literary Magazines: The Eighteenth and Nineteenth Centuries* (New York: Greenwood, 1986), pp. 50–7; Frank Luther Mott, *A History of American Magazines: 1850–1865* (Cambridge, MA: Harvard University Press, 1957), pp. 493–515; and Ellery Sedgwick, *The Atlantic Monthly 1857–1909: Yankee Humanism at High Tide and Ebb* (Amherst: University of Massachusetts Press, 1994).

27. *Harvard Memorial Biographies*, 2 vols, ed. T. W. Higginson (Cambridge, MA: Sever, 1867). James's brother, Wilky, had served in the 54th Massachusetts regiment under Robert Gould Shaw, who became a Union (and Harvard) icon after being killed in the assault on Fort Wagner. James's first signed fiction, 'The Story of a Year,' is clearly inspired by the experience of seeing Wilky brought home wounded from this battle.

28. Oliver Wendell Holmes, Jr, 'The Soldier's Faith' in *The Mind and Faith of Justice Holmes: His Speeches, Essays, Letters and Judicial Opinions*, ed. Max Lerner (Boston: Little, 1943), pp. 18–25; William James, 'The Moral Equivalent of War' in *The Moral Equivalent of War and Other Essays and Selections from Some Problems of Philosophy*, ed. John K. Roth (London: Harper, 1971), pp. 3–16.

29. Eric Haralson, 'Iron Henry, or James Goes to War,' *Arizona Quarterly* 53 (1997), 41–2.
30. This phrase is added in the 1879 Macmillan edition – James's first opportunity to make substantial changes – and is retained in the New York Edition.
31. W. D. Howells, 'A Foregone Conclusion,' *Atlantic Monthly* July–Dec. 1874; Henry James, Rev. of 'A Foregone Conclusion,' by W. D. Howells, *The Nation*, 7 Jan., 1875, pp. 12–13.
32. Henry James, 'The Story of a Year' in *Complete Stories 1874–1884* (New York: Library of America, 1999), pp. 23–4.
33. Gary Laderman, *The Sacred Remains: American Attitudes Towards Death, 1799–1883* (New Haven: Yale University Press, 1996), pp. 109–16.

2 Corpses and the corpus

1. Ronnie Bailie, *The Fantastic Anatomist: A Psychoanalytic Study of Henry James* (Amsterdam: Rodopi, 2000), p. 4.
2. Stevens, *Henry James and Sexuality*, p. 79.
3. Eve Kosovsky Sedgwick, 'Shame and Performativity: Henry James's New York Edition Prefaces' in *Henry James's New York Edition: The Construction of Authorship*, ed. David McWhirter (Stanford, CA: Stanford University Press, 1995), p. 235.
4. Barbara Leckie, *Culture and Adultery: The Novel, the Newspaper, and the Law, 1857–1914* (Philadelphia: University of Pennsylvania Press, 1999), pp. 154–201.
5. Gustave Flaubert, *Madame Bovary*, trans. Paul De Man (New York: Norton, 1965), pp. 237–41.
6. Stewart, *Death Sentences: Styles of Dying in British Fiction*, pp. 55–97.
7. 'The Middle Years' (1893) is the only example in James's fiction where the point of view follows the consciousness of a character up to the moment of death itself. The end of the story coincides, more or less, with the cessation of consciousness.
8. Lisa Downing, *Desiring the Dead: Necrophilia and Nineteenth-Century French Literature* (Oxford: Legenda, 2003), pp. 1–25.
9. Ibid., p. 5.
10. Henry James, 'The Altar of the Dead' in *Complete Stories 1892–1898* (New York: Library of America, 1996), p. 485.
11. Fiedler, *Love and Death in the American Novel*, pp. 282–3.
12. Bronfen, *Over Her Dead Body*, pp. 370–1.
13. Henry James, *Watch and Ward* in *Novels 1871–1880* (New York: Library of America, 1983), p. 10.
14. Ibid., p. 12.
15. Henry Wallis, *Chatterton* (Tate Gallery, London); Michelangelo [Michelangelo Buonarroti], *Pietà* (St Peter's, Rome).
16. Julia Kristeva, *Powers of Horror: An Essay on Abjection*, trans. Leon S. Roudiez (New York: Columbia University Press, 1982), pp. 3–4.

17. Ibid., pp. 2, 10.
18. Ibid., p. 3.
19. Palmer Arm and Leg Patent, advertisement, *Atlantic Monthly* Mar. 1865, back cover.
20. Susan M. Griffin, 'Scar Texts: Tracing the Marks of Jamesian Masculinity,' *Arizona Quarterly* 53 (1997), 64.
21. Philippe Ariès, *The Hour of Our Death*, trans. Helen Weaver (London: Penguin, 1981), pp. 560–601.
22. Ibid., pp. 561–2.
23. Ibid., pp. 609–11.
24. Henry James, 'The Beast in the Jungle' in *Complete Stories 1898–1910* (New York: Library of America, 1996), p. 535.
25. Bronfen, *Over Her Dead Body*, p. 369.
26. Jacques Derrida, '*Fors*: The Anglish Words of Nicolas Abraham and Maria Torok,' trans. Barbara Johnson, in Nicolas Abraham and Maria Torok, *The Wolf Man's Magic Word: A Cryptonomy*, trans. Nicholas Rand (Minneapolis: University of Minnesota Press, 1986), pp. xi–xlviii.
27. Ibid., p. xxxviii.
28. Ibid., p. xix.
29. Ibid., p. xxxviii.
30. Henry James, 'The Jolly Corner' in *Complete Stories 1898–1910* (New York: Library of America, 1996), p. 704; hereafter cited as *JC*.
31. Henry James, 'The Aspern Papers' in *Complete Stories 1884–1891* (New York: Library of America, 1999), p. 303.
32. Richard Salmon, *Henry James and the Culture of Publicity* (Cambridge: Cambridge University Press, 1997), p. 84.
33. Tim Armstrong, *Modernism, Technology, and the Body: A Cultural Study* (Cambridge: Cambridge University Press, 1998), pp. 43–58.
34. James, 'The Aspern Papers,' p. 320.
35. Henry James, 'The Death of the Lion' in *Complete Stories 1892–1898* (New York: Library of America, 1996), p. 388.
36. James, *The American*, pp. 871–2.
37. Henry James, *The Wings of the Dove*, 2 vols (New York: Scribner's, 1909), vol. 2, pp. 386–7; hereafter cited as *WD*.
38. James, *The American*, pp. 871–2. This is the first American book version (1877). In the New York Edition, a different repetition is used to create the closing cadence: Mrs Tristram's ' "poor, poor Claire!" ' emphasises Claire's disappearance from the world rather than the letter's; Henry James, *The American* (New York: Scribner's, 1907), p. 540.
39. Henry James life mask, *45Z-1a, Houghton Library, Harvard University.
40. Margaret Brooke, the Ranee of Sarawak, one of James's friends. Greg Zacharias identified this word.
41. Alice James, pencil draft of copy of a letter to Harry James, AHGJ1o, James Family Papers, Center for Henry James Studies, Creighton University. This extract is reproduced courtesy of Bay James.
42. Stanley Olson, *John Singer Sargent: His Portrait* (London: Macmillan, 1986), pp. 241–4.

43. Ibid., p. 249.
44. F. Hilaire d'Arois, photographs of Henry James in Portraits – H. James, Jr, Pf MS Am1094, Houghton Library, Harvard University; reprinted in Fred Kaplan, *Henry James: The Imagination of Genius, A Biography* (London: Hodder, 1992), facing p. 305.
45. Georg Kolbe, 'How Death Masks Are Taken' in Ernst Benkard, *Undying Faces: A Collection of Death Masks*, trans. Margaret M. Green (London: Hogarth Press, 1929), p. 44. Nietzsche's death mask is shown as plate 97 in Benkard's collection; Victor Hugo's is plate 86. Both can currently be viewed online at Thanatos.net's Deathmask Gallery (2002–3), URL: http://thanatos.net/deathmasks.
46. Jeremy Stubbs, 'Surrealism and the Death-Mask' in *Dying Words: The Last Moments of Writers and Philosophers*, ed. Martin Crowley (Amsterdam: Rodopi, 2000), p. 75.
47. Henry James life mask, *45Z-1b, Houghton Library, Harvard University.
48. David Lodge, *Author, Author* (London: Secker & Warburg, 2004).
49. Henry James Today, American University of Paris, July 2002; Katherine McClellan, photographs of Henry James in Portraits – H. James, Jr, Pf MS Am1094, Houghton Library, Harvard University.
50. Joyce's readings from *Ulysses* and *Finnegan's Wake* are available on *The James Joyce Audio Collection*, narr. James Joyce and Cyril Cusack, audio compact disk (New York: HarperAudio, 2002).
51. I take these terms from Ruth Leys, 'Death Masks: Kardiner and Ferenczi on Psychic Trauma,' *Representations* 53 (1996), 63.
52. J. Hillis Miller, *Versions of Pygmalion* (Cambridge, MA: Harvard University Press, 1990). One chapter is devoted to James's 'The Last of the Valerii.'
53. Ibid., p. 222.
54. Gay Wilson Allen, *William James: A Biography* (London: Hart-Davis, 1967), p. 491; William James death mask, *45Z-2, Houghton Library, Harvard University.
55. Benkard, p. 32.
56. Nicola Luckhurst, 'Proust's Beard' in *Dying Words*, ed. Crowley, pp. 104–11.
57. Henry James, *The Sacred Fount* (Harmondsworth: Penguin, 1994), pp. 34–6.
58. Edel, *Henry James: The Master, 1901–1916*, pp. 553–7; Henry James, *The Complete Notebooks of Henry James*, ed. Leon Edel and Lyall H. Powers (New York: Oxford University Press, 1987), pp. 581–4.
59. Kaplan, *Henry James: The Imagination of Genius, A Biography*, p. 566.
60. James, *The Complete Notebooks of Henry James*, p. 240.
61. W. H. Auden, 'At the Grave of Henry James' in *Collected Poems*, ed. Edward Mendelson (London: Faber, 1991), p. 310, lines 1, 17. For a more recent comment on James's grave see Heather O'Donnell, 'Stumbling on Henry James,' *Henry James Review* 21 (2000), 234–41.
62. Laderman, *The Sacred Remains: American Attitudes Towards Death, 1799–1883*, p. 163.
63. Stephen Prothero, *Purified by Fire: A History of Cremation* (Berkeley: University of California Press, 2000), pp. 20–1, 100–1.

64. Allen, p. 493.
65. Greg W. Zacharias and Pierre A. Walker (eds), *The Complete Letters of Henry James*, Center for Henry James Studies, Creighton University, URL: http://mockingbird.creighton.edu/english/hjcenter.htm.

3   *The Wings of the Dove* and the morbid

1. Susan Sontag, *Illness and Metaphor* (New York: Farrar, 1977), pp. 30–5; Jeffrey Meyers, *Disease and the Novel, 1880–1960* (London: Macmillan, 1985), pp. 4–8.
2. Diana Price Herndl, *Invalid Women: Figuring Feminine Illness in American Fiction and Culture, 1840–1940* (Chapel Hill: University of North Carolina Press, 1993), p. 191.
3. Athena Vrettos, *Somatic Fictions: Imagining Illness in Victorian Culture* (Stanford, CA: Stanford University Press, 1995), p. 16.
4. Stevens, *Henry James and Sexuality*, pp. 38–9.
5. Catherine Moloney, 'George Eliot, Henry James, and Consumption: A Shadow on the Lung of the Victorian Psyche' (unpublished dissertation, University of London, 1999), pp. 260–80.
6. John Stokes, *In the Nineties* (Hemel Hempstead: University of Chicago Press, 1989), pp. 26–7.
7. Max Nordau, *Degeneration* (London: Heinemann, 1895).
8. William Greenslade, *Degeneration, Culture and the Novel* (Cambridge: University of Cambridge Press, 1994), pp. 211–19.
9. Tambling, *Henry James*, pp. 58–62.
10. Henry James, *The Bostonians* in *Novels 1881–1886* (New York: Library of America, 1985), p. 810.
11. Ibid., p. 806. Boeotia was a Greek province, looked down upon by Athenians.
12. Auchard, *Silence in Henry James: The Heritage of Symbolism and Decadence*, p. 87.
13. Ibid., p. 47.
14. For further discussion of James's ambivalent relationship with the decadent movement, see Jonathan Freedman, *Professions of Taste: Henry James, British Aestheticism, and Commodity Culture* (Stanford, CA: Stanford University Press, 1990), pp. 202–57.
15. Leavis, *The Great Tradition: George Eliot, Henry James, Joseph Conrad*, pp. 161–2.
16. Henry James, Preface to *The Altar of the Dead, The Beast in the Jungle, The Birthplace, and Other Tales* (New York: Scribner's, 1909), p. ix.
17. Michel Foucault, *The Birth of the Clinic: An Archaeology of Medical Perception*, trans. A. M. Sheridan (London: Tavistock, 1973), pp. 149–73.
18. Ibid., p. 171. Note that this statement is antithetical to Ariès's argument, cited in Chapter 2, that death in the nineteenth century belonged primarily to the other rather than to the self. This difference in opinion illustrates the complexity of the history of attitudes towards death.
19. Henry James, *Washington Square* in *Novels 1881–1886* (New York: Library of America, 1985), p. 177; hereafter cited as *WS*.

20. Quoted in Stokes, *In the Nineties*, p. 27.
21. Freedman, p. 214.
22. Stevens, *Henry James and Sexuality*, p. 24.
23. Ibid., p. 32.
24. Lustig, *Henry James and the Ghostly*, p. 7.
25. Philip Page, '*The Princess Casamassima*: Suicide and "the Penetrating Imagination," ' *Tennessee Studies in Literature* 22 (1977), 162–9.
26. See, for example, Martha Banta, *Taylorised Lives: Narrative Productions in the Age of Taylor, Veblen, and Ford* (Chicago: University of Chicago Press, 1993), p. 75.
27. See, for example, Michael Anesko, *'Friction with the Market': Henry James and the Profession of Authorship* (Oxford: Oxford University Press, 1986), p. 143; Marcia Jacobson, *Henry James and the Mass Market* (Alabama: University of Alabama Press, 1983), pp. 18, 144.
28. Ariès, *The Hour of Our Death*, pp. 508–20, 611.
29. Walter Benjamin, 'The Work of Art in the Age of Mechanical Reproduction' in *Illuminations*, ed. Hannah Arendt, trans. Harry Zohn (London: Fontana, 1992), p. 219.
30. Maxwell Geismer, *Henry James and His Cult* (London: Chatto, 1964).
31. Denis Flannery, *Henry James: A Certain Illusion* (Aldershot: Ashgate, 2000), p. 192.
32. See, for example, Kenneth Reinhard, 'The Jamesian Thing: *The Wings of the Dove* and the Ethics of Mourning,' *Arizona Quarterly* 53 (1997), 115–46.
33. Sigmund Freud, 'Mourning and Melancholia' in *The Standard Edition of the Complete Psychological Works of Sigmund Freud*, trans. James Strachey, (London: Hogarth, 1953–66), vol. 14, pp. 243–58.
34. Gert Buelens, Introduction to *Enacting History in Henry James: Narrative, Power, and Ethics* (Cambridge: Cambridge University Press, 1997), p. 8. Reinhard takes a similar view of the reader's responsibility for mourning Milly.
35. Dorothea Krook, *The Ordeal of Consciousness in Henry James* (Cambridge: Cambridge University Press, 1962), pp. 220–1.
36. Peter Brooks, *The Melodramatic Imagination: Balzac, Henry James, Melodrama and the Mode of Excess* (New York: Columbia University Press, 1985), pp. 179–93.
37. Robert Weisbuch, 'Henry James and the Idea of Evil' in *The Cambridge Companion to Henry James*, ed. Jonathan Freedman (Cambridge: Cambridge University Press, 1998), p. 103.
38. Robert Pippin, *Henry James and Modern Moral Life* (Cambridge: Cambridge University Press, 2000), p. 177.

4 Afterlives

1. Jacques Derrida, 'Living on: Borderlines,' trans. James Hulbert, in *Deconstruction and Criticism*, by Harold Bloom *et al.* (London: Routledge, 1979), pp. 75–176.

2. A seminal statement is Donna J. Haraway, 'A Cyborg Manifesto: Science, Technology, and Socialist-Feminism in the Late Twentieth Century' in *Simians, Cyborgs, and Women: The Reinvention of Nature* (London: Free Association, 1991), pp. 149–81.
3. Seltzer, *Bodies and Machines*, pp. 196–7.
4. Ibid.
5. I introduce the idea of the cyborg in relation to James in 'A Virtual Henry James,' *Henry James E-Journal*, issue 6, June 2003, URL: http://www2.newpaltz.edu/~hathaway/cutting/ejourn6.htm.
6. Kittler, *Discourse Networks 1800/1900*, pp. 356–7.
7. Kittler, *Gramophone, Film, Typewriter*, p. 10.
8. Though there is an abridged audio-book: Henry James, *The Wings of the Dove*, narr. William Hope, audio compact disk (Munich: Naxos, 1997).
9. Daniel Pick, *Svengali's Web: The Alien Enchanter in Modern Culture* (London: Yale University Press, 2000), pp. 68–91.
10. Jonathan Crary, *Suspensions of Perception: Attention, Spectacle, and Modern Culture* (Cambridge, MA: MIT, 1999), pp. 60–3, 136, 215–18, 230–7.
11. Ibid., p. 75.
12. Bayadère: Hindu dancing girl or striped material – in other words, vulgar distractions.
13. Kittler, *Discourse Networks 1800/1900*, p. 193.
14. Edel, *Henry James: The Master, 1901–1916*, p. 95.
15. See, for example, Steven Connor, 'The Machine in the Ghost: Spiritualism, Technology, and the "Direct Voice"' in *Ghosts: Deconstruction, Psychoanalysis, History*, ed. Peter Buse and Andrew Stott (Basingstoke: Macmillan, 1992), pp. 203–25; Erik Davis, *Techgnosis: Myth, Magic and Mysticism in the Age of Information* (London: Serpent's Tail, 1998), pp. 60–5.
16. Roger Luckhurst, *The Invention of Telepathy: 1870–1901* (Oxford: Oxford University Press, 2002).
17. Ibid., p. 247.
18. Sharon Cameron, *Thinking in Henry James* (Chicago: University of Chicago Press, 1989), p. 157.
19. Henry James, 'Is There a Life after Death?,' p. 613.
20. Ibid., p. 614.
21. Ibid., p. 613.
22. Psalms, 55:6, 68:13.
23. Christopher J. Stuart, '"Is There a Life after Death?": Henry James's Response to the New York Edition,' *Colby Quarterly* 35 (1999), 90–101.
24. Ibid., p. 101.
25. M. M. Bakhtin, 'The Problem of the Text in Linguistics, Philology, and the Human Sciences: An Experiment in Philosophical Analysis' in *Speech Genres and Other Late Essays*, trans. Vern W. McGee, ed. Caryl Emerson and Michael Holquist (Austin: University of Texas Press, 1986), p. 126.
26. Adeline Tintner, *The Twentieth-Century World of Henry James: Changes in His Work after 1900* (Baton Rouge: Louisiana State University Press, 2000), p. 121.
27. Cameron, p. 162.

28. Ibid., p. 160.
29. Thurschwell, *Literature, Technology and Magical Thinking*, pp. 107, 114.
30. Ibid., p. 93.
31. Sigmund Freud, 'Totem and Taboo' in *Standard Edition*, vol. 13, p. 85.
32. Thurschwell, p. 7.
33. Pierre Bourdieu, *Distinction: A Social Critique of the Judgement of Taste*, trans. Richard Nice (London: Routledge, 1984), p. 72.
34. Bauman, *Mortality, Immortality and Other Life Strategies*, p. 55.
35. Ian Hamilton, *Keepers of the Flame: Literary Estates and the Rise of Biography* (London: Hutchinson, 1992), p. 214.
36. Michael Millgate, *Testamentary Acts: Browning, Tennyson, James, Hardy* (Oxford: Clarendon, 1992), p. 109. For Edel's discussion of James's will and codicil, see *Henry James: The Master, 1901–1916*, pp. 296, 565.
37. The quoted phrase comes from Coventry Patmore's popular poem, *The Angel in the House*, 2 vols (London: Parker, 1854–6).
38. Henry James, *The Tragic Muse* in *Novels 1886–1890* (New York: Library of America, 1989), pp. 760–1, 866–7, 871, 912, 1074.
39. Ibid., p. 1255.
40. Matthew Arnold, 'Up to Easter' in *The Last Word*, ed. R. H. Super (Ann Arbor: University of Michigan Press, 1977), p. 202.
41. See, for example, John Plunkett, *Queen Victoria: The First Media Monarch* (Oxford: Oxford University Press, 2003), which argues for the central role of mass print and visual culture in the making of the modern British monarchy.
42. David Amigoni, *Victorian Biography: Intellectuals and the Ordering of Discourse* (Hemel Hempstead: Harvester, 1993), p. 180, n. 27.
43. Ibid., p. 120.
44. Ian Small, *Conditions for Criticism: Authority, Knowledge, and Literature in the Late Nineteenth Century* (Oxford: Clarendon, 1991).
45. Ibid., p. 59.
46. Laurel Brake, *Subjugated Knowledges: Journalism, Gender and Literature in the Nineteenth Century* (Basingstoke: Macmillan, 1994), p. 188.
47. Small, pp. 60–1.
48. Henry James, *Hawthorne* (London: Macmillan, 1879), p. 43.
49. Brake, pp. 63–80.
50. See, for example, Kate Campbell, 'Journalistic Discourses and Constructions of Modern Knowledge' in *Nineteenth-Century Media and the Construction of Identities*, ed. Laurel Brake, Bill Bell and David Finkelstein (Basingstoke: Palgrave, 2000), p. 49.
51. Millgate, *Testamentary Acts: Browning, Tennyson, James, Hardy*, p. 180.
52. Adeline Tintner, *Henry James's Legacy: The Afterlife of His Figure and Fiction* (Baton Rouge: Louisiana State University Press, 1998).
53. Jacques Derrida, 'To Speculate – on Freud' in *The Post Card: From Socrates to Freud and Beyond*, trans. Alan Bass (Chicago: University of Chicago Press, 1987), pp. 257–409. Sigmund Freud, *Beyond the Pleasure Principle* in *Standard Edition*, vol. 18, pp. 7–64; this is the essay in which Freud introduces his idea of the death drive.

54. Derrida, pp. 298 ff.
55. Freud, p. 15.
56. Derrida, pp. 328–34.
57. Richard Dawkins, *The Selfish Gene* (Oxford: Oxford University Press, 1976), pp. 203–15.
58. Tim Armstrong, *Haunted Hardy: Poetry, History, Memory* (Basingstoke: Palgrave, 2000), pp. 10–16.
59. Posnock, *The Trial of Curiosity*, p. 4.
60. Hence the title of R. B. J. Wilson's reverential study, *Henry James's Ultimate Narrative: The Golden Bowl* (St Lucia: University of Queensland Press, 1981).
61. This aspect of James's later fiction points towards the modernist concern with impersonality and death, expressed for example in Maurice Blanchot, 'Rilke and Death's Demand' in *The Space of Literature*, trans. Ann Smock (Lincoln: University of Nebraska Press, 1982), pp. 120–59.
62. Salmon, *Henry James and the Culture of Publicity*, pp. 139, 147.
63. Henry James, 'The Papers' in *Complete Stories 1898–1910* (New York: Library of America, 1996), p. 634; hereafter cited as *TP*.
64. Roland Barthes, 'The Death of the Author' in *Image Music Text*, trans. Stephen Heath (London: Fontana, 1977), pp. 142–8.

5   Demography in *The Portrait of a Lady*

1. A. James Hammerton, *Emigrant Gentlewomen: Genteel Poverty and Female Emigration, 1830–1914* (Totowa, NJ: Rowman & Littlefield, 1979), pp. 28–32; Rita S. Kranidis, *The Victorian Spinster and Colonial Emigration* (New York: St Martin's Press, 1999), pp. 1–3.
2. Robert Woods, *The Demography of Victorian England and Wales* (Cambridge: Cambridge University Press, 2000), pp. 31–2; 170–1.
3. Maureen E. Montgomery, *'Gilded Prostitution': Status, Money, and Transatlantic Marriages, 1870–1914* (London: Routledge, 1989), pp. 6–8.
4. Henry James, 'The Next Time' in *Complete Stories 1892–1898* (New York: Library of America, 1996), p. 521.
5. Montgomery, pp. 71, 103–5.
6. Henry James, 'Professor Fargo' in *Complete Stories 1874–1884* (New York: Library of America, 1999), p. 33.
7. Henry James, 'Honoré de Balzac, 1902' in *Literary Criticism: French Writers, Other European Writers, The Prefaces to the New York Edition* (New York: Library of America, 1984), p. 93; hereafter cited as *HB*.
8. Terry Eagleton, *Criticism and Ideology: A Study in Marxist Literary Theory* (London: NLB, 1976), p. 142.
9. Ian Hacking, *The Taming of Chance* (Cambridge: Cambridge University Press, 1996), pp. 133–5. My discussion of statistics in the nineteenth century also draws on Theodore M. Porter, *The Rise of Statistical Thinking, 1820–1900* (Princeton, NJ: Princeton University Press, 1986).
10. Henry Thomas Buckle, *History of Civilization in England*, 2 vols (London: Parker, 1857).

11. Seltzer, *Bodies and Machines*, pp. 82–3.
12. Ibid., pp. 106–13. On 'heroines and the law of averages' in American naturalist fiction, see also Banta, *Taylorised Lives: Narrative Productions in the Age of Taylor, Veblen, and Ford*, pp. 175–93.
13. Lyall H. Powers, *Henry James and the Naturalist Movement* (East Lansing: Michigan State University Press, 1971). For further discussion of James's break from naturalism, see Dennis F. Tredy, 'Teaching the "Grandsons of Balzac" a Lesson: Henry James in the 1890's,' *Revue D'Etudes Anglophones* 2 (2004), URL: http://www.e-rea.org/.
14. Émile Durkheim, *Le Suicide: Étude de Sociologie* (Paris: Alcan, 1897). Stokes traces Durkheim's study back to Henry Morselli's statistical essay on suicide, which appeared in 1879; Stokes, *In the Nineties*, pp. 121, 185.
15. Henry James, 'Emile Zola' in *Literary Criticism: French Writers, Other European Writers, The Prefaces to the New York Edition* (New York: Library of America, 1984), p. 877; emphasis in original.
16. Henry James, *The American Scene* in *Collected Travel Writings: Great Britain and America* (New York: Library of America, 1993), pp. 424, 456; hereafter cited as *AS*.
17. Jacob Riis, *How the Other Half Lives: Studies among the Tenements of New York* (New York: Scribner's, 1890).
18. Blue-books were reports from governmental departments and commissions, often highly statistical in their content.
19. Charles Dickens, *Hard Times* (New York: Norton, 2001), p. 56.
20. Henry James, Preface to *The Golden Bowl*, 2 vols (New York: Scribner's Sons, 1909), vol. 1, p. vii.
21. Banta, pp. 75–9.
22. Ibid., pp. 77–9.
23. Henry James, *The Portrait of a Lady* in *Novels 1881–1886* (New York: Library of America, 1985), p. 629; hereafter cited as *POL*.
24. Henry James, 'Madame de Mauves' in *Complete Stories 1864–1874* (New York: Library of America, 1999), p. 903.
25. I owe this suggestion to Julia Kuehn.
26. On Kant, Burke, and the Romantic sublime, see Thomas Weiskel, *The Romantic Sublime: Studies in the Structure and Psychology of Transcendence* (Baltimore: Johns Hopkins University Press, 1976). For contrasting positions on the post-Romantic sublime, see Barbara Claire Freeman, *The Feminine Sublime: Gender and Excess in Women's Fiction* (Berkeley: University of California Press, 1995); Catherine Maxwell, *The Female Sublime: From Milton to Swinburne* (Manchester: Manchester University Press, 2001); Rita Felski, *The Gender of Modernity* (Cambridge, MA: Harvard University Press, 1995), pp. 115–44.
27. Henry James, *The Portrait of a Lady*, 2 vols (New York: Scribner's, 1908), vol. 2, pp. 437–8.
28. Henry James, *The Portrait of a Lady* (Boston: Houghton Mifflin, 2001); Eadweard Muybridge, *Walking and Opening a Parasol* in *Muybridge's Complete Human and Animal Locomotion*, 3 vols (New York: Dover, 1979), vol. 2, p. 940.

29. Seltzer, *Bodies and Machines*, pp. 100, 115; Hacking, *The Taming of Chance*, pp. 182–3.
30. Tambling, *Henry James*, pp. 56, 70.
31. See, for example, Beth Sharon Ash, 'Frail Vessels and Vast Designs: A Psychoanalytic Portrait of Isabel Archer' in *New Essays on* The Portrait of a Lady, ed. Joel Porte (Cambridge: Cambridge University Press, 1990), pp. 123–62.
32. Edgar Allen Poe, 'The Philosophy of Composition' in *Essays and Reviews* (New York: Library of America, 1984), pp. 13–25; Bronfen, *Over Her Dead Body*, p. 59.
33. Achille Guillard, *Éléments de Statistique Humaine, ou Démographie Comparée* (Paris: Guillaumin, 1855).
34. Woods, *The Demography of Victorian England and Wales*, pp. 17–19, 381.
35. Laura Peters, *Orphan Texts: Victorian Orphans, Culture and Empire* (Manchester: Manchester University Press, 2000).
36. William Veeder, 'The Portrait of a Lack' in *New Essays on* The Portrait of a Lady, p. 95.
37. Alfred Habegger, 'The Fatherless Heroine and the Filial Son: Deep Background for *The Portrait of a Lady*' in *New Essays on* The Portrait of a Lady, p. 53.
38. Gordon, *A Private Life of Henry James*, pp. 487–8.
39. Henry James, *The Ivory Tower* (New York: Scribner's, 1917), pp. 280–1.
40. Ibid., p. 291.
41. Jacques Derrida, 'Ulysses Gramophone: Hear Say Yes in Joyce' in *Acts of Literature*, ed. Derek Attridge, trans. Tina Kendall, rev. Shari Benstock (New York: Routledge, 1992), pp. 297–308.

Bibliography

Allen, Gay Wilson, *William James: A Biography* (London: Hart-Davis, 1967).

Amigoni, David, *Victorian Biography: Intellectuals and the Ordering of Discourse* (Hemel Hempstead: Harvester, 1993).

Anesko, Michael, *'Friction with the Market': Henry James and the Profession of Authorship* (Oxford: Oxford University Press, 1986).

Ariès, Philippe, *The Hour of Our Death*, trans. Helen Weaver (London: Penguin, 1981).

Armstrong, Paul B., *The Phenomenology of Henry James* (Chapel Hill: University of North Carolina Press, 1983).

Armstrong, Tim, *Haunted Hardy: Poetry, History, Memory* (Basingstoke: Palgrave, 2000).

——, *Modernism, Technology, and the Body: A Cultural Study* (Cambridge: Cambridge University Press, 1998).

Arnold, Matthew, 'Up to Easter' in *The Last Word*, ed. R. H. Super (Ann Arbor: University of Michigan Press, 1977), pp. 190–209.

d'Arois, F. Hilaire, Photographs of Henry James in Portraits – H. James, Jr, Pf MS Am1094, Houghton Library, Harvard University.

Ash, Beth Sharon, 'Frail Vessels and Vast Designs: A Psychoanalytic Portrait of Isabel Archer' in *New Essays on* The Portrait of a Lady, ed. Joel Porte (Cambridge: Cambridge University Press, 1990), pp. 123–62.

Auchard, John, *Silence in Henry James: The Heritage of Symbolism and Decadence* (London: Pennsylvania State University Press, 1986).

Auden, W. H., 'At the Grave of Henry James' in *Collected Poems*, ed. Edward Mendelson (London: Faber, 1991), pp. 310–12.

Bailie, Ronnie, *The Fantastic Anatomist: A Psychoanalytic Study of Henry James* (Amsterdam: Rodopi, 2000).

Bakhtin, M. M., 'The Problem of the Text in Linguistics, Philology, and the Human Sciences: An Experiment in Philosophical Analysis' in *Speech Genres and Other Late Essays*, trans. Vern W. McGee, ed. Caryl Emerson and Michael Holquist (Austin: University of Texas Press, 1986), pp. 103–31.

Banta, Martha, *Henry James and the Occult: The Great Extension* (Bloomington: Indiana University Press, 1972).

——, *Taylorised Lives: Narrative Productions in the Age of Taylor, Veblen, and Ford* (Chicago: University of Chicago Press, 1993).

Barthes, Roland, 'The Death of the Author' in *Image Music Text*, trans. Stephen Heath (London: Fontana, 1977), pp. 142–8.

Bauman, Zygmunt, *Mortality, Immortality and Other Life Strategies* (Cambridge: Polity, 1992).

Benjamin, Walter, 'The Work of Art in the Age of Mechanical Reproduction' in *Illuminations*, ed. Hannah Arendt, trans. Harry Zohn (London: Fontana, 1992), pp. 211–44.

Benkard, Ernst, *Undying Faces: A Collection of Death Masks*, trans. Margaret M. Green (London: Hogarth Press, 1929).

Biedler, Peter G., *Ghosts, Demons, and Henry James: The Turn of the Screw at the Turn of the Century* (Columbia: University of Missouri Press, 1989).

Blain, N. A., 'Ideas of "Life" and their Moral Force in the Novels of Henry James' (unpublished dissertation, University of Strathclyde, 1981).

Blanchot, Maurice, 'Rilke and Death's Demand' in *The Space of Literature*, trans. Ann Smock (Lincoln: University of Nebraska Press, 1982), pp. 120–59.

Bourdieu, Pierre, *Distinction: A Social Critique of the Judgement of Taste*, trans. Richard Nice (London: Routledge, 1984).

Brake, Laurel, *Subjugated Knowledges: Journalism, Gender and Literature in the Nineteenth Century* (Basingstoke: Macmillan, 1994).

Bronfen, Elisabeth, *Over Her Dead Body: Death, Femininity and the Aesthetic* (Manchester: Manchester University Press, 1992).

Brooks, Peter, *The Melodramatic Imagination: Balzac, Henry James, Melodrama and the Mode of Excess* (New York: Columbia University Press, 1985).

Buckle, Henry Thomas, *History of Civilization in England*, 2 vols (London: Parker, 1857).

Buelens, Gert, Introduction, *Enacting History in Henry James: Narrative, Power, and Ethics* (Cambridge: Cambridge University Press, 1997), pp. 1–15.

Cameron, Sharon, *Thinking in Henry James* (Chicago: University of Chicago Press, 1989).

Campbell, Kate, 'Journalistic Discourses and Constructions of Modern Knowledge' in *Nineteenth-Century Media and the Construction of Identities*, ed. Laurel Brake, Bill Bell and David Finkelstein (Basingstoke: Palgrave, 2000), pp. 40–53.

Cannon, Kelly, *Henry James and Masculinity: The Man at the Margins* (Basingstoke: Macmillan, 1994).

Cargill, Oscar, *The Novels of Henry James* (New York: Macmillan, 1961).

Chielens, Edward E. (ed.), *American Literary Magazines: The Eighteenth and Nineteenth Centuries* (New York: Greenwood, 1986).

Clark, Susan, 'A Note on *The Turn of the Screw*: Death from Natural Causes,' *Studies in Short Fiction* 15 (1978), 110–12.

Collins, Carvel, 'James' *The Turn of the Screw*,' *Explicator* 13 (1954–5).

Connor, Steven, 'The Machine in the Ghost: Spiritualism, Technology, and the "Direct Voice"' in *Ghosts: Deconstruction, Psychoanalysis, History*, ed. Peter Buse and Andrew Stott (Basingstoke: Macmillan, 1992), pp. 203–25.

Crary, Jonathan, *Suspensions of Perception: Attention, Spectacle, and Modern Culture* (Cambridge, MA: MIT, 1999).

Cutting, Andrew, 'A Virtual Henry James,' *Henry James E-Journal*, issue 6, June 2003, URL: http://www2.newpaltz.edu/~hathaway/cutting/ejourn6.htm.

Davis, Erik, *Techgnosis: Myth, Magic and Mysticism in the Age of Information* (London: Serpent's Tail, 1998).

Dawkins, Richard, *The Selfish Gene* (Oxford: Oxford University Press, 1976).

Derrida, Jacques, 'Living on: Borderlines,' trans. James Hulbert, in *Deconstruction and Criticism*, by Harold Bloom *et al*. (London: Routledge, 1979), pp. 75–176.

——, '*Fors*: The Anglish Words of Nicolas Abraham and Maria Torok,' trans. Barbara Johnson, in Nicolas Abraham and Maria Torok, *The Wolf Man's Magic Word: A Cryptonomy*, trans. Nicholas Rand (Minneapolis: University of Minnesota Press, 1986), pp. xi–xlviii.

——, 'To Speculate – on Freud' in *The Post Card: From Socrates to Freud and Beyond*, trans. Alan Bass (Chicago: University of Chicago Press, 1987), pp. 257–409.

——, 'Ulysses Gramophone: Hear Say Yes in Joyce' in *Acts of Literature*, ed. Derek Attridge, trans. Tina Kendall, rev. Shari Benstock (New York: Routledge, 1992), pp. 256–309.

——, *Specters of Marx: The State of the Debt, the Work of Mourning, and the New International*, trans. Peggy Kamuf (New York: Routledge, 1994).

Dickens, Charles, *Hard Times* (New York: Norton, 2001).

Dolin, Kieran, *Fiction and the Law: Legal Discourse in Victorian and Modernist Literature* (Cambridge: Cambridge University Press, 1999).

Dollimore, Jonathan, *Death, Desire and Loss in Western Culture* (London: Penguin, 1998).

Donadio, Stephen, *Nietzsche, Henry James, and the Artistic Will* (New York: Oxford University Press, 1978).

Downing, Lisa, *Desiring the Dead: Necrophilia and Nineteenth-Century French Literature* (Oxford: Legenda, 2003).

Durkheim, Émile, *Le Suicide: Étude de Sociologie* (Paris: Alcan, 1897).

Eagleton, Terry, *Criticism and Ideology: A Study in Marxist Literary Theory* (London: NLB, 1976).

Edel, Leon, *Henry James: The Untried Years 1843–1870* (London: Hart-Davis, 1953).

——, *Henry James: The Treacherous Years 1895–1901* (London: Hart-Davis, 1969).

——, *Henry James: The Master, 1901–1916* (London: Hart-Davis, 1972).

Ellmann, Richard, 'James Amongst the Aesthetes' in *Henry James and Homo-Erotic Desire*, ed. John R. Bradley (Basingstoke: Macmillan, 1999), pp. 25–44.

Felman, Shoshana, 'Turning the Screw of Interpretation,' *Yale French Studies* 55–6 (1977), 94–207.

Felski, Rita, *The Gender of Modernity* (Cambridge, MA: Harvard University Press, 1995).

Fiedler, Leslie, *Love and Death in the American Novel* (New York: Criterion, 1960).

Flannery, Denis, *Henry James: A Certain Illusion* (Aldershot: Ashgate, 2000).

Flaubert, Gustave, *Madame Bovary*, trans. Paul De Man (New York: Norton, 1965).

Fluck, Winfried, 'Power Relations in the Novels of James: The "Liberal" and the "Radical" Version' in *Enacting History in Henry James: Narrative, Power, and Ethics*, ed. Gert Buelens (Cambridge: Cambridge University Press, 1997), pp. 16–39.

Foucault, Michel, *The Birth of the Clinic: An Archaeology of Medical Perception*, trans. A. M. Sheridan (London: Tavistock, 1973).

Freedman, Jonathan, *Professions of Taste: Henry James, British Aestheticism, and Commodity Culture* (Stanford, CA: Stanford University Press, 1990).

Freeman, Barbara Claire, *The Feminine Sublime: Gender and Excess in Women's Fiction* (Berkeley: University of California Press, 1995).

Freud, Sigmund, *Beyond the Pleasure Principle* in *The Standard Edition of the Complete Psychological Works of Sigmund Freud*, trans. James Strachey (London: Hogarth, 1953–66), vol. 18, pp. 7–64.

——, 'Mourning and Melancholia' in *Standard Edition*, vol. 14, pp. 243–58.

——, 'Totem and Taboo' in *Standard Edition*, vol. 13, pp. 243–58.

Fussell, Edwin Sill, *The Catholic Side of Henry James* (Cambridge: Cambridge University Press, 1993).

Geismer, Maxwell, *Henry James and His Cult* (London: Chatto, 1964).

Girard, René, *Violence and the Sacred*, trans. Patrick Gregory (Baltimore: Johns Hopkins University Press, 1977).

Gordon, Lyndall, *A Private Life of Henry James: Two Women and His Art* (London: Chatto & Windus, 1998).

Greenslade, William, *Degeneration, Culture and the Novel* (Cambridge: University of Cambridge Press, 1994).

Griffin, Susan M., 'Scar Texts: Tracing the Marks of Jamesian Masculinity,' *Arizona Quarterly* 53 (1997), 61–82.

Guillard, Achille, *Éléments de Statistique Humaine, ou Démographie Comparée* (Paris: Guillaumin, 1855).

Habegger, Alfred, 'The Fatherless Heroine and the Filial Son: Deep Background for *The Portrait of a Lady*' in *New Essays on* The Portrait of a Lady, ed. Joel Porte (Cambridge: Cambridge University Press, 1990), pp. 49–93.

Hacking, Ian, *The Taming of Chance* (Cambridge: Cambridge University Press, 1996).

Hamilton, Ian, *Keepers of the Flame: Literary Estates and the Rise of Biography* (London: Hutchinson, 1992).

Hammerton, A. James, *Emigrant Gentlewomen: Genteel Poverty and Female Emigration, 1830–1914* (Totowa, NJ: Rowman & Littlefield, 1979).

Haralson, Eric, 'Iron Henry, or James Goes to War,' *Arizona Quarterly* 53 (1997), 39–59.

——, *Henry James and Queer Modernity* (Cambridge: Cambridge University Press, 2003).

Haraway, Donna J., 'A Cyborg Manifesto: Science, Technology, and Socialist-Feminism in the Late Twentieth Century' in *Simians, Cyborgs, and Women: The Reinvention of Nature* (London: Free Association, 1991), pp. 149–81.

Harvard Memorial Biographies, 2 vols, ed. T. W. Higginson (Cambridge, MA: Sever, 1867).

Henry James life masks, *45Z-1a and *45Z-1b, Houghton Library, Harvard University.

Herndl, Diana Price, *Invalid Women: Figuring Feminine Illness in American Fiction and Culture, 1840–1940* (Chapel Hill: University of North Carolina Press, 1993).

Hocks, Richard A., *Henry James and Pragmatistic Thought: A Study in the Relationship between the Philosophy of William James and the Literary Art of Henry James* (Chapel Hill: University of North Carolina Press, 1974).

Holmes, Oliver Wendell, Jr, 'The Soldier's Faith' in *The Mind and Faith of Justice Holmes: His Speeches, Essays, Letters and Judicial Opinions*, ed. Max Lerner (Boston: Little, 1943), pp. 18–25.

Hoople, Robin P., *Distinguished Discord: Discontinuity and Pattern in the Critical Tradition of* The Turn of the Screw (Lewisburg: Bucknell University Press, 1997).

Howe, Julia Ward, 'Battle Hymn of the Republic,' *Atlantic Monthly*, Feb. 1862, p. 145.

Howells, W. D., 'A Foregone Conclusion,' *Atlantic Monthly*, July–Dec. 1874.

Jacobson, Marcia, *Henry James and the Mass Market* (Alabama: University of Alabama Press, 1983).

James, Alice, Pencil draft of copy of a letter to Harry James, AHGJ1o, James Family Papers, Center for Henry James Studies, Creighton University.

James and the Sacred, Special issue of *Henry James Review* 22 (2001).

James, Henry, Rev. of 'A Foregone Conclusion,' by W. D. Howells, *The Nation*, Jan. 7, 1875, pp. 12–13.

——, 'Roderick Hudson,' *Atlantic Monthly*, Jan.–Dec. 1875.

——, *Hawthorne* (London: Macmillan, 1879).

——, *The American* (New York: Scribner's, 1907).

——, *Roderick Hudson* (New York: Scribner's, 1907).

——, *The Portrait of a Lady*, 2 vols (New York: Scribner's, 1908).

——, Preface to *The Princess Casamassima*, 2 vols (New York: Scribner's, 1908), vol. 1, pp. v–xxiii.

——, Preface to *The Altar of the Dead, The Beast in the Jungle, The Birthplace, and Other Tales* (New York: Scribner's, 1909), pp. v–xxix.

——, *The Ambassadors*, 2 vols (New York: Scribner's, 1909).

——, Preface to *The Golden Bowl*, 2 vols (New York: Scribner's Sons, 1909), vol. 1, pp. v–xxv.

——, *The Wings of the Dove*, 2 vols (New York: Scribner's, 1909).

——, *Notes of a Son and Brother* (London: Macmillan, 1914).

——, *The Ivory Tower* (New York: Scribner's, 1917).

——, 'Is There a Life after Death?' in *The James Family*, by F. O. Matthiessen (New York: Knopf, 1948), pp. 602–14.

——, *The Other House* (London: Hart-Davis, 1948).

——, *The American* in *Novels 1871–1880* (New York: Library of America, 1983), pp. 513–872.

——, *Roderick Hudson* in *Novels 1871–1880* (New York: Library of America, 1983), pp. 163–511.

——, *Watch and Ward* in *Novels 1871–1880* (New York: Library of America, 1983), pp. 1–161.

——, *Henry James Letters*, ed. Leon Edel, 4 vols (London: Macmillan, 1974–1980; Cambridge, MA: Belknap, 1984).

——, 'Emile Zola' in *Literary Criticism: French Writers, Other European Writers, The Prefaces to the New York Edition* (New York: Library of America, 1984), pp. 871–99.

——, 'Honoré de Balzac, 1902' in *Literary Criticism: French Writers, Other European Writers, The Prefaces to the New York Edition* (New York: Library of America, 1984), pp. 90–115.

——, *The Bostonians* in *Novels 1881–1886* (New York: Library of America, 1985), pp. 801–1219.

——, *The Portrait of a Lady* in *Novels 1881–1886* (New York: Library of America, 1985), pp. 191–800.

——, *Washington Square* in *Novels 1881–1886* (New York: Library of America, 1985), pp. 1–189.

——, *The Complete Notebooks of Henry James*, ed. Leon Edel and Lyall H. Powers (New York: Oxford University Press, 1987).

——, *The Princess Casamassima* in *Novels 1886–1890* (New York: Library of America, 1989), pp. 1–553.

——, *The Tragic Muse* in *Novels 1886–1890* (New York: Library of America, 1989), pp. 701–1255.

——, *The American Scene* in *Collected Travel Writings: Great Britain and America* (New York: Library of America, 1993), pp. 351–736.

——, *The Sacred Fount* (Harmondsworth: Penguin, 1994).

——, 'The Altar of the Dead' in *Complete Stories 1892–1898* (New York: Library of America, 1996), pp. 450–85.

——, 'The Beast in the Jungle' in *Complete Stories 1898–1910* (New York: Library of America, 1996), pp. 496–541.

——, 'The Death of the Lion' in *Complete Stories 1892–1898* (New York: Library of America, 1996), pp. 356–92.

——, 'The Jolly Corner' in *Complete Stories 1898–1910* (New York: Library of America, 1996), pp. 697–731.

——, 'The Next Time' in *Complete Stories 1892–1898* (New York: Library of America, 1996), pp. 486–524.

——, 'The Papers' in *Complete Stories 1898–1910* (New York: Library of America, 1996), pp. 542–638.

——, 'The Turn of the Screw' in *Complete Stories 1892–1898* (New York: Library of America, 1996), pp. 635–740.

——, *The Wings of the Dove*, narr. William Hope, audio compact disk (Munich: Naxos, 1997).

——, 'The Aspern Papers' in *Complete Stories 1884–1891* (New York: Library of America, 1999), pp. 356–92.

——, 'Madame de Mauves' in *Complete Stories 1864–1874* (New York: Library of America, 1999), pp. 828–903.

——, 'Professor Fargo' in *Complete Stories 1874–1884* (New York: Library of America, 1999), pp. 1–35.

——, 'The Story of a Year' in *Complete Stories 1874–1884* (New York: Library of America, 1999), pp. 23–66.

——, *The Portrait of a Lady* (Boston: Houghton Mifflin, 2001).

The James Joyce Audio Collection, narr. James Joyce and Cyril Cusack, audio compact disk (New York: HarperAudio, 2002).

James, William, 'The Moral Equivalent of War' in *The Moral Equivalent of War and Other Essays and Selections from Some Problems of Philosophy*, ed. John K. Roth (London: Harper, 1971), pp. 3–16.

Kaplan, Fred, *Henry James: The Imagination of Genius, A Biography* (London: Hodder, 1992).

Kittler, Friedrich, *Discourse Networks 1800/1900*, trans. Michael Metteer with Chris Cullens (Stanford, CA: Stanford University Press, 1990).

——, *Gramophone, Film, Typewriter*, trans. Geoffrey Winthrop-Young and Michael Wutz (Stanford, CA: Stanford University Press, 1999).

Kohan, Kevin, 'James and the Originary Scene,' *Henry James Review* 22 (2001), 229–38.

Kolbe, Georg, 'How Death Masks Are Taken' in Ernst Benkard, *Undying Faces: A Collection of Death Masks*, trans. Margaret M. Green (London: Hogarth Press, 1929), pp. 41–5.

Kranidis, Rita S., *The Victorian Spinster and Colonial Emigration* (New York: St Martin's Press, 1999).

Kristeva, Julia, *Powers of Horror: An Essay on Abjection*, trans. Leon S. Roudiez (New York: Columbia University Press, 1982).

Krook, Dorothea, *The Ordeal of Consciousness in Henry James* (Cambridge: Cambridge University Press, 1962).

Laderman, Gary, *The Sacred Remains: American Attitudes Towards Death, 1799–1883* (New Haven: Yale University Press, 1996).

Lawrence, D. H., *Women in Love* (London: Heinemann, 1921).

Leavis, F. R., *The Great Tradition: George Eliot, Henry James, Joseph Conrad* (London: Chatto & Windus, 1948).

Leckie, Barbara, *Culture and Adultery: The Novel, the Newspaper, and the Law, 1857–1914* (Philadelphia: University of Pennsylvania Press, 1999).

Leys, Ruth, 'Death Masks: Kardiner and Ferenczi on Psychic Trauma,' *Representations* 53 (1996), 44–73.

Lodge, David, *Author, Author* (London: Secker & Warburg, 2004).

Luckhurst, Nicola, 'Proust's Beard' in *Dying Words: The Last Moments of Writers and Philosophers*, ed. Martin Crowley (Amsterdam: Rodopi, 2000), pp. 95–113.

Luckhurst, Roger, *The Invention of Telepathy: 1870–1901* (Oxford: Oxford University Press, 2002).

Lustig, T. J., *Henry James and the Ghostly* (Cambridge: Cambridge University Press, 1994).

Maxwell, Catherine, *The Female Sublime: From Milton to Swinburne* (Manchester: Manchester University Press, 2001).

Mazzella, Anthony J., 'James's Revisions' in *A Companion to Henry James Studies*, ed. Daniel Mark Fogel (London: Greenwood, 1993), pp. 311–33.

McClellan, Katherine, Photographs of Henry James in Portraits – H. James, Jr, Pf MS Am1094, Houghton Library, Harvard University.

Meyers, Jeffrey, *Disease and the Novel, 1880–1960* (London: Macmillan, 1985).

Michelangelo [Michelangelo Buonarroti], *Pietà* (St Peter's, Rome).

Miller, J. Hillis, *Versions of Pygmalion* (Cambridge, MA: Harvard University Press, 1990).

Millgate, Michael, *Testamentary Acts: Browning, Tennyson, James, Hardy* (Oxford: Clarendon, 1992).

Moloney, Catherine, 'George Eliot, Henry James, and Consumption: A Shadow on the Lung of the Victorian Psyche' (unpublished dissertation, University of London, 1999).

Montgomery, Maureen E., *'Gilded Prostitution': Status, Money, and Transatlantic Marriages, 1870–1914* (London: Routledge, 1989).

Moore, Geoffrey, Introduction to *Roderick Hudson*, by Henry James (Harmondsworth: Penguin, 1986), pp. 7–32.

Mott, Frank Luther, *A History of American Magazines: 1850–1865* (Cambridge, MA: Harvard University Press, 1957).

Muybridge, Eadweard, *Walking and Opening a Parasol* in *Muybridge's Complete Human and Animal Locomotion*, 3 vols (New York: Dover, 1979), vol. 2, p. 940.

Nordau, Max, *Degeneration* (London: Heinemann, 1895).

O'Donnell, Heather, 'Stumbling on Henry James,' *Henry James Review* 21 (2000), 234–41.

Olson, Stanley, *John Singer Sargent: His Portrait* (London: Macmillan, 1986).

Page, Philip, '*The Princess Casamassima*: Suicide and "the Penetrating Imagination,"' *Tennessee Studies in Literature* 22 (1977), 162–9.

Palmer, Arm and Leg Patent, Advertisement, *Atlantic Monthly*, Mar. 1865, back cover.

Patmore, Coventry, *The Angel in the House*, 2 vols (London: Parker, 1854–6).

Peters, Laura, *Orphan Texts: Victorian Orphans, Culture and Empire* (Manchester: Manchester University Press, 2000).

Pick, Daniel, *Svengali's Web: The Alien Enchanter in Modern Culture* (London: Yale University Press, 2000).

Pippin, Robert, *Henry James and Modern Moral Life* (Cambridge: Cambridge University Press, 2000).

Plunkett, John, *Queen Victoria: The First Media Monarch* (Oxford: Oxford University Press, 2003).

Poe, Edgar Allen, 'The Philosophy of Composition' in *Essays and Reviews* (New York: Library of America, 1984), pp. 13–25.

Poirier, Richard, *The Comic Sense of Henry James: A Study of the Early Novels* (London: Chatto, 1960).

Porter, Theodore M., *The Rise of Statistical Thinking, 1820–1900* (Princeton, NJ: Princeton University Press, 1986).

Posnock, Ross, *The Trial of Curiosity: Henry James, William James, and the Challenge of Modernity* (New York: Oxford University Press, 1991).

Powers, Lyall H., *Henry James and the Naturalist Movement* (East Lancing: Michigan State University Press, 1971).

Prothero, Stephen, *Purified by Fire: A History of Cremation* (Berkeley: University of California Press, 2000).

Reinhard, Kenneth, 'The Jamesian Thing: *The Wings of the Dove* and the Ethics of Mourning,' *Arizona Quarterly* 53 (1997), 115–46.

Riis, Jacob, *How the Other Half Lives: Studies among the Tenements of New York* (New York: Scribner's, 1890).

Rowe, John Carlos, 'Henry James and Critical Theory' in *A Companion to Henry James Studies*, ed. Daniel Mark Fogel (London: Greenwood, 1993), pp. 73–93.

Salmon, Richard, *Henry James and the Culture of Publicity* (Cambridge: Cambridge University Press, 1997).

Schopenhauer, Arthur, *The World as Will and Representation*, 2 vols, trans. E. F. J. Payne (New York: Dover, 1966).

Sedgwick, Ellery, *The Atlantic Monthly 1857–1909: Yankee Humanism at High Tide and Ebb* (Amherst: University of Massachusetts Press, 1994).

Sedgwick, Eve Kosovsky, 'Shame and Performativity: Henry James's New York Edition Prefaces' in *Henry James's New York Edition: The Construction of Authorship*, ed. David McWhirter (Stanford, CA: Stanford University Press, 1995), pp. 206–39.

Seltzer, Mark, *Henry James and the Art of Power* (Ithaca: Cornell University Press, 1984).

——, *Bodies and Machines* (New York: Routledge, 1992).

Small, Ian, *Conditions for Criticism: Authority, Knowledge, and Literature in the Late Nineteenth Century* (Oxford: Clarendon, 1991).

Smith, Robert, *Derrida and Autobiography* (Cambridge: Cambridge University Press, 1995).

Sontag, Susan, *Illness and Metaphor* (New York: Farrar, 1977).

Stevens, Hugh, *Henry James and Sexuality* (Cambridge: Cambridge University Press, 1998).

Stewart, Garrett, *Death Sentences: Styles of Dying in British Fiction* (Cambridge, MA: Harvard University Press, 1984).

Stokes, John, *In the Nineties* (Hemel Hempstead: University of Chicago Press, 1989).

Stuart, Christopher J., ' "Is There a Life after Death?": Henry James's Response to the New York Edition,' *Colby Quarterly* 35 (1999), 90–101.

Stubbs, Jeremy, 'Surrealism and the Death-Mask' in *Dying Words: The Last Moments of Writers and Philosophers*, ed. Martin Crowley (Amsterdam: Rodopi, 2000), pp. 69–94.

Sussman, Henry, *The Hegelian Aftermath: Readings in Hegel, Kierkegaard, Freud, Proust, and James* (Baltimore: Johns Hopkins University Press, 1982).

Tambling, Jeremy, *Henry James* (London: Macmillan, 2000).

Thanatos.net Deathmask Gallery (2002–3), URL: http://thanatos.net/deathmasks.

Thurschwell, Pamela, *Literature, Technology and Magical Thinking, 1880–1920* (Cambridge: Cambridge University Press, 2001).

Tintner, Adeline, *Henry James's Legacy: The Afterlife of His Figure and Fiction* (Baton Rouge: Louisiana State University Press, 1998).

——, *The Twentieth-Century World of Henry James: Changes in His Work after 1900* (Baton Rouge: Louisiana State University Press, 2000).

Tredy, Dennis F., 'Teaching the "Grandsons of Balzac" a Lesson: Henry James in the 1890's,' *Revue D'Etudes Anglophones* 2 (2004), URL: http://www.e-rea.org/.

Trilling, Lionel, 'The Princess Casamassima' in *The Liberal Imagination: Essays on Literature and Society* (Harmondsworth: Penguin, 1970), pp. 69–101.

Veeder, William, 'The Portrait of a Lack' in *New Essays on* The Portrait of a Lady, ed. Joel Porte (Cambridge: Cambridge University Press, 1990), pp. 95–121.

Vrettos, Athena, *Somatic Fictions: Imagining Illness in Victorian Culture* (Stanford, CA: Stanford University Press, 1995).

Wallis, Henry, *Chatterton* (Tate Gallery, London).

Weisbuch, Robert, 'Henry James and the Idea of Evil' in *The Cambridge Companion to Henry James*, ed. Jonathan Freedman (Cambridge: Cambridge University Press, 1998), pp. 102–19.

Weiskel, Thomas, *The Romantic Sublime: Studies in the Structure and Psychology of Transcendence* (Baltimore: Johns Hopkins University Press, 1976).

William James death mask, *45Z–2, Houghton Library, Harvard University.

Wilson, R. B. J., *Henry James's Ultimate Narrative: The Golden Bowl* (St Lucia: University of Queensland Press, 1981).

Woods, Robert, *The Demography of Victorian England and Wales* (Cambridge: Cambridge University Press, 2000).

Wordsworth, William, Preface to *Lyrical Ballads*, 1802 in *Lyrical Ballads, and Other Poems, 1797–1800*, ed. James Butler and Karen Green (Ithaca: Cornell University Press, 1992), pp. 741–60.

Zacharias, Greg W. and Pierre A. Walker (eds), *The Complete Letters of Henry James*, Center for Henry James Studies, Creighton University, URL: http://mockingbird.creighton.edu/english/hjcenter.htm.

Index

Printed in the United States
137693LV00001B/143/A